say you will

M. MALONE

Say You Will © August 2014 M. Malone

Editor: Daisycakes Creative Services

Proofreading: Leah Guinan

CrushStar Romance
An Imprint of CrushStar Multimedia LLC

ISBN-13: 978-1-938789-17-5

Birthday Cake

"I really enjoyed this one...There was a fabulous twist at the end that I didn't see coming, but it was the absolutely *perfect* way to end the book. Just fun and sexy!"
--Smitten By Reading

"Trent and Mara have enough chemistry to fuel a rocket ship. Mara's seduction of Trent is classic and hysterical. I mean this guy is out of his depth with this girl but hey the great thing is that he wants her as bad as she wants him. When they finally give in it's explosive! Teasing Trent is hot hot hot!"
--Joyfully Reviewed

He's the Man

"A story full of smart, compelling characters, and a strong storyline...will keep you coming back for more."
-- Romantic Reads

This book has angst, humor, sexy times, and love. What more could you ask for? I hope there are going to be more in this series and you can bet I will be first in line.
-- S.W. & More Book Reviews

One More Day

I am now officially in love with the Alexander family. There was so much about this book that worked for me. First and foremost, I loved the romance between Jackson and Ridley. They had fabulous, explosive chemistry. I loved that Jackson works and lives the music industry. When he sang his song to her, I honestly melted.

--Smitten by Reading

Ridley and Jackson explode with passion on the pages of One More Day... this is a pure romance! Ridley and Jackson are a sweet and sensational couple and I can't wait to find out what happens in their future. Malone has a winner with The Alexanders series! Please keep them coming!

--Joyfully Reviewed

The Things I Do for You

"Malone does an exceptional job ... showcasing how two very different people can fall in love."

-- RT Book Reviews

"Nicholas is perfect leading man material."

-- Romance Junkies

Ms. Malone does an excellent job of taking an unconventional way of coming together and developed it into a true love story. The sexual chemistry between the hero and heroine was off the charts

--BookKraze Reviews

The book is full of great characters - my favorite had to be Jackson - he is sweet and sexy yet cautious with his heart since he lost his wife in a car accident. The story is well written with plenty of twists... I can't wait to read the next installment of the Alexander brothers.

--Fairy Tale Ending Reviews

All I Need is You

I traveled through this book feeling a gamut of emotions: hurt, embarrassment, despair, anger, love, joy, and happiness. In the end, I loved the story and would recommend this book to anyone looking for a happily ever after ending jam-packed with lots of steamy love and intrigue

-- Twin Sisters Rockin' Reviews

contents

say you will

part one

"God hath given you one face,
and you make yourself another."
— *Hamlet, William Shakespeare*

SAYING good-bye never seemed to get any easier.

"You won't forget about us, will you?" Travis gazed up at him with blue eyes the same shade as his own.

"I could never forget about you or your mother. I'll be back as soon as I can, buddy. Be good for your mom, okay?"

"Okay. Here's my picture." The little boy thrust a piece of construction paper at him.

Trent looked down at the lumpy figures on the page.

Travis pointed at each one. "That's me. That's you. And that's mom." He had written across the bottom of the picture in crayon "My familee" and added his name under his likeness.

Trent folded it carefully and put it in the inner pocket of his suit jacket. "I'll keep it right here with me. This is too important to pack in a suitcase."

Travis hugged him fiercely, then with typical toddler nonchalance raced back to the television. The sounds of his favorite cartoon resumed a few seconds later.

"He's been working on that drawing for you all week."

Avery stood in the doorway to the kitchen, watching him. Tears shone in her eyes.

"I can hardly believe he's old enough for preschool. It really puts things in perspective."

She wiped her hands on the dish towel tucked into her waistband. "You're all packed?"

"Yeah. I think I got everything this time." His eyes swept the room, looking for anything he might have missed when he packed last night. He couldn't afford to accidentally leave anything behind since he wouldn't be here for a while.

He'd been coming to see them for the past few months, and it was harder and harder to leave every time. Soon all the lies would be over and he'd be able to get back to his life.

Just a little bit longer.

He stood and slung his duffel over his shoulder. The weight of it barely registered. Packing light was a requirement for traveling under the radar. He'd been on the road so much lately that he could pack and unpack in his sleep.

Avery followed him as he walked to the front door. "He misses you so much when you leave. So do I."

Trent pushed her dark hair away from her face. She wouldn't meet his eyes, which was a bad sign. She always did this. Just when she got her life back on course, she'd backtrack and end up in the same place.

"This is the way it has to be for now. It'll all be over soon. Hang in there. I'll be back to see you in a few weeks if I can get away."

Avery bit her lip and looked away. "I didn't think it would be this hard. I'm lonely living here all by myself."

"It's hard on me too. I miss you. You know I love you more

than life." He kissed her on the forehead, the same way he'd done for years.

Her smile never faltered, but as she watched him leave, he could tell she was crying.

Just a few more weeks and this will all be over.

one

MARA SIMMONS WOULD HAVE NEVER DESCRIBED herself as a badass. But to her coworkers at Lawson, Westbrooke & Hyde, she was a vigilante. A fearless crusader. Either that or they all just thought she was too stupid to be afraid.

"I really appreciate this. He keeps asking for these files, and I've been making excuses until you got here." Her coworker, Lanie Roberts, hovered outside the door to her boss's office with a frightened look on her face.

Ethan Westbrooke had everyone in the company terrified of him. The only person he couldn't intimidate was Mara, which was how she'd gotten stuck working for him. Usually he went through executive assistants at an alarming rate.

The woman before Mara had lasted only three days before calling down to HR in tears, asking to be reassigned.

Mara had been with him for a little over a year.

"It's okay, Lanie. I'll take them in to him. I was just going in to bring him his coffee anyway."

"Mara! Where are the contracts Lawson sent up?" Ethan's loud bellow carried through his office door.

Lanie wrung her hands as Mara took the folder the girl had been holding in a death grip. "Okay. I'll just, ah, wait out here."

Mara smothered a smile. Then, after a perfunctory knock on her boss's door, she pushed it open with her hip.

"Here's your coffee and those contracts you've been waiting on." Mara set the folder she carried on the edge of his desk and his coffee to the right of the report he was currently reading.

He barely glanced up, just answered with a muffled grunt. The only thing visible was his perfectly styled dark hair. She held in a sigh. Grunting was better than growling. He was in a decent mood today. That was something.

As soon as she left the office, Lanie appeared at her elbow. "Did you give it to him?"

"I did. Now that he has the contracts, he shouldn't need anything else for a while."

Lanie visibly relaxed. "Thank you so much. I almost cried this morning when you weren't here. You're the only one he likes."

"He doesn't like me. He yells at me too. I just don't listen," Mara replied as she settled into her desk chair.

"Anyway, I was thinking we should do happy hour tonight. Or maybe a movie? I need to get away from Jesse. He's driving me crazy."

Mara chuckled. She'd heard all the ins and outs of the saga of Lanie and Jesse. Those two had enough drama to fuel a reality show. But she couldn't handle that tonight. She had her own drama to deal with.

"I can't. I have a family dinner tonight. Plus I want to stick close to home. Trent's been traveling a lot lately."

Lanie smiled knowingly. "Say no more. I get it. You need a little quality time with your man. Take care of business at home." She winked and walked back to the elevator bank to go back to her floor.

As soon as the elevator doors closed, Mara's practiced smile fell. If only it were a night of hot sex waiting for her. Lately Trent had been so distant and too tired to do much after work. He was also traveling more than ever. Except he was strangely closemouthed about the projects he was working on and what he was doing during the time he was gone.

There was no one thing she could point to that was off, but Mara just knew.

He was lying to her.

"*If you're done gossiping.*" A deep voice interrupted her thoughts.

She was so startled that she jumped and knocked over her own coffee cup. The dark liquid quickly spread across her desk, snaking under her keyboard and soaking the pad of sticky notes next to her phone.

"Damn it." She hopped up, unsurprised to see a dark stain on the front of her pale pink skirt. She inched the material up her legs, holding it away from her body. "This is just great. There's no way this stain is coming out."

When she looked up, Ethan stood as still as a statue, his dark eyes locked on her legs. Then he looked up at her. A muscle in his jaw tensed.

Stunned by the feral look in his eyes, she immediately dropped her skirt. "Mr. Westbrooke. You startled me."

Normally he would have had some cutting remark to make or chastised her for stating the obvious and wasting his billable hours. Instead, he just blinked at her.

Then he said in a deceptively soft voice, "These contracts don't contain any of the changes I requested. Find out why."

He ran his fingers through his hair, sending the dark strands into disarray. With one last piercing look, he retreated back into his office.

———

LATER THAT DAY, Mara raced around her living room, straightening the pillows on the couch and collecting stray items of clothing she'd discarded in her frenzy to get to work that morning. Trent had originally been scheduled to fly in late, but she'd gotten a text right before leaving work that he'd be home early.

By the time she made it back to her bedroom, she had a pair of gym shoes in her arms, the cardigan she'd decided not to wear that morning thrown over her shoulder, and an earring that had been missing for months in her hand.

Suddenly she stopped right in the middle of the room. "Why am I even bothering with all this stuff? I haven't seen him in a week. I seriously doubt he'll care about any of this."

She dropped everything in her arms next to the bed and then went into the bathroom. After yanking out her ponytail, she flipped over and fluffed her hair out, then applied another layer of lip gloss. Just as she finished, she heard the front door open.

Anticipation quickened her steps as she trotted down the hallway. Trent looked up when she entered the living room.

With a squeal, she flung herself into his arms. "I'm so happy to see you!"

He fell back slightly until he hit the wall, accepting her

noisy kisses all over his face. "I'm happy to see you too. I really missed you, baby."

The low rumble of his words spread through her. It made her heart soar to hear him say the same thing she was feeling. She looked at his suit in surprise. Usually he just wore slacks and maybe a tie. Since he was such a casual guy, he probably wouldn't like it if he knew how arousing she found his corporate look.

"I missed you too. And I'm really looking forward to having you home for a while."

"Come with me while I unpack. I just want to look at you."

She followed him into the bedroom. He sat on the edge of the bed, and in that moment, she could see how exhausted he was. It was all over his face, in the tight line of his lips and the pinched skin around his eyes. He looked awful.

"Why don't you take a shower? I can help you unpack."

A smile lifted the edges of his lips. "I think I'll do that. Thanks. You're the best."

He stood and yanked his shirt over his head. She followed him with her eyes, enjoying the flex and play of the muscles in his back as he disappeared into the bathroom.

She turned back to his duffel and unzipped it. Layers of clothes sprang from the bag. With a muffled curse, she forced them back inside and tried to arrange them in some semblance of order. The sight of the jumbled clothes reminded her of the conversation they needed to have. Trent was usually a neat freak.

It was confirmation of what she knew instinctively.

Something wasn't right.

She folded the clothes as the sounds of the shower filtered out of the bathroom behind her. By the time the water turned off, she'd created three neat piles—one for underwear, one for his dress shirts, and another for casual clothes.

"Hey, baby."

Trent stood in the doorway to the bathroom, a towel tucked snugly around his waist. Even as her mouth watered, she had to remind herself of her plans. Dinner first, then they needed to talk.

She was determined to keep her head on straight so they could have a conversation. It wouldn't do to get lost in passion and ignore the lingering tension between them. So Trent and his mouthwatering abs would just have to wait for a few hours.

"Matt and Penny are coming over for dinner. I have to go to the store to pick up a few things. If I'd known you were coming in so early, I would have done it last night."

"That's fine. You. Go. On." He punctuated each word with a mind-drugging kiss.

By the time he was done, Mara was ready to rip his towel off. Especially since his skin was appealingly warm and still slightly damp from his shower.

"I'm going to get some work done while you're gone, then I can give you my undivided attention tonight. Actually, can you bring me my laptop case? I must have left it on the couch."

He pulled her up on her toes to meet his kiss, anchoring her against him in the way that never failed to turn her to mush. He was so handsome with his sun-kissed blond hair and those piercing blue eyes that always made her melt.

By the time he released her, she could barely remember her own name, let alone what he'd asked her to do.

Laptop, then grocery store. I'm supposed to be going out.

"Okay, I'm going. I love you."

She hugged him tighter, suddenly overcome with emotion.

It was easy to assume the worst when he wasn't home, but she just couldn't believe the emotion he showed toward her was feigned. No one had ever treated her the way he did or so openly showed his affection.

There was probably something bad going on with work which would explain why he was suddenly traveling so much.

Guilt tightened her belly. She'd been stewing in her own insecurity this whole time and assigning him false motives when he was likely just trying to keep from losing his job.

Trent had always had weird hang-ups about money. Her brother had given her a sizable loan to buy the town house, and when Trent found out about it, he'd been furious.

Like a lot of men, he seemed to think that if he couldn't financially support her, she wouldn't love him. But Mara didn't need that from him. She'd been supporting herself since she was old enough to work.

Trent pulled her closer and kissed her forehead the way he always did. "Be careful out there. You know I love you more than life."

A smile on her face, she left the room and headed back down the hallway to the living room to grab her handbag.

When she spotted his laptop bag and suit jacket on the chair, she remembered that he'd asked her to bring his stuff. The jacket was one of her favorites on him, a pale gray pinstripe that brought out the intense color of his eyes.

She folded it over her arm carefully. Something bulky poked out of the fabric.

With one hand, she slung the laptop case over her shoulder and then reached into the inner pocket. Her hands met what felt like heavy paper. She pulled it out. It unfolded in her hands, showcasing the bright colors of what was obviously a child's drawing.

But that wasn't what turned her heart to ice. It was the childish scrawl at the bottom, *My familee*, right above a painstakingly written name.

Travis.

Quickly, she pulled her cell phone out of her pocket and took a photo. Her hands shook as she refolded the drawing and tucked it into the inner pocket of the jacket where she'd found it. She dropped the laptop case and coat jacket back on the chair and then grabbed her own handbag. Her mind was in a whirl as she let herself out, locking the door behind her.

Different scenarios ran through her head as she drove through the familiar streets of New Haven. She soothed herself with the sight of the cheerful red awnings of the businesses on Main Street and the graceful arch of the trees that bordered the road.

It wasn't until she pulled into the parking lot of the grocery store that she spoke the words aloud that had been screaming through her brain for the entire drive.

"Trent's middle name is Travis."

———

AS SOON AS he heard Mara drive away, Trent opened his laptop and got to work. Running a company in absentia was one of the hardest things he'd ever had to do. But the knowledge that he wasn't doing it for his own benefit was what bolstered him.

His older brother had borne the brunt of his father's expectations for years. He could take the reins for a short time, at least until his father was back on his feet.

He logged in to Townsend Industries remotely and spent a few minutes catching up on e-mail. His assistant, Gina, usually responded on his behalf to anything that wasn't pressing and sorted the rest of his correspondence into folders.

There was always a pile of e-mail after he'd been visiting Avery. When he was there, he wanted to spend as much time as possible with Travis. As a result, his own work tended to slide. Now that he was helping his father out after a health scare, his work was compounded.

As he read through some of the documents his assistant had forwarded on, he thought of how it must be killing his father to have to step back. James Townsend III had taken over Townsend Industries from his own father twenty years ago, and Trent didn't think he'd missed a day of work since. Having a heart attack was probably the only way to make him miss a day at the office.

After a call to Gina to clarify a few things, he applied his digital signature to several proposals from department heads. There was one in particular that Gina had flagged as urgent. It was a request from the head of HR to expand employee benefits. He glanced at the time. It was already after business hours, but if he called the guy now, he could take care of it before Mara got back home.

Bernie had worked for TI for years and seemed to live and breathe business just like his father did. It was surprising that he'd sent the proposal to Trent at all. Everyone knew he was only acting CEO while his father was on leave.

He dialed Bernie's direct office number. After several rings, he answered.

"Bernie. It's Trent. I'm looking over the proposal you sent now."

After a moment of startled silence, the other man stammered out a greeting. "Yes, sir. I wasn't expecting to get a call back so soon. I was so sorry to hear about your father. How is he doing?"

"He's still recovering," Trent stated succinctly. He definitely didn't want to get into a conversation about his father. "I won't be back in the office for a few weeks, but I'm still working remotely. Tell me about your proposal."

"Well, it's a response to our latest employee satisfaction survey. Exit interviews show that quality-of-life concerns are the number one reason some of our best employees have left. They've taken jobs that are closer to home so they can spend more time with family. If we had a daycare on site, that would be a substantial perk."

Trent stood and massaged his temples. Before he'd left home, he'd had no idea just how sheltered he really was. He'd learned more living on his own than he ever had at his father's side. He'd learned about compassion and that the people they employed were so much more than just cogs in the machinery of their empire.

The people were what made the company run.

He listened as Bernie rattled off numbers and construction estimates. Finally the other man stopped talking long enough for him to get a word in edgewise.

"Do it. If you get started immediately, it'll be done before the summer."

"Really?" Bernie's shock was palpable even across the phone lines.

"Absolutely. I think it sounds great."

"Yes. It is, of course," he stammered. "It's just that I presented this proposal to your father last year and he denied it."

Trent grimaced. "Well, I think we've already established that I am *not* my father."

After several other updates, Bernie finally hung up. Trent composed an e-mail to his assistant with a summary of what they'd decided so that if Bernie needed assistance, she'd know what was authorized.

He was sure that his father wouldn't be pleased when he found out how much the new daycare would cost, and the thought of his imminent displeasure made it all the sweeter. Knowing his father, he wondered how long before he'd hear about it.

The phone rang twenty minutes later, and Trent laughed out loud. Predictable.

"Good evening, Father."

"Why did Bernie just send a request to legal regarding some daycare permits? I already vetoed that."

"And I just approved it."

"Waste of time, money, and resources. That space could have been used—"

The sound of the front door opening galvanized Trent into action. Mara was home and he definitely didn't have time to spend arguing with his father.

"You wanted me to come back. I did what you asked. Don't find fault with every decision I make."

He could almost hear his father's rage simmering from hundreds of miles away.

"It would only take one phone call to topple the little world you've built over there. *One phone call.* How long do you think they'll stick by you then?"

Trent closed his eyes. He would love to deny it or tell his father he was wrong. His friends loved him, but he'd learned over and over again that love could only cover so much.

And money had a way of tainting everything. Even friendship.

Especially friendship.

"I don't know. But I've already proven to you once that I don't respond well to threats. Last time I left home and didn't come back. Try me again and see what happens."

two

LATER THAT EVENING, Mara crushed another clove of garlic and then tipped the mortar to release the fragrant herbs into a mixture of rosemary and thyme she'd already prepared. Then, using a small brush, she painted the mixture over the lamb chops she'd arranged carefully in a baking dish.

Family dinner night was something she looked forward to every week.

It was a tradition that she'd started with her brother after he'd mentioned how much Penny missed her family. They had dinner with their friends the Alexanders regularly, which was how Mara had gotten the idea to do their own family dinner night.

Even if their parents weren't local, there wasn't anything to stop her from hosting a small dinner of her own each week. Plus, it gave her the opportunity to do something she loved more than almost anything else.

Cook.

"Hey, do you need any help?" Trent poked his head around the door to the kitchen.

His blond hair was sticking up on top. He must be having a hard time with whatever he was working on. He always yanked at the top lock of his hair when he was frustrated. Mara thought it was adorable.

"No, I've got it. Finish your work."

"Okay. Thanks. I'll be done in just a few. Then we can talk wedding dates and stuff. Did you ever decide about who you're going to ask to be your maid of honor?"

Her good mood fell slightly. "Nope. I'm going to have to make a decision soon though. If we're serious about doing this within the next year."

"And we are," Trent interrupted with a dark look that thrilled her.

It was an unbelievable comfort to be marrying a man who wasn't running from commitment but instead seemed to embrace it.

"Then I need to make sure that my whole wedding party has the date and is available for it. You have to do the same thing."

He shrugged. "I already know my wedding party. Matt will be my best man. Jackson, Nick, and my older brother James will be groomsmen. Easy."

At her scowl, he wisely retreated back down the hallway to finish his work.

She hummed as she finished basting the lamb chops and placed the heavy dish in the oven. The entire kitchen was filled with the fragrant smell of the rice pilaf simmering on the stove. She lifted the lid and stirred it, noting the consistency.

Trent's casual mention of his brother had her thinking about his family. Trent had both a brother and a sister. It had seemed odd to her that they didn't have more contact at the beginning of their relationship, but over time she'd accepted that Trent simply wasn't that close to his family.

Her relationship with Matt was different than most other siblings. It wasn't often that she went long without talking to her brother. And now that Penny was a part of his life, it was like she'd gained a sister. They were constantly on the phone, talking and laughing and making plans for the weekend.

Trent seemed to only talk to his family on holidays. She wasn't trying to judge, but their relationship seemed so cold.

A staccato knock on the front door pulled her from her thoughts. After checking her pilaf one last time, she put the lid on the pan and ran to open the door.

"You're here!" She hugged Penny and held the door open so that she and Matt could come in.

Matt shrugged out of his coat and handed her one of the long baguette loaves she loved so much. "It was the last one they had. You're lucky I got it."

"I am lucky." She hugged him, perhaps a bit longer than usual, because he immediately pulled back and stared at her with eyes that saw too much.

"Are you okay, sis?"

She pulled the bread tighter against her chest, inhaling the soft, doughy smell. "Of course I am. Just hungry."

They followed her back to the kitchen.

"What can I do to help?" Penny asked. "I'm no gourmand like you, but I can make a mean salad. Just ask your brother." She gave Matt a look that Mara was sure she wasn't meant to see.

"Okay, okay. You two keep the lovey-dovey to a PG level please?" Trent laughed.

"Hey, man, what's going on?" Matt stood and extended a hand.

They clasped hands in the strange and complicated blend of handshake, fist bump, and side-hug that men seemed to do so seamlessly. Penny was greeted with a kiss on the cheek.

"Not much. The usual work crap. What about you? Any interesting cases lately?"

Her brother had been working for Eli Alexander, who owned a security company, for quite a while now and always had entertaining stories. He guarded everyone from entertainers to politicians, even a local chef who'd gotten threats while competing on a national television show.

Mara had begged endlessly for him to introduce her to the handsome chef. Not that she'd do anything, of course, but the man was just dreamy. And his pumpkin risotto recipe had made her a fan for life.

"Not much. I'm probably going to be traveling more, which is kind of a bummer."

"Which is a *total* bummer," Penny interjected. "But we've got our routine down now. We do video chats and text when we can." She turned to Trent. "You travel a lot for work too, right?"

Mara's hand paused on the handle of the pan of rice, desperately interested in Trent's answer. It was one thing to read stuff into their interactions when they were alone, but she was pretty good at deciphering body language in other people's conversations.

Matt leaned over, breaking her concentration. "Hey, sis, give me a knife and I'll start slicing this bread."

Absently, she withdrew one of the knives from the butcher

block, but her attention was on Trent and Penny across the room.

"I have been traveling a lot more lately," Trent was saying. "It's definitely not fun. All the packing and unpacking is what really gets you. And all the time spent in transit. I've spent more time in cars and on planes lately than I have at home."

"What are you working on now? New clients?" Penny leaned forward in interest.

Mara leaned forward too.

"Mara? Mara!"

Startled, Mara pulled back and turned to face her brother. He jumped back and she dropped the knife she'd forgotten she was holding. As it fell, out of sheer instinct she grabbed at it. The pain as it sliced over the soft flesh of her palm was like a lick of fire.

"Ouch!" She yanked her hand back, too late. The knife clattered to the floor at her feet.

Trent and Penny stood at the commotion. Matt put his arms around her shoulders and gently drew her back away from the stove area. Mara still had her hand curled protectively into a fist against her chest.

When she straightened her fingers, the amount of bright red blood on her hand scared her so badly she actually felt light-headed.

"My hand," she said weakly.

Trent took one look at her hand and paled. He barreled past Penny and grabbed her by the arm.

"What did you do? *What the hell did you do?*"

He pulled her against him, and when he did, she could feel that he was trembling. Stunned at his response, Mara just stared at him, the pain in her hand forgotten.

"It was an accident. I didn't mean to..."

"Just hold on. We'll get you to the hospital. It'll be fine. *Just hold on.*" He looked around at the others.

Matt stared at him, obviously as stunned as Mara felt.

"We need to get pressure on it." Penny took over with the comfortable assurance only someone with medical training could have in the midst of crisis.

She grabbed a dish towel as she passed the oven and wrapped it gently around Mara's hand.

"She should go to the hospital. We don't know how deep it is," Trent insisted.

"No! I don't want to sit in a hospital waiting room for an hour so they can tell me that I need to keep it clean and dry. I don't think it's that bad."

Penny gave her a look. "If it looks deep, then I'm going to browbeat you until you go."

"Fair enough."

She slowly opened her hand. Now that the bleeding was under control, it didn't look so scary. Penny must have thought so too, because she no longer looked as worried. She tugged Mara over to the sink and gently used a damp paper towel to clean some of the blood off her hand. Just the soft press of the towel on her palm made her wince, but Mara got her face under control before Penny noticed. Or Trent.

She glanced over at him. He stood back a few feet but watched them intently. When their eyes met, he moved forward and put his arm around her, his eyes searching her face as if he wasn't convinced she was really okay.

"Well, it doesn't appear to be that deep," Penny announced. "It looks like just a surface slice, but I still think you should see someone, okay? Make an appointment with your general physician to make sure this doesn't get infected."

"Yes, *mother*. I will." She grinned at her friend, a feeling of relief coursing through her.

"I just found these bandages in the hall bathroom. There are still some of the extra-large ones left." Matt held out the box to Penny along with some antibacterial spray.

Penny shook the container. "This is probably going to hurt worse than the slice."

Mara turned her head and buried her face in Trent's shirt. "Go ahead," she said, her voice muffled.

As Penny sprayed the cut, Mara gritted her teeth against the burn. The pain was the least she deserved since the whole thing had happened because she was letting her imagination get away from her.

All because she was turning into a typical jealous shrew and thinking her man was cheating just because he wasn't home with her every second of his spare time.

Pathetic.

At her shiver, Trent held her closer. She glanced up at him, and when he noticed her looking, he kissed her forehead. Mara was glad the cut wasn't very deep, not just for her own sake but also because she didn't think Trent was up to a visit to the emergency room. He looked like he was on the verge of falling apart as it was.

Although it scared her to see him so emotional, at the same time she was truly moved by his concern for her. Any doubts she'd ever had about his feelings vanished. No one could fake that kind of reaction.

He loved her.

In that moment, she made a decision to stop worrying so

much and just live in the moment. She had a man who adored her and was actually excited about their wedding.

Yes, he had some weird family issues and spent a little too much time at work, but for once, she wasn't going to overanalyze and nitpick things to death. It was time to let it go and just be thankful.

Her life was as close to perfect as it could get.

———

ONCE PENNY FINISHED COATING Mara's hand with antibacterial spray, she bandaged the cut. Mara made faces and squirmed throughout the entire process, and Trent held her close, allowing her to burrow into his shirt. Part of him wanted to scoop her up and force her into his car so he could take her to the hospital.

But a tiny rational part of his brain agreed that sitting in a waiting room for a scratch on the hand made no sense.

Then she picked up the bloody towel that had fallen to the floor, and he knew he was seconds away from losing it.

He grabbed the box of bandages. "I'll go put these away," he muttered before escaping the kitchen.

He barely made it to the hallway before his breath started coming fast and hard, choking him. Images of Mara, bloody and pale, swam before his eyes. The box of bandages fell from his fingers and hit the floor as he leaned against the wall.

Nothing could happen to her.

Not again.

Slowly, the sounds of laughter and conversation infiltrated his jumbled thoughts. His breathing slowed down and his memories, both past and present, converged. Instead of white tile beneath his feet, it was the tan carpeting that Mara had decided was most practical. The wall next to his cheek was a soft buttercream instead of blue.

He was at home with his friends.

Mara was fine. He would take care of her the way he'd been doing for years. And nothing would take her away from him.

As his heart rate settled, he leaned down to pick up the box of bandages that he'd dropped. When he straightened, Matt stood in front of him watching him.

"You okay, man?"

Trent nodded, swallowing hard with a throat that felt like it had been coated with sandpaper. He held up the bandages. "I just dropped these."

"Yeah, I see that." Matt continued watching him as he walked down the hall, ducking into the bathroom to put the box away.

While he was there, he splashed his face at the sink, allowing the cool water to rinse away the sheen of sweat that made his skin feel clammy to the touch. As he dried his face with a hand towel, he looked up, his eyes meeting his own reflection.

Blond hair sticking up in the middle. Blue eyes. Pale skin.

The face that stared back at him could have been a mirror image of how he'd looked years ago on the day his world had stopped spinning. Except everything was different now and he couldn't allow any of the ugliness of his *before* to taint his *now*.

"She's fine. And she's going to stay that way," he stated aloud.

He would make sure of it.

OVER THE NEXT FEW WEEKS, Trent was moody, distracted, and always too tired for sex. Although she'd initially thought he was hiding job troubles, his behavior over the past few weeks told her what was really going on.

There was only one condition that produced these symptoms in a healthy, twenty-something male.

Another woman.

Tears welled in her eyes, and she hastily wiped them away with the back of her hand. It was devastating to even think of Trent leaving her to be with someone else, but there was no other explanation.

And since he'd left a few days ago on "business" with another pitiful explanation, it was time to face a harsh reality. There was something going on.

There had to be.

Obviously he wasn't going to be honest about it. And she had to know. Had to. It pained her to admit it, but she couldn't walk away without ironclad proof of his wrongdoing. The part of her that had loved him since college wouldn't allow it.

It was time to get some outside help.

She parked in front of her friend Ridley's sprawling white colonial home. There was already a bunch of cars out front, so she must be one of the last to arrive. Girls' night out was always the first Friday of the month. Mara's usual circle of troublemakers included her brother's girlfriend, Penny, and the Alexander twins, Ridley and Raina.

Despite being aware of the standing date, the men in their lives always found some way to invite themselves along or otherwise sabotage their attempts to go out. Although it was funny to watch her friends from college and her brother acting so jealous over the women in their lives, their co-opting of Girl's Night usually bugged her.

But not tonight.

Tonight she was thrilled to see all the guys' vehicles in front of the house because it meant that Eli was probably there. That was far preferable to having to call him and explain her problem over the phone.

This was already guaranteed to be humiliating enough.

Especially since she didn't want the rest of her friends to know about her problems with Trent. He was their friend too. It wasn't fair to put them in the middle, especially when she wasn't really sure what was going on.

As she walked up the steps, the front door opened. Ridley stood in the entryway, one hand on her rounded belly.

"Mara! I'm so glad you're here." Ridley grabbed her by the arm and pulled her over the threshold.

Several children raced by, followed by the sounds of shrieking. Something crashed in the distance. Her friend didn't even blink. Mara followed as Ridley tugged her toward the kitchen.

"The guys were supposed to take the kids out so we could have a quiet night in, but then Jada got sick, and Nick didn't want to take her too far. So now everyone somehow ended up here. Katie came over to help with the kids and brought Hunter and Matthew. Then Laura's husband, Pete, brought Annabelle and Isabelle."

By this time, they'd reached the kitchen, which was just as loud as the entryway. Nick stood in the corner, bouncing his daughter Jada in his arms. She wasn't impressed by his efforts if her screams were any indication.

Ridley dropped onto one of the kitchen stools with a heavy sigh. "It's chaos in here, and I'm too tired to keep up with it all.

Hunter asked me to find his mom, and I couldn't even search the first floor without getting tired."

Mara felt a tug on the edge of her sleeve. When she turned, she recognized one of the neighborhood kids. Brown skinned and curly haired, he looked a lot like his mother.

Ridley held out her hand. "This is Katie's youngest boy, Hunter."

"Pleased to meet you, Hunter." She held out her hand, very formal, and managed to keep a straight face as he shook it solemnly.

"Can you help me find my mom?" he asked.

Ridley sighed. "Katie was just here a few minutes ago. Would you mind looking for her?"

"Of course. It's no problem. You stay here and catch your breath. Hunter and I will go on an adventure."

She offered Hunter her hand. After a moment, he took it, glancing up at her with big, trusting eyes.

They explored the lower level, peeking into the living room and the massive home gym. When she glanced out in the backyard, she saw several children running around and recognized Bennett, the oldest of the Alexander brothers, talking to a group of people she didn't know.

That explained why most of the rooms were empty. Everyone was outside enjoying the spring weather.

When they got upstairs, they came upon several young boys in one of the bedrooms. Hunter suddenly screeched, "There's my brother!" and raced forward.

"Do you want to stay here and play while I look for your mom?"

Hunter nodded eagerly, his attention already on the other children. Jackson's oldest son, Chris, offered him another toy.

"It's okay. I can watch the *little* kids. My dad said that I can be in charge."

Mara grinned back. "Excellent. I will leave them in your capable hands then, Mr. Alexander."

Chris's chest puffed out as he turned back to the other kids. "Okay, let's play with the robots first. And everyone has to *share*."

Mara walked back out into the hallway and then hesitantly pushed open the door to the master bedroom. It was dark, the curtains drawn, so the entire room was in shadow.

Just as she was about to leave, she heard a soft sniffle. She peered around the bed. Down on the floor next to the window, Katie sat with her head on her knees.

Mara crouched down low. "Katie? Are you okay?"

Her head lifted and their eyes met. The other's woman's eyes were bloodshot and swollen. She quickly wiped her face with the back of her hand.

"Sorry. I just needed a minute away from all the noise."

"I get that. It is pretty crazy down there. Hunter was looking for you."

"Is he okay?"

"He's fine. The other boys are showing him their robot toys. I think he forgot I existed as soon as he saw that. Typical men, huh?"

Katie laughed softly. "Yeah, some things never change, I guess."

"Any reason you're up here hiding out? I mean, I know why I'm hiding out."

"Are you? Hiding, I mean?" Katie peered at her curiously.

Normally she wasn't given to dumping her problems on strangers, but she recognized a woman on the edge. Sometimes when you were at the end of your rope, you just needed someone who was open to listening and sharing. Even if they weren't a close friend, just being there was enough.

"Well, yeah. I have some hard decisions to make today. And I'm probably going to hurt some of my friends and family when I make them."

Katie was nodding along. "Me too. Actually, I already made my decision." She looked away. Her shoulders shook with an involuntary shiver. "I'm officially divorced as of today. My husband doesn't even care. He didn't fight for us. What's worse, he didn't even fight for our kids."

"I'm sorry." Mara moved closer so her head could rest back against the wall.

"I'm not crying over him. I'm crying that my kids have a father who couldn't care less about leaving them behind. And also that I have no way to support them. Don stopped paying child support and I have no idea how I'm going to pay the mortgage."

"That is so wrong. He can't do that. Have you told Jackson? Maybe he knows someone who can help."

"I'll be okay. I can't tell Jackson and Ridley because they'll try to pay it for me. I can't have people giving me charity. I'll figure something out." Katie glanced over at her. "What about you? What's your story?"

Mara leaned back against the wall. "I think my fiancé is cheating on me?"

"Do you guys have kids?"

"No. Not yet."

"Well, figure it out now. Don't end up like me. Make note of everything so that the next time it happens, no one can say you're just being hysterical or imagining things."

"It's nothing. Just a hunch more than anything. And the fact that he's suddenly traveling a lot more."

Katie sat up, the fervor in her voice increasing with every word she spoke. "Even if it's just a hunch, follow it. If he's flying somewhere, get his flight number. Get the number to the hotel where he's supposed to be staying. Use seduction to scramble his brain and then ask him questions. Do everything you can to figure this out, because if it's not going to last, it's better to know that now than after two kids."

three

TRENT PUSHED OPEN the double doors leading to the pediatric wing of the hospital. After a few days visiting Avery and Travis, he'd left for the airport, only to get a message from Avery that Travis didn't feel well.

When he'd first read the message, he'd assumed Avery was just being overprotective. The stress of worrying about when James would come back had made her moody and needier than usual.

Then she'd texted again to say they were at the hospital.

He'd come straight there from the airport, thankful he'd been running behind and hadn't taken off yet.

There was truly no reason for his heart to be beating so fast or for his pulse rate to feel like it was about to explode. From experience, he knew that it was probably just Travis's asthma and that the little boy would be fine.

But experience didn't keep his heart out of his throat.

The nurse behind the desk looked up when he stopped and leaned his arms on the counter. "I'm here for Travis Townsend."

Her brow furrowed. "Name please?"

"Trent Townsend. I'm his uncle."

At that she perked up. "Of course. His mother told us to expect you. Follow me." She rounded the counter and led him down the hall, her shoes squeaking slightly on the linoleum floor. "Your family has been so generous, Mr. Townsend. The new asthma research study funded by the Townsend grant has made such a difference already. My granddaughter has asthma."

Trent nodded along, but everything she was saying faded away as soon as they crossed the threshold into one of the patient rooms. Travis turned and Trent let out the breath he didn't even know he'd been holding.

"Uncle Trent! You came back!" Travis raised one of his hands, but it didn't get far off the bed before he let it drop.

Trent sat gently on the side of the bed and kissed the top of his nephew's blond head. "Of course I came back." He glanced over at Avery. "Is he okay?"

She came to stand on the other side of Travis's bed. "The doctor just left. Travis was having trouble breathing and making these strange wheezing sounds. The inhaler only helped a little, so I brought him in. They want to do some tests."

Trent turned around at the sharp tug on his shirtsleeve. Travis watched him with his big blue eyes. "Is my daddy coming home now?"

Trent swallowed against another tide of anger at his brother. His negligent, party-loving, irresponsible brother. "I'm still trying to find him, buddy. But I'm going to do everything I can, okay? Right now I want you to just rest for a bit."

"Okay." Travis rubbed his face with one chubby hand and

then clutched the stuffed elephant he took with him everywhere.

Trent got up, motioning with his head for Avery to follow. After one last kiss to her son's head, she came to stand next to him, facing the doorway.

She sniffled and then delicately wiped beneath her eyes. "About what you said... I guess that means he isn't coming back then?"

In that moment Trent would have given anything to be able to lie to her. Because having to tell one of his best friends that the man she'd loved forever had no intention of being there for her sucked in a major way.

When she finally smiled, he kissed her on the forehead and released her.

"I'm so sorry to keep pulling you away from home. How does your fiancée feel about all this? And why haven't you brought her to meet me yet? It's not like you to be so secretive."

Trent shook his head. "I'm not being secretive."

"Yes, you are," she insisted. "You've always been so strange about girls. Remember when you liked that foreign exchange student during freshman year of high school? You were so funny. Every time she talked to you, you'd turn beet red and act like you couldn't understand what she was saying. Even though I was friends with her, you never asked for an introduction."

Trent laughed. "I don't even know who you're talking about."

Avery smirked. "Sure you don't. Well, I remember perfectly. Her name was Genevieve, and she wore sweaters so tight you could practically see her rib cage. And you blushed whenever she talked to you. If you'd wanted to impress her you could have easily. Your French was better than mine even back then. But you never did."

For a moment she looked pensive, then her gaze came back to rest on Travis. "It's amazing how much has changed since then. But you're still the best friend I've ever had."

She hugged him, and he tried to pretend he didn't feel her shoulders shaking as she cried quietly.

"I am so sorry."

Sorry that his brother was an ass. Sorry that she had to sit in this hospital and watch her baby struggling to breathe. There were so many things that he'd fix for her if he could, but just like always, he was forced to watch it all unfold. Everything out of his hands.

He felt almost as helpless as he'd felt as a freshman struggling to find the words to tell Genevieve Marchant that she was pretty.

"I'm so sorry. I swear I would kick his ass for you if I only knew where he was."

"It's okay. None of this is your fault. And I feel so bad every time I have to call you. Every time I have to take you away from your life to help me out. I should be able to deal on my own."

Trent squeezed her arms gently. "I don't want you to do that. I love you and Travis, and you know I'd do anything for you. You shouldn't have to do all this stuff alone. Don't worry about things for me. I'll deal."

"Why don't you just bring her with you? I would love to meet her."

"I'm planning to bring her home soon," Trent hedged.

Suddenly her eyes narrowed and her fingers tightened around his forearms. Painfully. "Trent Townsend. What are you not telling me?"

He didn't meet her eyes. Ever since they were children, Avery'd had the uncanny ability to suss out when he was lying about something. She'd corner him and badger the truth out of him if necessary.

"It's nothing. I just haven't introduced her to the family yet."

"What do you mean she hasn't met the family? I've been hearing about this girl for years. You're getting married." She stared at him, her gaze penetrating him until he felt like he was being held under a laser beam.

"She doesn't know about the money," he admitted finally.

Avery's mouth fell open. "Um... okay? What the hell does that mean?"

He grabbed his hair with both hands, tugging on the strands as if pulling his hair out would lessen the sudden pressure behind his forehead.

"You know about what happened with my father after high school, right?"

She shrugged. "Yeah, James told me about it. Your father told you that there was no way you could make it in the world without your family's influence. You walked away and didn't come back."

He nodded along at her summary. "Basically. However, the most important part of that story is that when I left, I created a new life for myself far away from Manhattan. I could have gone to school any number of places, but if I'd chosen any of the Ivy Leagues, there would have undoubtedly been someone who connected the Townsend name with our family. I would have never been able to escape it."

"That's why you chose Virginia?"

"Yes. I wanted someplace small with access to the water so

I could surf in the summer. I was checking out college campuses and just stumbled across the perfect fit one day."

"That still doesn't explain why you haven't brought Mara home yet."

"Avery, when I'm in Virginia, my life is completely different than it is here. I live in a two-bedroom town house. If we want to take a vacation, we can't just go. She has to ask for permission from her boss."

Her eyes had gotten bigger and bigger with every word. "Well, okay. I understand that you think this would be overwhelming for her."

He shook his head. She still wasn't getting it. "We have a mortgage that we pay every month. If Mara lost her job, she'd worry over how to pay it."

Then he spoke the words that he knew would drive the point home. "She drives a Honda, Avery. Your last spa weekend cost more than her car. It's an entirely different world. The people there don't know how much money I have. Apparently, they like me for no reason at all."

Avery blinked. It appeared that for the first time since they were children, she was speechless.

"James said you'd gone rustic, but I didn't really know what he meant." She peered at him curiously. "And you're happy?"

He thought back to his last argument with Mara. The way they'd been over the past few weeks. He'd been keeping this from her for so long, hurting her with lies of omission. The past few years had been some of the best of his life and had literally made him into a man.

He'd had valid reasons for starting over, and keeping his life in New York a secret had been a necessity to that.

He wouldn't give up the years of anonymity and peace he'd

gained for anything. But Mara was his soul mate, and it was time for him to show her his beginnings. Things would finally come full circle, and the life he'd run away from would allow him to provide her with every luxury.

He could finally treat her the way she deserved.

"Happier than I've ever been," he replied with total honesty.

———

BY THE TIME Mara came back downstairs, everyone else had arrived.

"Mara, there you are. Kaylee just got here, so that's everyone," Ridley announced.

Mara looked around, finally noticing Kay across the room. Kaylee Wilhelm was a talented local pop singer Ridley's husband, Jackson, had signed to a music deal the prior year. Mara had always liked her, even though their personalities were like night and day.

Kay was shy and sweet and easily flustered, which strangely enough made her the perfect partner for the gruff Eli Alexander.

Ridley struggled to her feet, one hand on her distended belly. Before she could stand completely, Kay was there at her elbow. "Sit down. You're supposed to be staying off your feet."

Ridley accepted the gentle scolding with a smile. "How are you? It feels like I haven't seen you in a while."

They all moved over so Kay could sit down. "It's been hectic. I had a gig in Vegas, and now your husband is keeping me in the studio. He's determined for us to finish our duets album before the baby is born."

Ridley let out a little sigh. "I'm so happy he's singing again."

"I think the world is happy he's singing again," Kay agreed.

Mara tried to smile appropriately as the conversation turned to all the baby preparation Ridley was doing. Normally she'd have been all over a conversation about decorating a nursery, but this time she had her mind on other things.

Such as the possibility of her future husband being a cheating scum bucket.

"Did Eli come with you?" she asked Kay as casually as she could manage.

Kay stopped talking mid-sentence. "Uh, yeah. He's over there somewhere." She gestured toward where Ridley's husband, Jackson, stood talking to his parents. "Were you looking to torture him some more?"

Mara winced. When Kay and Eli were getting together, she'd had the bright idea of making Eli jealous by hooking Kay up on a blind date. The date itself had been a disaster and the follow-up date had been even worse since Eli's truck had literally exploded before it was over.

"I take responsibility for torturing him with thoughts of you doing the horizontal mambo with another guy, but I had nothing to do with the crazy stalker who blew up his truck."

Kay grinned. "I'm sure he knows that. Logically."

Mara excused herself and stopped off in the kitchen to get another soda. Just as she was about to take a sip, Eli stepped into the kitchen. She reached back into the refrigerator and pulled out a beer.

He took it slowly, as if afraid it would detonate in his hands. "This is for me?"

Mara ignored his look of shock. "Of course. You look thirsty."

He popped the cap and took a long pull. "Thanks. This is exactly what I needed."

"Long day?"

"No longer than any other." He didn't elaborate.

Mara figured she'd have to draw him out. Eli wasn't much of a conversationalist even when he was trying.

"It must be so hard, doing all that secretive investigative stuff and not being able to talk about it with anyone. Or maybe you talk about it with the other guys you work with, like Tank and Matt. Is that how you guys do it? Talk it over together, or do you ever do stuff that you don't share with the team?"

Eli clamped his lips together. He carried a usually stern expression most of the time, so she wasn't sure what to make of it. It almost looked like he was... laughing?

"No offense, Mara, but you have no future in espionage. Now what is it that you want to investigate without your brother finding out?"

Busted.

Mara dropped down on the kitchen stool next to him. "It's Trent."

Eli didn't move or say anything in reaction, but she could almost feel the air around them go still. "You want Trent investigated?"

"Yes," she whispered, feeling like a complete traitor.

Images flew through her mind. Trent had been a part of her life since college. Pretty much every major memory of her adult life, he was there. Matt considered him one of his best friends.

What if she was wrong? She couldn't chance damaging their friendship without proof.

"I think something's going on with him. He's been on business trips every few weeks, and he never used to travel this much. Also, whenever I ask about what he did while he was gone, he's so shifty. I know something isn't right."

Eli didn't try to convince her that she was wrong or just imagining things. Mara wasn't sure if she found that comforting or not.

"How far do you want me to go with this? There's a chance that he's not actually doing anything shady while on these trips. But if I start digging, I might find other stuff you didn't know about. Should I just look into his travel over the past few weeks or dig into his entire life?"

Mara looked over her shoulder. The girls were all gathered around Ridley. Penny had a hand on her friend's extended belly. Suddenly they all burst into laughter. Raina adjusted her daughter on her shoulder, holding her tight to her chest like the precious gift that she was.

That's what I want, Mara thought. *I want to raise my babies, surrounded by friends and family. But only with a man I trust completely.*

"Mara?"

She turned back to Eli, who watched her with narrowed eyes. "Go all the way."

He nodded once. "I'll have a report for you in a few days."

"So quickly?" It was stupid, but the thought that she'd know one way or the other so soon was terrifying.

Maybe it made her a coward, but she'd like a little longer to wallow in the bliss of her ignorance.

Eli stood and patted her shoulder. "If he's clean, it'll be even quicker. The dirty ones always take a little longer."

———

TRENT HAD it on good authority that he was one lucky bastard. Of course, this wasn't news to him but it was never more apparent than when coming home after a trip.

He'd stayed an extra day to make sure Travis was doing better and then caught the first available flight home. The experience had only reminded him of why he shouldn't have used his father's private jet in the first place.

After flying private again for the first time in years, it was extremely difficult to go back to flying commercial. He was exhausted and needed a drink. Something stronger than the cheap spirits he'd been served on board.

"How was your flight?" Mara stood in the hallway leaning against the wall, her hand on a curvy hip in a seductive pose. "Did you make a lot of deals?"

His brain ground to an immediate halt, all thoughts of his father and the hassles of flying obliterated by the sight of his sexy-as-hell future wife wearing a sheer nightgown the color of peaches. In fact, it took him more than a few minutes for the appropriate area of his brain to translate the meaning of what she said at all.

Then the words brought him back to reality with a crashing halt.

Deals.

The fake business trip she thought he'd been on.

Right.

"Everything went smoothly. I'll probably get a promotion soon. Do you remember I told you about that?"

She tilted her head slightly and twirled a finger around one of the thick, shiny brown curls tumbling over her shoulder. "I think I vaguely remember something like that."

Her shoulder dipped and the strap of her gown slid down her arm until her entire shoulder was bare.

Trent gulped. "I might have to be taking more trips to New York. Does that sound familiar?"

She sashayed forward, her gown slipping down even more until one of her plump breasts was in danger of popping out of the satin material. Her index finger wedged underneath his tie, tugging at the knot. After she loosened it enough to slip it over his head, her hands dropped to his belt buckle.

"I remember. At least then maybe you wouldn't have to travel so much. Especially not during storm season. I was so worried you'd get stuck in Detroit."

Her hands made quick work of his belt, and she was stroking him in such a way that he could barely remember his own name. "Storms. What storms?"

Her hands stilled. "There have been crazy storms throughout most of Michigan for the past few days. There was even a period of time when the airport grounded all planes. Which you would know if you'd actually been there."

Most of his blood still wasn't in his brain, but Trent had enough of his wits left to recognize the signs. And these signs were neon orange with DANGER AHEAD printed all over them.

"Mara, wait. Let me explain."

All he got before she turned on her heel and stomped down the hallway was a brief glimpse of the stricken look on her face. The bedroom door slammed.

"Fuck!" He kicked his duffel bag.

four

TRENT THREW his stuff down on the fluffy comforter of the hotel bed. He'd spent the past hour trying to convince Mara to talk to him and had finally given up when he heard the water start in her bathroom. She loved a good long soak in the tub. It could be hours before she came out.

So he'd grabbed his things and left.

He'd contemplated going to Jackson or Nick's house, but they'd want to talk and he wasn't in the mood. He'd eventually ended up at a hotel. His thoughts raced back over the events of the night, trying to figure out where everything had gone so wrong.

He'd give Mara the night to cool off, and then he'd come back and explain everything. Once she understood, not only about his background but also about his need to succeed on his own, she would understand. It would be an incredible weight off his shoulders for her to know the truth.

Then he could finally start taking care of her the way he'd wanted to for years.

He hadn't even had a chance to unpack, he thought

bitterly. He pulled out his cell phone and dialed his brother's number. James answered on the first ring.

"Miss me yet, brother?"

The smug attitude in James's voice grated on Trent's already shredded nerves. "I'm waiting for you to come to your senses and get back here. You have a family to think about."

"Dad can kiss my ass," James drawled.

"Not him. Your family. Avery and your son. Travis needs you. He deserves to have a father around."

"From what I hear, you're taking care of that for me too."

"I can't be there all the time. I have my own life. Or did that not occur to you? That my own fiancée might not appreciate me leaving her behind to clean up your messes."

It was ridiculous that he'd actually thought that appealing to his brother's sense of morality would work. He'd hoped that if James knew that helping him out was ruining Trent's life, he'd come back.

Unfortunately it seemed his older brother was tired of even attempting to play nice.

"Let's face it, bro, this is your role, not mine. I was never cut out to be the heir. If fate had any sense of justice at all, you'd have been born first." There was a bunch of noise in the background, and James yelled something that Trent couldn't make out.

"Where are you?"

"South Beach. If you get tired of dancing to our father's tune, you should join me. Until then, I'll be having fun for once."

"Don't hang up on me. James!" Trent cursed as the line went dead.

He put his phone in his pocket before he could follow his

urge to throw it across the room. Or to call Mara, which was what he really wanted to do.

It sucked to be here in this damn hotel room when she was only a few miles away, her naked, tempting body covered in suds. The only thing keeping them apart was one little conversation.

Once she knew why he'd kept his family a secret, she'd understand. She'd forgive him. Then things could go back to the way they'd always been.

Perfect.

His phone buzzed in his pocket. When he drew it out and saw the name on the display, his fingers tightened around the case. His father's voice was the last thing Trent felt like hearing right now.

"This really isn't a good time," he said in lieu of a greeting. His cold reception didn't seem to register with his father at all.

"It's time for you to come home."

"We've had this discussion. I'm helping out while James is gone but that's it. I'm going to talk to James again. Try to get him to see reason."

"Your brother is an idiot. We don't have time for this now. The board is circling, and there are rumors that they're trying to oust me."

It shouldn't have hurt. But the sudden realization of why his father was so determined to get him home cut him to the core. His father wasn't trying to get him to come back out of sentimentality or a desire to bring their family together. He was trying to keep a figurehead in place that he could control. He was trying to keep a Townsend at the head of Townsend Industries.

He was afraid.

"I'll keep acting as interim CEO until either James comes back or your doctors say you're okay to work again. But that's it."

"It's time for you to stop messing around. Just bring the girl with you if that's what the problem is."

His father's casual mention of Mara made his skin crawl. He didn't want Mara anywhere near the moral cesspool of Townsend Industries.

"You've been spying on me again, I see."

There was no response.

"I can't come home yet. I need more time." He hung up and lay back on the comforter.

But Trent had a feeling his time had run out.

———

MARA SLAMMED the drawer of her desk. After a sleepless night, she'd awoken to find that Trent had sent her a text message that he would be back today so they could talk. No phone call, no voice mail. Nothing personal at all. Just a text, as if she was an afterthought.

He couldn't even put in the effort to fight with her properly?

"Calls keep diverting to my phone!" Ethan's voice roared from behind his closed office door.

Mara bit the inside of her cheek to repress a growl. Everyone had given her a wide berth today, for which she was grateful. Everyone except the one person she needed to leave her alone the most. She wasn't in the mood to placate her boss today of all days.

Ethan had definitely picked up on her mood though

because he wasn't making as many ridiculous demands as usual. He was still talking to her however, which meant that her scowl wasn't as effective as she'd hoped it would be.

The door in front of her desk opened. Ethan poked his head out. "Did you hear what I said?"

"I'm pretty sure the whole building heard you," she replied as politely as possible.

Guilt kept her from snapping back. She'd been so disorganized today that several calls she normally would have answered had slipped through.

"I was away from my desk this morning checking on something. I meant to divert them to Ada's phone," she said, referring to his partner's administrative assistant who usually covered for her when she couldn't be at her desk.

"Your job is to answer the phones so I don't have to talk to anyone!" His voice echoed up and down the hallway.

"I'm doing the best I can here." She could hear the defeat in her own voice, and normally it would have mortified her.

The only reason she'd lasted as long as she had swimming with a shark like Ethan Westbrooke was by showing no fear. If he thought for even a moment that she couldn't handle the pressure, he'd probably fire her with no remorse. And getting fired and not having a way to pay her mortgage would just be the perfect capstone to her craptacular month.

To her horror, tears sprang to her eyes.

She quickly got busy looking at something on her desk, hoping that Ethan hadn't seen. He didn't say anything at first, but she could feel him still standing there.

Finally he simply said, "Noted." Then he walked back into his office.

Mara sniffled and decided to do some filing. That was at least one thing that she could do without screwing up.

Ethan opened the door of his office and strode out. "I asked for the contract changes days ago! Where are they?"

"They haven't come back yet."

He crossed his arms. "Why not?"

"I don't know."

Ethan reared back as if she'd slapped him. "You don't know?"

Finally she couldn't take it anymore. "No, I don't know. Perhaps if you'd actually allow your underlings to question you without biting their heads off, they could do their jobs properly. Instead, they're all terrified of you, so they take ages to do every single thing for fear that they'll be fired."

"That's it." Ethan rounded the desk and pulled her up by the arm.

He held her elbow only in a light grip, so he wasn't hurting her at all, but she was so stunned that she didn't even protest. She just allowed him to herd her into the inner sanctum of his office.

It wasn't until the heavy door clicked shut with an ominous sound behind her that she spoke up.

"What the hell is going on?"

"That's what I was going to ask you. You've always challenged me, but you've never been rude. What's happened?"

"I apologize. You're right. Don't I get to have a bad day?"

"No, you don't get to have a bad day. I need you too much for that."

"You don't need anybody."

Ethan sent her a dark look. He paced across the room, then stopped and stood with his hands clenched at his side.

"Unfortunately, I do. I'm a miserable, misanthropic bastard and apparently you are the only one who makes me feel human."

He didn't sound even remotely happy about it. But the way he was looking at her was warm and completely at odds with the harsh statement. If Mara was hard pressed to put a word to it, she would have to say affectionate.

Ethan Westbrooke was looking at her with... affection.

What in the world was she supposed to do with that?

"I'm truly sorry about today. I'll do better. Things are just... I'm having some personal issues right now. But I promise there won't be a repeat of what happened today."

"Personal issues." Ethan stood staring at a spot on the floor. He finally raised his eyes to hers. "Boyfriend trouble?"

"With all due respect, sir, that's none of your business."

"You're right, it isn't." He stalked behind his desk and stood at the window, gazing out over the city skyline.

Norfolk wasn't a major city like New York or LA, but it was a bustling port of commerce. Mara had always liked the view from Ethan's office. When she'd first been transferred to this floor, she'd used every opportunity she could to take a peek out of that window.

"It sounds like he doesn't know what to do with a beautiful woman."

"You think you'd do so much better, huh?

His smile was pained. "No, I don't. I would hurt you far worse. But that doesn't make it okay."

He pulled a card from his inner pocket and then scribbled something on the back. He held it out to her. Obviously he wasn't going to walk over and give it to her but expected her to come take it.

Mara sighed. Finally she rose and walked over to his desk. "What is this?"

He pressed the card into her hand. "I want you to take this. If you ever need me, call."

"I already know your number. I answer your phone line, remember?"

"My cell number is on the back."

That got her attention. Although Ethan was a bone fide workaholic, he was notoriously private. When she'd worked for his partner, Daniel Lawson, she'd called Daniel on his cell phone all the time with work-related matters. She'd come to Ethan expecting him to be the same way.

It had been a shock to find out that he guarded his time away from the office ruthlessly and never gave out his personal information.

And now she had his cell phone number.

"Thank you for trying to help. It's really very kind of you."

"I'm not doing this out of the goodness of my heart." Ethan smirked, but there was a certain sadness behind the expression. "There is no goodness in my heart. I'm doing this because for whatever reason, you make me feel things. I am simply using you for my own ends."

Despite the harsh words, Mara smiled back at him. "Thanks for the warning. At least you're honest."

When she got back to her desk, the message light was blinking on her phone.

Eli's voice grumbled over the line. "Mara. I have the report for you. I'm sorry it took a little longer. But then, I warned you."

She put the phone down and turned to her computer screen. Ethan stood watching from the door to his office. She wasn't sure what to make of his strange confessions or even of

Eli's cryptic message. All she knew was there was a mound of work waiting in her in-box and that it wasn't going to complete itself.

That, at least, she knew she could handle.

"Bad news?" Ethan asked.

Her fingers paused over her keyboard. It was useless to pretend she was fine when they both knew otherwise. But pretending was preferable to breaking down and crying like a toddler. Which was what she really wanted to do.

"I'll ask about those contract changes you requested. You'll have it before the end of the day. I'll make sure of it."

He nodded once, then he was gone.

———

THE REST of the afternoon was better. Mara diverted her calls to Ada, who'd assured her that she didn't mind, so that she could get a handle on things. Nothing made her feel better than a clear in-box, so for the rest of the day she blocked out everything and focused on completing her work.

Ethan didn't come out of his office except to greet his appointments. She breathed a sigh of relief when one of the attorneys from another floor entered his office and closed the door. As long as he was occupied, she didn't have to think about their strange conversation or how he'd looked at her.

As if her life wasn't screwed up enough lately.

What was she going to do? It was the major question that she'd been trying to avoid all day.

Her entire life was set to go in one direction. Marry Trent and live happily ever after. For once in her life, she'd actually done something to make her mother happy. She'd found a man who was steady and dependable and loved her.

Or so she'd thought.

Just thinking about the prior night made her alternately angry and sad. She hadn't felt like this in a long time. Hopeless and despondent and shattered.

The last time she'd had her entire world crushed had been at her quinceañera party when she'd learned that her mother had only married her father because of his money. When she'd been told that her mother was proud of her because her beauty was sure to take her far in life.

Which by her mother's definition meant a rich husband with a big house.

She glanced at the time in the top corner of her computer screen. It was almost time to leave, and she doubted that she'd accomplish anything of use at this point. After gathering her things, she stopped at Ada's desk to thank her for her help and then rode the elevator down to the lobby.

To her surprise, when the doors opened, the first thing she saw was her brother.

"Matt? What are you doing here?"

He stood and dropped the magazine he'd been reading back on the waiting room table. She glanced around, noticing that several of the women in the lobby were eyeing him.

It always amused her to see the way women responded to her brother. Of course, she thought he was about as perfect as a guy could be so she didn't blame them, but it was still funny to imagine her brother as some kind of heartthrob.

Typical Matt, he seemed oblivious to the looks and stares directed at him anyway. When one of the women placed herself directly in front of him, he moved around her with a barely polite nod and headed straight for Mara. He didn't look happy.

Her mind immediately went to Trent. Had something happened to him? Her heart sped up.

"What's happened? Is Trent okay?"

Matt's scowl only deepened, which did nothing to reassure her. He was typically serious, but Mara had long gotten used to that. It had been worse since his time overseas, but he'd been getting better in the past year.

Or at least, she'd thought he had been getting better. He seemed to have lightened up a lot and found his sense of humor since dating Penny.

"Trent is fine as far as I know. But there's something you should know."

He glanced behind him. No one stood close enough to overhear, but that didn't seem to make him feel any better. He put an arm around her shoulders and led her outside.

"Come on. I'll drive you to my place."

Mara clutched her things closer to her chest when he tried to take her bag. "But I need to go home. Trent left last night and never came back. We had a fight," she admitted.

She hated to put her brother between her and Trent. It wasn't fair. They'd been friends far longer than she and Trent had been a couple, and he didn't deserve to be put in the middle.

But surprisingly Matt didn't seem shocked at her words at all. If anything, his features only grew grimmer.

Mara had the sudden feeling that she wouldn't be going home for a while.

"We need to talk, sis."

five

TRENT WOKE to complete and utter darkness. He blinked, disoriented, trying to figure out what had woken him up. He'd come home a little after six o'clock, surprised to find that Mara wasn't home from work yet.

He'd sent her a message telling her that he'd meet her here after work. She hadn't responded, but he'd assumed it was because she was still pissed.

As the hours passed, he'd started to get worried, so he'd called her cell phone and several of their friends. Finally she'd responded and told him that she was spending the night at her brother's house. She'd sent her message loud and clear. She didn't want to talk to him.

But they needed to talk, and there was no getting around it. He'd gone to sleep in their bed, figuring that she couldn't avoid her own house forever.

He turned his head at a slight movement to his left. When he caught sight of the dark, man-sized shape in the corner, his heart skipped a beat. He shot up in the bed, the sheets tangling around his legs.

Once his eyes adjusted and he recognized Matt's face, his heart slowed down.

Slightly.

"What the hell, man? You scared the shit out of me."

Matt didn't respond, and Trent leaned over and turned on the light.

"What's going on?"

In the light, he could see what had been hidden in the dark. Matt was furious.

He knows, Trent thought dimly. For once in his life, his father hadn't been bluffing.

A pair of jeans hit him in the face.

"Get dressed and meet me in the kitchen. You have two minutes."

By the time he snatched the fabric off his face, Matt was gone.

Fuck.

His brain still wasn't firing on all cylinders, but he knew enough to get dressed. Quickly. Knowing his best friend, he wasn't going to give him more than sixty seconds or he'd be back. And it was doubtful that he'd come out here to confront him alone.

Trent sighed.

That meant he'd probably have an angry Jackson or Nick to deal with as well. He'd face a boardroom of angry shareholders any day before taking on his friends. Mainly because he actually cared what they thought of him.

But you knew when you chose to get involved with his sister that there was a very real chance this would end badly.

When he emerged into the kitchen, he bit back another curse. Matt stood against the counter with Elliott Alexander.

Any hopes of convincing his friend of his sincerity went out the window.

"You know why we're here?" Eli asked.

Trent nodded. He'd always known that things would come out. But when you were in the midst of living a lie, you convinced yourself that you were invincible. That no one would ever figure out your game.

Until the terrifying moment when it ceased to be a game and became the thing you wanted most in the world.

"When did my father call you?"

Matt glanced over at Eli, who looked similarly confused. "What the hell are you talking about? Why would your father call us?"

Now that gave him a moment of doubt. During this entire thing, the one wild card was his father. He'd assumed that he would eventually tire of waiting for Trent to come to his senses and would out him. Eli noticed the look on his face and seemed to understand instantly.

"You think your father told us? No. I investigated you at Mara's request. She thought you were cheating on her."

He dropped down into one of the kitchen chairs. Despite everything, he'd never meant to hurt Mara. He'd never meant to hurt anyone. But he supposed it had been foolish to think that he could have his cake and eat it too.

Such a silly expression, he thought to himself. After all, what were you supposed to do with cake if not eat it?

"I never meant to hurt her."

Matt let out a disgusted sound. "Right. Just like you never meant to lie to her about your entire life. Was any of that shit you told us true? Your parents live in the Midwest? You grew up on a farm? Did you just make up the most generic all-

American thing you could think of and decide to go with that?"

"Yes. That's exactly what I did."

Stunned into silence, Matt sat in one of the chairs across from him.

Trent leaned forward. "There's no way to spin this so I come off looking good. Despite all evidence to the contrary, I really don't like lying and rarely do it. But when I was eighteen, I had a chance to start over. To live on my own and experience life like everyone else."

"You mean everyone else not in the one percent?" Eli commented.

"Exactly. I'm not going to bore you with any poor-little-rich-kid stories. At this point, it doesn't even matter. I lied to you about my background, and I've been lying by omission ever since."

"Why?" Mara appeared in the doorway to the kitchen.

At the sight of her face, his stomach dropped out. There was no other word to describe how she looked other than ravaged. Her eyes were so red and puffy she looked like she'd been punched in the face. Blotches of pink across her cheeks showed where she'd rubbed at them over and over again.

At his stare, she rubbed the top of her hair, trying to tame the strands sticking out of the top of her ponytail. "I know I look awful."

He stood to go to her only to have Matt block his path. "Stay where you are."

"Look, Matt. I know you're angry, but I'm still the same person. I'm still me."

"Are you? Because the guy I've known for years doesn't look anything like the guy we've been investigating this past week. The Trent that I know has family on a farm out in the Midwest somewhere. His favorite thing to do on the weekends is go surfing or hang out and throw some steaks on the grill." He picked up the folder from the counter. "I don't know this guy. This guy with a penthouse in Manhattan who regularly gives away more money than any of us will see in a lifetime."

"It's still me. Yes, my family has a lot of money, but I'm still the same guy you've known for years."

In light of everything else they'd found out so far, Trent was relieved that they hadn't found Avery. That was something he needed to tell Mara about directly. Lots of women didn't like it when their man had a close female friend, but he knew Mara wasn't like that.

Once she understood that he'd grown up with Avery and that, more importantly, she was his brother's girl, she would understand.

Mara moved closer, pushing past when Matt tried to stop her. "No, I want to hear what he has to say. Don't I deserve that much?"

Matt didn't look happy about it, but he let her pass.

"I know I lied to you, and there's nothing I can do to take that back. But I love your sister, and if she still wants me, I'm not walking away."

"If you love me, then you'll tell me the truth. Where did you get this?" Mara pulled out her cell phone and held it up.

He recognized the picture Travis had given him a few weeks ago. His heart dropped at the shattered look on her face.

"My nephew drew that for me."

A visible shudder went through her. She clasped her arms around her middle. "Your nephew? So you've been going home to see your sister?"

Matt moved forward. "Hold up, sis. Before you get your hopes up again, that may be his nephew, but this is definitely not his sister."

He held up a picture of Avery.

———

MARA CLUTCHED HER ARMS TIGHTER, wondering if it was possible for your heart to literally just fall to pieces. After Matt had taken her back to his house, he'd shown her all the information they'd dug up on Trent. She'd spent hours looking through his real estate holdings, old pictures, and even a listing of his family's charitable contributions.

It had been like reading a book about a different person. Part of her had even held out an irrational hope that it was all a mistake. That there was another Townsend family with a handsome, blue-eyed son named Trent who lived a charmed life on the Upper East Side of Manhattan.

Because that life, the life she'd gotten only a glimpse of through written reports, didn't belong to her Trent. The boy she'd bumped into on her first day of college and fallen into crazy stupid love with. The boy who'd both annoyed her and captivated her, fueling plenty of her late-night dirty dreams when she was alone in her small dorm room.

The boy she'd watched grow into an exceptional man.

And now her brother had brought out the one piece of the puzzle that she'd been trying to avoid thinking about. Matt still held up the picture of the pretty brunette who was currently living in Trent's New York apartment.

Matt hadn't even wanted her to come along for this

confrontation. He was trying to protect her even now, but she didn't have the heart to tell him the damage was already done.

Viewing the pictures of his other life, his "real" life with his other girlfriend, had shattered whatever composure she'd had left. Her heart was already broken. All she was trying to do at this point was salvage some of the pieces.

"You know about Avery?" Trent closed his eyes briefly and Mara had to resist the urge to scream.

After all they'd accused him of, the only thing he was worried about was that they'd identified his mistress?

"Hell yeah, we found out," Matt growled. "Sorry to blow your cover."

She could tell her brother was on the verge of violence. She put a hand on his arm, hoping to calm him down. He glanced at her and nodded once.

"It isn't like that," Trent countered. "I'm not cheating on Mara." His gaze shifted to hers. "I would never do that. And I was going to tell you everything before we got married. It just never seemed like the right time."

Matt laughed. "I'm sure it didn't. You were right at home. Why bother with a little thing like the truth?"

Trent dropped his head forward into his hands. "I know it looks bad, but Avery is just a friend. One of my oldest friends. I grew up with the Maxwells. My older brother, James, my little sister, Sophia, and I used to play with the two Maxwell kids, Avery and Preston, all the time. Our parents weren't exactly friends, but we ran in the same social circles and went to the same private school, so it was inevitable that we would see each other at times."

"If you're estranged from your family, why have you been

sneaking home to see them so much?" Mara truly wanted to understand.

Because it was becoming more and more clear that Trent wasn't estranged from his family. He apparently just didn't want her to meet them.

"My nephew has been ill. He's the main reason I went back. He's just a kid, and he doesn't understand why his father isn't around. My brother should have been there with his son while he was sick. Instead, he ditched his responsibilities to go play in Miami."

"So that makes it okay for you to ditch my sister and go play house with this chick behind our backs?" Matt made a disgusted sound.

Trent squeezed his head between his hands. "I know this sounds bad, but I swear it's not like that. Avery and Travis are family. She'd be my sister-in-law if my brother weren't such a screwup. I couldn't just leave her to deal with Travis's medical issues on her own."

"I don't believe you," Matt stated.

Trent's lips quirked up into a half smile. "See, that's one of the things I've always liked best about you. You say what you think and you don't give a shit whether anyone else likes it. Most of the people I meet who know about my family's wealth, they don't say stuff like that to me. They say what they think I want to hear. They flatter me, they say whatever they think will make me like them. Then the requests start. Can I borrow this? Or I'm a little short until payday, can you help me out?"

Mara came a little closer. "You didn't think we would do that, did you?"

He grabbed her hand, holding tight when she tried to tug it back. "I didn't think so, but I really didn't want to take a chance and be wrong. Which has happened before. I've never been happier in my life than I am with you."

Matt shoved between them. "Stay away from her. You've done enough damage as it is. I just brought her here so she could see that it was true. So she'd know for sure that you're a liar. Now it's time for you to go."

Trent's jaw tightened, but he stood, holding up his hands in surrender.

"I'll go. I know I screwed up and it'll take time, but I just want you to know that I'm sorry. And that even if you don't understand my reasons, I don't regret anything. Knowing all of you for these past years has been the best part of my life."

Matt stood unmoved between, but Mara couldn't tear her eyes away from Trent. Even though his words were directed to all of them, she could feel that he was talking directly to her.

Asking her to understand.

Asking her to forgive.

Just before he reached the doorway to the kitchen, he turned back to her.

"I know I don't deserve your trust. Or you. But I love you, and I am going to prove to you that I'm for real."

———

BUTTING out wasn't an easy thing to do, and Matt Simmons was discovering that it was even harder when a situation involved people you knew and loved.

Or people you thought you knew, anyway. He wasn't entirely sure he knew Trent at all. The thought made him feel both strangely hurt and murderously angry at the same time, so he was trying not to think about it.

His fingers tightened around the steering wheel as he drove away from his sister's town house. In the rearview mirror, he watched as the lights on the lower level went dark.

He turned to the man in the passenger seat of his truck, who sat looking out the window into the night. Eli Alexander was more than just his boss. He was a mentor and a friend. He was also a master at weeding through bullshit.

"Do you think he meant any of that? About being sorry or whatever?"

Eli glanced over at him. "It's hard to say. Liars tend to be convincing. And it's hard to believe any guy when he says the woman living in his house is 'just a friend.' If I had a sister, I wouldn't be thrilled about her dating this dude."

"I want you to keep digging. There's so little about him before the age of eighteen."

"Maybe he was a quiet kid," Eli suggested.

Matt considered the idea. But it just didn't wash with the Trent he'd come to know over the years. People could lie about their background, but it was harder to fake a certain personality for years. Trent hadn't exactly been a choirboy throughout college. His personality type tended to have the kind of teenage years that parents feared.

"He's never been quiet. I'm thinking he wouldn't be this clean unless he'd intentionally buried something. And we know from experience that he has no problem hiding things when he wants to."

"Is any of that really necessary though? Your sister seemed pretty mad."

Matt scoffed. He wished it were that simple, but when it came to Mara and her emotions, nothing was straightforward.

"Mara is a softie underneath it all. I knew the first day they met. Shit, I knew it was going to be a problem. After I got to know Trent, I was okay with it. But I shouldn't have ignored that gut feeling I had in the beginning that he wasn't right for her."

"Like you didn't think he was a good guy?" Eli asked.

"Nah. It wasn't that. I can't really explain what it was. He just seemed... remote. Like he didn't really give a shit about anything. Freshman year we were all partying pretty hard, but I never really saw him with any girls. There was just something weird about it. I actually thought he was gay for a while, but then I saw the way he looked at Mara, so..."

Eli chuckled. "It takes a lot to surprise me, but I have to admit this one got me. Finding out that dude was some kind of bazillionaire was not what I was expecting to find when Mara asked me to check into him."

Matt grunted. "I can't believe she went behind my back like that."

It made him feel soft that he was so upset that she hadn't told him about her suspicions. Yes, he was friends with Trent first, but she was his sister. His twin. He would do anything for her, so it had rankled to find out she'd approached Eli when she needed help.

"You know why she did that. She's worried about you. And probably a little embarrassed."

"Well, she has nothing to be embarrassed about. He lied to her. She didn't do anything wrong."

Eli shook his head. "I know that. You know that. But in her shoes, I would feel strange that I was going to marry someone only to find out they weren't who I thought they were."

Matt parked the car in his driveway. A minute later, the front curtains twitched.

He glanced over at Eli. "Do you mind coming in so you can assure Penny that I didn't kill anybody?"

The curtains fell into place, but Matt knew if he didn't come in within the next few minutes, Penny would come out to the car and drag him out. He thought back to his state of mind that evening.

For the first time, Penny had witnessed his overprotective big brother tendencies in full effect. After he'd driven Mara to their place, he'd had the unhappy task of showing her the things they'd found. He'd been on the razor's edge of violence as Mara had cried quietly over the file. Especially the pictures of the brunette currently living in Trent's other place.

His blood pressure started to rise again just thinking about it.

Another rare smile covered Eli's face. "She was a little worried, huh?"

"Yeah. That would be an understatement."

six

THE NEXT MORNING, Mara rolled over and stared at the empty pillow on the other side of the bed. After their long, exhausting conversation the night before, Trent had gone to a hotel. Her brother and Eli had stayed after he left to make sure he didn't come back.

Even though she knew Matt was just worried about her, it truly pained her to see the animosity between him and his former best friend. Especially watching him treat Trent like a criminal. Then she mentally kicked herself for feeling sympathetic.

Trent had lied to her. To all of them, really. She wasn't the one who should be feeling sorry.

That didn't stop her from missing him so much it physically hurt.

It was a chore to get ready for work. The tasks that usually brought her so much pleasure, like looking through her closet and choosing which pair of heels made her feel the most fierce, left her completely cold today.

In an uncharacteristic move, she grabbed a ruffly white

blouse, black slacks, and plain gray cardigan and spread them out on the bed. Then she wrinkled her nose. She was depressed, but this outfit was only going to make it worse.

So she went back into her closet and pulled out her brightest pair of red high heels that she usually only wore clubbing. When paired next to the simplicity of her clothes, the shoes really made a statement.

She hoped that statement was something along the lines of *I'm not as gullible as everyone seems to think.*

She carried the thought with her as she hurried through a quick shower and then pulled her damp hair back. The entire drive to work she thought about how she was going to approach Mr. Westbrooke.

It was simple. She would have to arrange for some time off. Her personal life was a mess, and she needed time to figure things out. But Ethan was such a workaholic and had never taken a vacation in the entire time that she'd worked for him. She honestly wasn't sure how he was going to react to her sudden request for a week off.

Her thoughts drifted to their strange conversation in his office. It would be the ultimate in flattery to think that he liked her, but she was too smart for that.

Mara knew she was beautiful. It was impossible to grow up with a beauty queen for a mother and not be aware of the effect her face had on men.

But beauty didn't count for much with men like Ethan, simply because he was surrounded by beautiful women all the time. She'd seen him at company functions, and he'd always had a woman who looked like a supermodel on his arm. It wasn't that there was anything special about her.

Except for the fact that she wasn't afraid to yell back at him.

But for whatever the reason, he'd told her to ask for help if she needed it. Well, it was time to test whether he'd been serious about that.

She pulled into the employee parking lot and marched into the building, then stopped short when she saw Lanie hovering by her desk.

"Mara! Thank God the rumors aren't true."

"What rumors?" She set her things down on her desk and booted up her computer.

The entire time she kept her eye on Ethan's door. He must be in a meeting, but as soon as whoever was in there came out, she would go in and state her case. Originally she'd thought to wait until the end of the day and then make her request so she could escape home if he didn't take it well. But she couldn't stand the uncertainty of worrying about it all day.

"I heard that you got fired yesterday," Lanie whispered.

"What?" Mara forgot to keep her voice down and Ada looked up in alarm.

Mara smiled sheepishly and then pulled Lanie around the corner and into the employee break room. Aaron, one of the mail-room guys, stood at the sink stirring a cup of coffee. With only a cursory glance in his direction, she whirled around to face Lanie.

"Spill it."

"Well, yesterday afternoon someone said they saw Mr. Westbrooke yelling at you and then he called you into his office. They said they heard more yelling and then you ran out and got your stuff and left."

Mara ran her hands over the low ponytail she'd pulled her

hair into that morning. "The rumor mill around here is ridiculous. That's not at all what happened. Ethan was yelling, but that's just how he communicates. I was having a bad day and left a little early. I wasn't fired."

"So why were you in his office so long?" Lanie asked innocently.

Mara glanced over her shoulder again. Aaron still stood at the sink sipping his coffee. When he noticed both of their glares, he lowered his eyes and shuffled past them and out the door.

As soon as he was gone, Lanie turned back and raised an eyebrow. "You two aren't—"

"No! Lanie, I'm not sleeping with my boss."

"Oh don't act like it's so unheard of. He's gorgeous. And rich."

"Another rich man is the last thing I need right now."

Lanie's expression instantly brightened. "Now it's your turn to spill. What do you mean by that?"

Mara bit her lip. It probably wasn't a good idea to talk about the situation, but how was she supposed to figure things out if she couldn't tell anyone?

It was impossible to get an unbiased opinion from her usual group of friends because they all knew Trent as well. It wasn't fair to put them in the middle and ask them to choose sides. And she needed to talk to someone about this strange situation.

"Have you ever heard of a guy pretending to be poor? Like instead of flashing his wealth around, he lives like a normal person, driving a normal car and stuff, even though he has a lot of money?"

"Um, no. Most guys do the opposite. They buy a car they

can't afford and dress flashy so they can make women think they have more money than they actually do."

"Right. I didn't think so. But it turns out Trent comes from a wealthy background but he never told me."

"Oh. Well, maybe his last girlfriend was a gold digger," Lanie suggested.

"Maybe."

"Is that why you've looked so sad lately?" At Mara's nod, Lanie put an arm around her shoulders. "I'm sure he had a good reason. He probably thought he was just being cautious."

"You're right. That's what I've been telling myself." Even though she didn't really feel it, Mara forced herself to smile.

It worked because Lanie instantly looked relieved. "It'll all work out in the end. I've seen the way he looks at you. He's crazy about you." She glanced at her watch. "I'd better get to my desk. I'll treat you to lunch today. You look like you could use a break."

———

TRENT CLIMBED the stairs to Matt's house and rubbed his hands. There were really only two ways this could go, and he was trying to ignore the gut feeling that it was going to end painfully.

Maybe with blood.

He pressed the doorbell and then leaned against the stair railing. His friend had purchased the one-story ranch house in a quiet, middle-class neighborhood. He'd been so proud when he bought it.

Trent had several properties around the world, but he'd

been more excited to help his best friend move into this modest home than about anything he'd ever purchased for investment.

After a few more minutes, he shifted restlessly. He didn't hear anything but figured someone was home because both Matt's truck and Penny's sedan were in the driveway. Whether they'd open the door when they saw it was him wasn't certain.

Finally the door swung open and Matt stood in the door-frame, a scowl on his face as he looked at Trent.

"All bets are off now, huh?"

Trent must have looked as confused as he felt because Matt looked at his outfit with disdain and clarified, "Nice monkey suit. No more pretending to be normal?"

Trent looked down at the suit he'd forgotten he was wearing and sighed. He knew Matt could get angry, but he'd never been on the receiving end of his friend's volatile temper before.

"I was never pretending with you. Any of you. I guess it might seem that way but I wasn't."

"Yeah? I've never seen you look like an insurance salesman before."

Matt snickered, but he moved aside so Trent could enter the house. He had to count that as progress. The television was set to a news station, and there was a beer on the coffee table. Matt ignored him and sat back down in front of the TV.

"I'm only wearing this because I need to go into the city. This is what I wear when I do that. Mara can tell you that."

Matt shrugged and kept his eyes on the screen. "So why are you here?"

"I have to go back to New York. I want to take Mara with me."

"You're asking permission now?"

Matt didn't move, but Trent could feel the frustration coming off him in waves. Knowing his friend as well as he did, Trent figured it had to be killing him not to say any more.

Matt had always been crazy overprotective of his sister, especially when it came to the guys she dated. Hell, he'd helped Matt intimidate more than a few of them. Which was why Matt's tacit approval of his relationship with Mara had meant so much to him.

There was no greater vote of confidence than for Matt to think that he was good enough for his sister.

Even though he knew he wasn't.

"No, I'm not asking for permission. I'm just asking you not to shoot me in the back when I do."

Penny appeared in the doorway and gave Trent a soft smile. "Hey, Trent."

He returned her smile. It was a small ray of sunshine not to feel like everyone hated him.

She crossed the room to Matt and hugged him. "I have to go to work. Your sister loves him, so be nice." She whispered the last part before shooting Trent another hesitant smile.

As soon as the door shut behind her, Trent turned back to his friend. Matt had his attention fixed on the television with the kind of marked determination only achieved when you were ignoring someone.

"I'm not going away."

Matt slammed his beer bottle back on the table and stood. "Yes, you are. You spent years lying to her, and Mara isn't just going to take you back because you're Mr. Moneybags now. You fucked up, and there's no taking that back. We're talking about years, Trent."

His friend had a point and he knew it. It was going to take a hell of a lot more than an apology before Mara could forgive him. That was why he needed her to agree to go to the city with him. There was no way to explain what he'd been running from. She had to experience it to understand.

"I know that. That's why this trip is so important. I want her to understand why I left. And over time I hope you'll understand too. Our friendship is important to me. I've admired you for years. We played beer pong together. You've had my back in more than one bar fight. I mean, shit, you taught me how to do laundry."

Matt laughed, and for a moment things were the way they'd always been. Then his expression got grave.

"Look, I still don't understand everything that's going on, but I have to look out for Mara. I can't let you hurt my sister."

"I would never do that. I love her."

"You won't mean to, but that doesn't mean it won't happen anyway. You thought you were protecting her before, and look how that turned out." Matt looked almost as frustrated as he felt.

Trent couldn't really argue against the point since he knew that he'd shattered her trust once already.

"I want to take Mara to New York and introduce her to my parents."

"Well, she's not going anywhere without me."

"You're more than welcome to come along."

Matt stared at him, then seemed to come to a conclusion. He pulled out his cell phone and hit a button. "Tank? I know you're out on leave right now, but I need a favor. I need you to cover my shifts."

———

MARA SHUT the last filing cabinet and stood, massaging the ache in her lower back. If Ethan wasn't so anal, she could have one of the file clerks help her, but he insisted that no one else touch his stuff. She rolled her eyes and hit the button for the elevator to take her back to her floor.

Lanie had insisted that they go out of the office for lunch today. Originally, she hadn't been too enthusiastic about it, but after an hour of handling files, she needed a break. A little sunshine and fresh air would probably do wonders for her mood after being stuck in that dark storage room.

The elevator doors opened and she narrowed her eyes. Trent stood next to her desk talking with Lanie. Her friend's high-pitched giggle was audible even from across the room. It sounded tinny and fake. Then she leaned forward and play-fully batted at Trent's arm.

He stiffened and took a step back, but Lanie moved closer, keeping the contact.

"Trent, what are you doing here?"

At the sound of her voice, Lanie stood up straight and hastily pulled her hand back from where it had been resting on Trent's arm.

Mara walked forward slowly, the ache in her back completely forgotten. Trent had only come by her office a few times, but Lanie had met him before. She hadn't been nearly this friendly then. Or this giggly.

"I came to take you to lunch." Trent moved away from Lanie and stood next to her. She got the sense that he was happy to get away from her friend and into "safe" territory.

"Actually, I already made plans with Lanie." She glanced

over at her friend, annoyed to see Lanie staring at Trent like he was covered in chocolate.

Lanie brushed away a nonexistent wrinkle in her skirt and giggled again. "Oh well, I'll take a rain check." When she met Mara's eyes finally, she blushed slightly. "It's no big deal. I'll see you later, Mara."

Mara watched in disbelief as her friend trotted away. When she got on the elevator, she sent Trent one last smile before the doors closed.

"If you'd rather not have lunch, I understand." Trent watched her from beneath lowered lashes.

"No, it's not that."

And it really wasn't a problem. As angry as she'd been, over the past few hours she'd had nothing to do but think. And question. The only way she'd get the answers to her questions was by talking to him.

She grabbed her purse and then motioned for him to follow her. They rode the elevator down to the main level and then she led him to the bridge.

"Uh, did you tell her about us? Your friend, I mean?" He motioned with his head back at her building.

Guiltily, Mara looked away. "Yeah. I shouldn't have. I mean, I can't believe Lanie was hanging all over you like that. Was that what you meant about people changing?"

Trent stopped at a hot dog stand and raised an eyebrow.

She nodded and smiled at the vendor. "Sure, this is fine."

The vendor looked between them eagerly. "Two with the works?"

Trent nodded his acceptance. Mara took a steaming hot dog wrapped in foil. Trent grinned as she took a greedy bite. He knew her love affair with boardwalk food. She appreciated fine cuisine, but there would always be a special place in her heart for hot dogs and funnel cakes.

Trent accepted his own hotdog and then handed the vendor a twenty-dollar bill. "Keep the change."

They walked over the bridge and stood at the rail, looking out over the water. Their arms brushed as they walked, and Mara soaked up the casual intimacy. She'd gotten so used to having the right to touch him whenever she wanted. It was petty, but she wanted to rub her hands all over him, to erase the image of her friend's flirty touches.

Trent leaned against the railing, turning so the sun wasn't directly in his eyes.

"Women respond differently when they know. But I don't want to make it seem like it's just women. Men too. Suddenly they have a business proposal they want to run by you. Or they start talking about their brother who lost his job and how he might lose his house."

"Or women giggle like idiots and rub themselves up against you," Mara interjected before taking another huge bite of her hot dog.

Trent shook his head ruefully. "Yeah, that tends to happen. I don't want it to seem like I'm made of stone. Of course you'd want to help everyone you could if possible. But you have no idea how refreshing it is to be around people who have no reason in the world to like you but somehow do anyway. For the past few years, that's what you have given me. Hanging with you and Matt and Jackson and Nick." He broke off and looked out over the water.

People strolled by on the pathways below, and Mara fixed her eyes on them as they passed. People-watching was one of her favorite activities during her lunch break. Jogging mothers pushed strollers that looked as complicated as her car, couples meandered arm in arm, as if they had no clear destination in mind. Several boats glided lazily by in the distance.

Trent stood silently next to her, his eyes fixed on the horizon. It was clear that his thoughts were far away from what was happening on the crystalline water.

"It's been a gift, this time I've had with all of you. I've just been Trent. Not a Townsend and not the boss's son, but just myself. I couldn't have ever guessed how valuable that time would be. Especially now that it's over."

"What does that mean?" Fear rose until it felt like it would choke her.

As angry as she was, it hadn't occurred to her until now that they might not work this out. Trent was a part of her and had been since they'd first met.

The idea of him just being... gone?

"My father is ill. My brother has taken off. I have to take control of the company temporarily. I have to go back."

"So that's it? 'I lied to you and now I'm leaving.' Is this really how things are going to end?"

"Not if I have anything to say about it."

Trent drew her close, and when his lips brushed over hers, she opened up to the kiss, melting against him. When he opened his eyes, they were bright with excitement.

"Tell me you don't feel that. You belong to me, and you know it. I know you're angry, and you have every right to be, but let me show you my world. Come with me to New York."

Mara looked up at him, trying to read his eyes. He sounded so sincere, but then again he'd always sounded like this. Even when he was lying to her.

But the truth was, she would never get over this until she understood why.

Why had he hidden this side of his life from her?

He was a rich guy. That was usually something men bragged about, something they used to their advantage. Why would he keep everything about him a secret and make her think he was struggling financially?

It didn't make sense, and even though she knew her curiosity was going to lead her into trouble, she couldn't help it.

She wanted to know.

"Okay."

———

AS SOON AS Mara pulled into her driveway that evening, Trent got out of his car. He hadn't wanted to give her a chance to change her mind this afternoon, so as soon as she'd agreed to accompany him to New York, he'd left. He'd used the time to arrange the details of their trip.

He'd been scheduled to fly back to New York that evening. Now that Mara was coming with him, he had Gina reschedule things so that he would fly out the next day instead. She would handle everything, including booking a suite in one of his family's hotels for Matt to stay in while he was there.

He wasn't sure how long his friend intended on sticking around, but he'd be in perfect comfort for however long he was there. In fact, he should have asked Matt to bring Penny along. As he walked up the driveway to where Mara stood watching him, he made a mental note to suggest the idea.

Mara watching him warily and nervously shifted the tote bag she carried on her shoulder as he got closer.

"You didn't have to wait out here. I wouldn't have minded if you used your key."

He followed behind her as she walked up the steps and unlocked the door. "I didn't want to presume. You've given me a chance to make things right, and I don't want to screw up again."

She didn't meet his eyes as he passed her, moving through the entryway and into the living room. It was strange to look around the familiar room and think that he might not be living there anymore. So much was riding on this trip to the city.

What if he couldn't make her understand?

What if she didn't forgive him?

"Why don't I make you some dinner?" He didn't think she'd kick him out immediately, but at least if they ate together, he'd get a guaranteed few more hours with her.

"Is that really the best way to get on my good side?"

They laughed together. Trent had to concede that point. "Probably not."

"I can make us something," Mara finally said. "Nothing fancy. I'll need time to get ready. I have to pack, and don't I need to book an airline ticket for tomorrow? What if I can't get a flight to join you this late?"

"All of that has been taken care of. You don't need to worry about any details. I'll pick you up in the morning. Matt is coming with us."

Her eyes rounded at that bit of news, but she didn't comment on it. "What should I pack? I mean, I'm planning to bring a nice outfit for when I meet your parents but what about the rest of the time?"

"Anything is fine. We'll do some sightseeing, and it's still pretty chilly at night there, so you'll need a coat. But don't worry about forgetting anything. If you need something you don't have while you're there, we'll just buy another one."

Trent had planned to take her shopping while they were there anyway but figured that was best left as a surprise. Mara loved shopping, and if things weren't going well, he hoped taking her down Fifth Avenue might make up for it.

Mara placed a hand over her stomach and then smiled tightly. "Okay. I wasn't sure if we'd be going out or anything. I don't want to embarrass you."

His stomach dropped. She suddenly wouldn't look at him, and he could have sworn he saw the slight sheen of tears in her eyes. Incredibly moved, Trent pulled her closer. When she still wouldn't meet his eyes, he tipped her chin up with one finger.

"You could *never* embarrass me. You are perfect."

He wanted to tell her that his life before her was like walking through a black-and-white movie. He wanted to show her in whatever way he could that she brought color and warmth into his world and kept him from descending back into the loneliness that had haunted him before.

But nothing he could say would express the enormity of what she'd given him just by loving him, so he was going to attempt to show her.

"Please don't worry about anything. This trip is for you. Because there's no way you can understand why I left that life until you experience it. The good and the bad."

Her head fell forward against his chest, and she snuggled against him, her breath washing against the side of his neck.

"I'm going to try to understand." After a final squeeze, she flashed a quick grin. "I'll get started on dinner. It's probably safer if you don't help."

Trent kissed her on the forehead and then allowed her to pull away. "I'll just watch something on television."

Mara disappeared down the hallway leading to the bedroom and reappeared a few minutes later wearing a long-sleeved shirt and leggings. He looked up from his perch on the sofa as she passed. Once he heard the familiar rattle of pans, he got up and moved to the hallway.

As he pulled his cell phone out of his pocket, he thought of the one detail that he hadn't trusted Gina to handle for him. If he didn't call now, there was a chance it wouldn't be taken care of before they arrived.

And this was something he couldn't leave to chance.

The concierge of his building answered on the first ring. "East Side Towers."

"Walter, it's Trent Townsend. I have a favor to ask."

The other man paused for a moment, betraying his surprise, but when he spoke again, his voice didn't convey anything other than consummate professionalism.

"Yes, sir. Anything."

Trent knew he meant that. Considering all the headache of moving Avery in and out over the past few months, Walter had more than earned a sizeable Christmas bonus for the year.

"Gina told me that she coordinated with you on relocating Miss Maxwell to my brother's residence. Now that she's gone, I need you to go through my penthouse and take down any personal pictures."

"Sir?"

"I know it's an odd request, but it's *very* important. Leave the artwork on the walls, but any pictures featuring my family or friends must be removed."

"Of course, sir. Should I hold them downstairs until your return?"

"Actually, if you would just seal them in a box and put it in my closet, that would be fine."

"Consider it done, sir."

Trent hung up and then wandered back out to the living room. As he passed the entrance to the kitchen, he paused to observe Mara as she chopped vegetables. He let himself soak up the joy of being in her presence. He ignored the hot shard of guilt at all the things he was still keeping from her.

So much was riding on this trip, and he couldn't afford any more missteps.

There were some things she wasn't ready for yet.

seven

IF MARA HAD EVER DOUBTED the rich were different, her experience the next morning confirmed it. She'd always loved traveling and the excitement and sense of adventure when going somewhere new, but she hated the hassle of flying.

They'd been running behind, and she'd been surprised the flight hadn't left without them. That was when Trent had finally clued her in that the plane wouldn't leave without them because they were the only passengers. It was a private jet owned by his father's company.

That was the moment it all started to sink in.

Her future husband was a wealthy man. Wealthy in a way that was both foreign and intimidating.

After getting over her shock that they had an entire plane to themselves, she'd been further flummoxed to find out they didn't even need to rush. To her surprise, there weren't even security lines for the wealthy. Oh no. They'd arrived at a separate part of the airport, and then a driver had taken them directly onto the tarmac right next to their plane.

She'd flown plenty of times before, but never on a private jet. Mara glanced around the cabin again, taking in the details she'd previously been too overwhelmed to notice.

The plane wasn't huge, but it was lavishly decorated in a cream-and-gray color scheme. The seats were all covered in butter-soft leather, and the carpet on the floor was nicer than what she'd purchased when she bought her house. Trent had given them a brief tour before takeoff, showing them the bathroom and even a small bedroom. She hadn't even been aware that you could have a bedroom on a plane.

She glanced over at Trent. He sat to her left, working on his laptop the way she'd seen him do a million times. But now everything about him looked different. Or maybe it was just that she was finally paying attention to the right things.

Her eyes roamed over him greedily, taking in the slightly too long blond hair and the bump on his nose that kept his profile from being too perfect. The face that she loved so much now represented something so frightening that she couldn't even put it into words.

The idea that someone you loved could turn out to be a virtual stranger wasn't something she knew how to process.

He looked up from the screen and blinked when he realized she was staring at him. "Are you okay? If there's anything you need, let me know."

She shook her head and went back to gazing out her window. It was easier to watch the skies fade away than to look at a man she wasn't sure she knew anymore. But after a few moments, her eyes were drawn back to him. It was impossible not to be curious.

Who was this guy?

The Trent she knew was more comfortable in board shorts

and covered with sand than a suit. But this new Trent looked like he'd been born in Hugo Boss. The suit he wore was definitely custom-made and fit him perfectly. Then there was the way everyone had treated him.

The morning had been a flurry of activity as they tried to get themselves together for the trip. Mara was used to travel being a hassle. It wasn't so much the packing she hated but all the minutiae—scheduling flights and rental cars and all the other details that had to be taken care of.

But traveling with Trent was an entirely different story.

With one phone call, he had taken care of everything from where Matt and Penny would stay to how they would get around when they got there. He wore power like a mantle that he could slip on and off.

When they'd gotten on the plane, everyone had immediately deferred to him. Everything had been "Yes, Mr. Townsend" and "Whatever you need, Mr. Townsend."

And every word spoken made her feel farther and farther away from the man she knew.

Someone tapped on her shoulder, so she twisted around in her seat. Matt had moved so he sat directly behind her. His brown eyes searched her face.

"Is everything okay, sis?" He glanced over at Trent with a scowl.

It had to be killing him to put their differences aside, but he had agreed to do it for her. However, that didn't mean he was going to be nice about it. If she knew her brother, he was going to take every opportunity to make Trent's life hell.

Not that she blamed him. After all, she wasn't the only one who'd been deceived.

"I'm okay. What about you?" As tough as he was acting, she

knew he'd been hurt too. To find out his best friend for years had been lying to him had to be a shock at best and a complete betrayal at worst.

"I'm fine; don't worry about me. This is about you. I'm here for you. And if you ever want to get the hell out of here, just say the word."

Mara smiled to herself. Even if nothing else in her life made sense, she could always count on her brother.

She turned around to find Trent watching her. "So where are we going again?"

"I keep a penthouse in the city."

"Of course you do." Mara tried not to feel bitter. He had an entire residence that she'd never seen.

He opened his mouth to say something, but she held up her hand. The last thing she wanted was to argue. They'd done enough of that over the past twenty-four hours. He wanted a new start and she'd agreed to that.

She could only hope that this trip didn't backfire.

Because so far every single new thing she'd learned about him just made him seem like a stranger.

———

THEIR EXPERIENCE once the plane landed mirrored boarding except instead of the mildly balmy and humid Virginia air she was used to, they stepped out into a dry heat that made her sinuses tingle. Trent motioned them toward a black town car.

Mara climbed in and then looked up in surprise when Matt slid in next to her.

By the tense line of Trent's mouth, she realized the men

still weren't speaking. Also that her brother had no intention of leaving her alone with Trent any more than necessary. Penny got in next, giving Mara a reassuring smile.

Mara tried not to gawk as they passed the towering skyscrapers she'd previously only seen on television. Her hands twisted in her lap. She refused to press her face against the window the way she really wanted to.

That was the worst part about how things had been different since she'd found out about Trent's background, this crushing insecurity that he was somehow "slumming" by being with her.

At that thought, she sat up straight and looked out the window unashamedly. She hadn't done anything wrong, and she was definitely not going to allow any situation to make her feel less than.

They pulled up to the curb next to a tall building, and the door next to her opened. The older gray-haired man who had driven them nodded to her pleasantly before moving to the trunk to deal with their bags.

Unsure of what to do with herself, Mara thumbed the strap of her purse and watched him heft out the luggage. She wasn't so much of a rube that she thought she was supposed to help him, but it felt so strange, so foreign, to just stand there and be waited on.

"Come on. It's time you saw your new place." Trent took her elbow gently and steered her toward the entrance. Another man in a crisp black suit opened the door for them.

"Welcome back, Mr. Townsend."

Trent smiled, the first true smile she'd seen on him so far. "Thanks, Ernesto. How's the grandbaby?"

"Getting bigger every day, sir."

"Just wait. She'll be wearing makeup and asking to borrow the car keys before long."

They swept into the building, the older man's chuckles following them. As soon as they entered the lobby, Mara couldn't keep up the sophisticated veneer of boredom she'd been trying so hard to project.

"Oh wow. This is where you live?"

"This is where *we* live. Or, it's one of the places we might live if you decide you like it."

She could tell he was trying hard to make her feel welcome and included, but there was nothing in her past to prepare her for the elegance of the marble lobby floor or the diamond-bright cut of the crystal in the chandeliers.

Even the elevator was some sort of technological marriage of steel and chrome and glass. She held on to Trent's arm and he turned his dazzling smile on her. He seemed so pleased, and truthfully she was just hanging on to him because he seemed like the only safe, normal thing in this strange new place.

Trent inserted a white card into a slot in the elevator and then pushed the button for the penthouse. Besides their party, there was only one other person on the elevator, a young woman wearing a tank top and shorts who looked like she'd just been jogging. After she got off, they were alone.

She chanced a glance over her shoulder. Penny looked a little dazed. Matt raised his eyebrows as if to say *"Would you look at this place?"*

It made her feel a little better. At least she wasn't the only one who felt more than a little out of place surrounded by all this opulence.

The doors slid open and they stepped directly into an

elegant entryway. A living room with a stunning wall of windows was directly ahead.

"Wait... this is it?" Mara glanced around in confusion.

She'd been expecting a hallway and then to have to open the door of their place with a key. Trent must have read her expression because he gestured for her to follow him.

"The elevator won't access our floor without a special keycard. Walter is bringing yours up as we speak."

"Oh, Walter. Right."

She had no idea who that was or if she was supposed to care. Probably one of his many staff that seemed to be always just out of sight.

"Do you guys want a tour?" Trent looked between them, and when no one else seemed inclined to say anything, Mara nodded.

He was trying so hard, and it was painful to keep up this silence. Even though she was still hurt, she'd promised to give him this weekend to explain. This was his chance to show her his world and for her to decide if she wanted to be a part of it. It was time she took that promise seriously.

"You guys can go back to the hotel, Matt. I'm okay here."

Her brother cast one last look out the expansive window and then crossed the room to her side. He looked at her so long that for a moment she wasn't sure he was going to leave at all.

Then he nudged her arm and said, "I'm starting to understand what he meant when he said knowing about his background makes people uncomfortable. I'm afraid to touch anything in this place."

A soft laugh escaped before she could stop it. "I know, right? Everything looks so perfect."

He kissed her on the head and murmured, "Give him hell before you take him back at least."

As he entered the elevator where Penny waited, he was smiling.

Once the doors closed behind him, Trent walked back out of the kitchen. He'd been giving her space this whole time, only touching her when necessary and not expecting her to talk to him. But now he came and stood directly in front of her.

"Are we going to be able to get past this, Mara? Because just the thought that you won't even let me try is killing me. You're too good to toy with me deliberately, so I'm asking you now—do I even have a chance?"

She looked around the room, her eyes skimming over the hardwood floors covered with rugs that were probably worth more than her house. The late-afternoon sunlight cast everything with a golden glow, including Trent. Standing in the light with the sun setting his hair aflame, all she could see was her man.

The same man who'd cheered her on, held her while she cried, and promised her that he wanted forever.

Maybe it was time to let him prove it.

———

TRENT WATCHED as Mara walked the perimeter of the room, trailing her fingertips over the back of the long sectional sofa, touching briefly the small sculptures on the side table and the granite of the kitchen breakfast bar.

The thing about Mara was that for all her boisterous enthusiasm, she could be maddeningly self-contained sometimes. She smiled, but was it because she was happy or because she was used to showing a happy face to the world? Was her tactile exploration a sign of acceptance, an interest in her new home, or was it merely curiosity? Polite interest?

He had no idea, and the pressure of wondering whether he was getting through to her or whether his entire plan had already crashed and burned was driving him crazy.

"I have a confession to make."

That finally got her to stop moving. She glanced over at him, her amusement evident in the small lift of her lips. "Just one? Why stop now—you seem to be on a roll."

He laughed. If she could make jokes then things weren't as bad as he feared. He motioned around the room. "I brought you here to impress you."

"You don't say." She'd done a full circuit of the room and finally made her way back to him. This was as close as she'd gotten to him voluntarily all day. Her eyes sparkled as she smiled up at him. "Well, I'm impressed. I can't deny that."

"I'd hoped that if I dazzled you with all that I have, all that I would gladly lay at your feet, that you'd be willing to overlook the dark side of this life. And I'm just selfish enough to hope that you're too tightly bound to me by the time you notice that this life can sometimes feel like living in a gilded cage."

"This is some cage," she muttered.

He reached out and grabbed her hand. The words he would say next were so important, and if he could go forward with any semblance of his conscience intact, he had to know that she'd really considered the pitfalls.

"When people know your net worth, there's always a risk that someone will try to harm you. Privacy becomes nonexistent. Being a Townsend is like having a target on your back."

"But I'm not a Townsend," Mara protested.

"If you marry me, you will be."

Although she'd stopped moving, he still couldn't tell what she was thinking. When he'd imagined showing her his world, this wasn't what he'd expected. He'd wanted to impress her, and so far, she seemed more distant than ever.

"This is my chance to treat you like the precious jewel you are."

Mara looked up at him and her eyes softened, her breasts rising and falling under the thin material of her blouse. He moved behind her, inhaling her sweet scent. After a moment, she leaned back against him with a sigh.

Unable to resist any longer, Trent buried his face in her hair. He didn't touch her anywhere else, sure that if he allowed himself the luxury of touching her that he'd never stop.

But then she made a soft, needy purr in the back of her throat, the helpless sound ricocheting through him and grabbing him by the balls. He hardened instantly and took a shallow breath, hoping she wouldn't move against him, because there would be no way to disguise his reaction to her. There would be nothing to hide the fact that just being near her inflamed him.

She'd always had that effect on him, inciting his deepest passions and making him feel like a feral animal.

"I don't need any of that," she whispered.

"I know you don't," he choked out. "But I would shower you with gifts just to see the glitter of diamonds against your perfect skin. You have no idea how hard it's been to hold back, to not buy you the things you deserve. That ends now. I am going to take care of you. And you are going to let me."

Trent knew it was a risk. Mara was so independent that from the very beginning he'd had to curb the arrogance that came from being born into one of the nation's richest families. He was used to doing whatever he wanted and having things exactly the way he liked.

But with Mara, he'd had to learn to temper that part of himself for fear that he'd scare her away. But now the curtain had been pulled back, his true nature revealed, and he found he couldn't stop himself from telling her exactly how things would be.

Instead of pulling away, she arched her back, brushing her curvy bottom against his erection. Trent groaned and his hands on her arms tightened. Maybe it had been an accident. She truly didn't know how she affected him sometimes, and he couldn't fall on her like an animal when she was likely just moving against him inadvertently.

Then she did it again. Rubbed that sexy ass back against him, and he lost it.

"Damn it, you know exactly what you do to me, don't you?"

She opened her mouth to respond, but whatever she was about to say was covered by the sound of a loud chime.

"What was that?" Mara glanced around warily.

Trent was tempted to lie but knew there was no use. Few people visited him here, so if his visitors were who he assumed, they wouldn't go away until they'd seen him.

"It's the front desk calling up. I must have visitors." He crossed the room and snatched up the phone. It took all his patience not to snarl into the damn thing.

"Yes, Walter?"

"Sir, your parents are here to see you."

"Of course they are. Can you give me a moment?"

"Yes, sir."

He set the phone down on the counter. Mara watched him warily from the other side of the island.

"Who is it?"

"Apparently my staff isn't as loyal as I'd hoped. It's my parents. I'd hoped we'd have a little more privacy before we had to deal with them."

She didn't say anything, but he could tell the thought of meeting his family held as little appeal for her as it did for him right then. Especially when she glanced down at her outfit. That was his girl.

"I can tell them to leave. They'll have to understand that we just got in and we're exhausted."

"But they already came out here. I'm sure they've missed you." Mara's fingers clenched around the fabric of her top. Then she smoothed it out as if just conscious of the nervous habit. "Besides, that's why we're here, right? So that I can become a part of your life. It's time to stop hiding."

There was wisdom in those words, but that didn't mean he couldn't also feel the disaster that was about to happen, the chaos and discord that his family seemed to generate as a matter of course. He was related to them and as such had to deal with their drama, but she wasn't used to it. He'd hoped to shield her for as long as he could.

However, it was only a matter of time, so perhaps it was better to get it over with. He only hoped she wouldn't turn around and leave as soon as she met them.

"All right. I just want you to remember that all this stuff"—he gestured around them—"is just that. *Stuff*. It's not who I am. I'm still the same guy who has loved you for years."

Mara hugged him tightly and then released him. "I know. Now let them in. It's about time I met my future in-laws."

He knew Mara thought he'd been keeping her a secret and that the belief had hurt her. It killed him that this beautiful, vibrant woman could have ever thought he was hiding her, although he knew his own actions had led her to that conclusion.

Because despite what Mara thought, she wasn't the one he was ashamed of.

part two

"And, after all, what is a lie?
'Tis but the truth in masquerade;"
— *Don Juan, Lord Byron*

MARA'S first thought when the elevator doors opened was that Trent's parents looked like mannequins.

His father was tall with light brown hair streaked through with silver. He wore a crisp black suit and a red tie, the quintessential image of a CEO. He was a handsome man despite his stiff demeanor. She could easily see Trent's features in his face.

His mother's blond hair was even lighter than her son's and every single strand was perfectly in place. Like her husband, she was formally dressed in a slim black sheath that showed off her trim figure, and a single strand of pearls was around her neck.

With envy, Mara glanced at her shoes. The distinctive red sole told her they were by one of her favorite designers. One of the designers that she knew she'd never be able to afford but drooled over in every fashion magazine.

"Darling! You're finally back." His mother came forward, sweeping past Mara with her arms outspread to pull Trent down into a hug.

Trent hugged her back stiffly before exchanging a terse nod with his father.

When his mother noticed Mara standing there, she beamed a bright smile. Then she handed over her handbag and the shopping bag she carried.

"Please put these away somewhere. And I'll have a glass of tea, *por favor*." She emphasized the Spanish words, saying them slowly but still managing to mangle the pronunciation.

For a moment, Mara just stood there, her arms filled with packages. Trent turned to her with a carefully blank look. His eyes closed briefly before he took the stuff out of her arms and set it off to the side next to the sofa.

His mother watched the interaction between them with confusion. She was probably wondering why Mara wasn't hopping to and fixing her drink.

She felt like being wicked and speaking back in Spanish, but the ironic thing was, despite his mother's assumption, her Spanish wasn't very good. Her mother was Colombian, but they'd always spoken English at home.

Note to self: learn more Spanish to use when making pretentious people feel uncomfortable.

When Trent put his arm around her waist, a single frown line appeared on his mother's forehead, marring the otherwise perfectly smooth skin of her face. Clearly this wasn't going to be the family bonding session Mara had hoped for. She was starting to understand why Trent hadn't brought her home sooner.

"Mom, Dad, this is my fiancée, Mara Simmons. Mara, these are my parents, James and Antonia Townsend."

She glanced up at him before smiling at his parents. No one said anything for a moment, so she awkwardly stuck out her hand in his mother's direction. "Hello, it's so nice to finally meet you both."

A look of disdain crossed his mother's face, which was quickly masked by a polite but cool smile. "Of course, yes. Your fiancée."

Mara noticed that while her words were perfectly polite, they also didn't extend any welcome or congratulations.

So that was how it would be. She pulled her hand back since his mother didn't seem inclined to shake it and instead snuggled closer to Trent, putting her arm around his waist as well.

At her touch, he visibly relaxed. "I wish we'd known in advance you were coming. We've only just arrived ourselves."

Mara froze and glanced at Trent from the corner of her eye. While polite, his tone definitely implied that his parents weren't welcome. Not that they seemed to care. His mother simply sniffed and perched on the edge of the couch. His father hadn't moved during the entire exchange.

As stiff as he was, he could be asleep with his eyes open for all the interest he showed in the conversation.

"If we'd told you we were coming, you would have just avoided us. You've been hiding out in the country for ages, darling. Do you blame me for being excited when I heard that you're finally moving back home?"

Trent's arm tightened around her waist. "I'm not moving back, Mother. I'm only here to visit. And to show Mara around, of course."

His mother's lips turned down slightly. Nothing else on her face moved. "Well, you aren't going to stay down there forever, surely. What about your family? Your friends? Your life?"

Trent pinched the bridge of his nose. He looked at her

apologetically. "My life is in Virginia now. Just as it has been for years."

When Trent's father finally moved, it startled Mara. He came to stand next to his wife, placing a hand on her shoulder. Antonia reached up to grasp it. They looked like a portrait of affluence. She could almost see their picture in a magazine with the caption "The Townsends of New York relaxing at their son's Manhattan penthouse."

"Your mother is just concerned for you, Trent. As am I. Your place is here. We need you. Especially in light of your brother's recent actions."

No one said anything, and Mara had to resist the urge to fidget. She got the sense that there was more than one conversation going on and she was only privy to the surface one.

"Would anyone like something to drink?" she asked, interjecting into the tense silence.

No one said anything, so she made her way over to the kitchen and busied herself inspecting the contents of the refrigerator. There wasn't much there, but when she opened the freezer she found several containers, each one carefully labeled. Lasagna. Chicken casserole. Minestrone soup.

She hadn't asked Trent if he had a housekeeper, but she could only assume he did. Things were too clean and perfect for him not to.

After about five minutes, Mara figured she probably couldn't hide out in the kitchen any longer. She'd spent as long as possible looking in the refrigerator, choosing between the various designer brands of sparkling water.

It was probably rude as hell, but she wasn't ready to go back out there and deal with more dismissive looks from Trent's parents.

This whole trip was supposed to be a new beginning, but she was already wondering if it was a mistake. Trent had told her his family was difficult and he preferred to spend as little time with them as possible. At the time she'd thought that was cold and unfeeling.

But now that she'd met them, she had to admit she already understood better a few things about Trent . If those were her parents, would she be anxious to go home often? Probably not.

And she hadn't even met his siblings yet. She shivered, imagining mini-versions of James and Antonia. She closed the refrigerator and squared her shoulders. She'd said she wanted to meet his parents, so she had to at least back Trent up. But when she walked into the living room, it was empty.

"Trent?"

He emerged from the hallway. His shirt was unbuttoned and he'd already pulled off his tie.

"Where are your parents?"

"I sent them home. I'm tired, and I'm sure you are too."

Her shoulders slumped. "I'm exhausted."

The corners of his lips twitched. "You don't have to pretend. If that had been my first time meeting my parents, I would have needed a time-out too. And a fifth of scotch."

Mara grimaced. "Was I that obvious?"

The amused grin on his face told her she had been, but he didn't seem bothered. He walked over and put a gentle hand on the small of her back.

"Come on. I haven't even shown you our room yet."

She followed him down the hallway, stopping briefly so he could point out a bathroom and a guest room.

"How big is this place?" she whispered as they passed another guest room.

She'd been talking to herself, but Trent answered anyway. "It's about five thousand square feet. There's a home theater, a billiards room, and an office on the other side of the living room."

Then he led her into a room in the back that was easily the size of her living room back home. A king-sized bed covered in a dove-gray comforter dominated the center of the room. The windows were similar to the ones up front, providing a stunning view of the bustling city scene.

"I don't even want to know how much a view like this costs."

Trent glanced at her and then looked away. "Ah, no, you probably don't."

She walked up to the glass and looked down. In the fading light of evening, the people and cars below were so small they looked like toys.

"Oh crap, now I'm curious. If I'm going to live here, I should probably not be completely ignorant. So how much would a place like this cost if I wanted to buy one?"

He didn't meet her eyes when he answered. "I bought this years ago, but at current market value, a penthouse in this area starts at about twenty million."

Mara swallowed. "Right."

He must have sensed her discomfort, so he held out his hand. When she took it, he led her to a door on the left side of the room. "This is your closet."

She stepped inside the large space, turning around to take in the full effect. Mara knew that her mouth was hanging open, but there was no way to avoid it. One wall was outfitted with cubbyholes for shoes, bags, and belts. The other wall held the standard rack for hanging dresses, skirts, and coats.

A chandelier dangling with assorted sizes of cut glass sparkled merrily over a circular custom-built dresser. She pulled out one of the drawers. There were built in dividers in the top shelves. A bench sat in the corner of the room next to the window.

Her closet was so big that it had a window.

"I can tell you like this room." Trent smirked as she ran her fingers over the custom cabinetry.

"Oh yeah. This almost makes dealing with your family worth it. Because that meeting was enough to make me want to slit my wrists!"

Trent paled and vaulted away from the doorframe. "Don't say that. *Don't ever say that.*"

Mara's breath seized in her lungs at the look on his face. She placed her hands on his chest and pushed back slightly so she could see his face. His pupils had dilated, making his eyes appear darker. She'd never seen him look so... destroyed.

"I should have never brought you here, subjected you to them. We can leave in the morning. Immediately."

When he pulled her into his arms, she allowed him to just hold her. Beneath her ear, his heart banged rapidly inside his chest. His hold on her arms was so tight it was almost painful, but she held still, just stroking the skin over his heart that was revealed by the opening in his shirt.

"Trent, I was just... it was a bad joke. I didn't mean anything by that."

Her words didn't seem to help. If anything, he just squeezed her tighter. His lips moved against her hair as he kissed the top of her head.

"You are my life. If anything ever happened to you... If anything *ever* took you away from me."

She ran her hands over his arms soothingly and allowed him to pull her closer. He seemed manic, holding her against him like he was afraid to let her go. It was disconcerting to see him like this, just another side to him that she wasn't used to.

He took her mouth, crushing her against him, holding her so tightly that she could barely move. She squirmed in his arms, alarmed by his sudden intensity. When she went lax, he pulled back, his breath coming hard and fast in a wash of air against her cheek.

"I'm sorry, I'm so sorry." His hands roamed over her face, her hair, petting gently.

She allowed it, sensing that the touching was soothing to him. When he finally calmed, she looked up into his eyes.

"I'm okay. And I'm not going anywhere."

When he lowered his head this time, it was slowly. Steadily. She tilted her face up into the kiss, one hand curling behind his head. Mara gave herself up to emotion, to being taken by the only man who had ever made her feel this way.

Trent had taken care of her when she was sick and comforted her when she was sad. He was the only one she had ever imagined forever with.

The only one she'd ever *wanted* to imagine forever with.

"Sometimes I think you don't know how much you mean to me," he whispered. "Everything about you is perfect. The way you move. The way you smell. The way you taste."

His fingers hooked into the sides of her jeans and tugged, working the material over her hips. Her underwear was pulled down too, and Mara watched helplessly as he tossed it aside.

His head descended and then his tongue connected with her core. Her loud moan echoed around them as he pulled her wet flesh between his lips. There was no buildup, no foreplay.

He just went for it, and unprepared, Mara wasn't ready to stifle her cries.

"Tell me you want me," Trent demanded.

He lifted his head, and captivated by the feral look in his eyes, Mara couldn't look away. She was standing half-naked in her brand-new closet with her legs spread. She was past the point of wanting.

But she knew he wouldn't touch her without the words. He wasn't himself. This was not the easygoing Trent she knew. This man was dominant and exacting.

And he wanted *her* with single-minded intensity.

"I want you," she panted. She could barely get the words out.

Immediately his thumb pushed into her wet heat, and she contracted around the thick digit. The orgasm took her off guard, flashing through her bright and hot. She squeezed her eyes shut and rode the shattering waves that left her feeling completely wrung out when they ended.

Boneless, she collapsed against him. He caught her, helping her to the floor. He moved over her, his hands working at his own belt, tugging at the zipper.

"Aah, yes," she cried out when he finally thrust inside her, pushing through her still-contracting muscles.

"Tell me you're mine," he growled against her neck, the sound one of desperate longing.

She arched as his fingers found her nipples. Her shirt was pushed roughly out of the way, and his thumb found her through her bra. The sensations were heightened through the slightly scratchy lace.

All the while, his hips worked a grinding rhythm, slowly screwing her halfway to insanity. Her own hips lifted with every thrust, accepting him, taking him as deep as possible.

"I need you," he mumbled.

She almost didn't hear the soft words, too distracted by the kisses he dotted over every inch of skin he could reach. Mara wrapped her legs around him, rocking up into his thrusts. He panted, harsh breaths against the side of her neck as he worked himself deeper, his hips fusing to hers again and again.

Her hands clutched at his shoulders, his back, his hair. Anything she could reach. Trent was usually a very gentle lover, allowing her to take the lead. But this was a side of him she'd never seen before.

A dominant, forceful side of him that alternately thrilled and worried her.

"Say you'll never leave me. Promise me." His eyes didn't leave her face the entire time.

She was suddenly hit with an overwhelming sense of protectiveness. What had set him off she didn't know, but she would do whatever he needed, say whatever he needed, to be okay.

Because that was loving someone, Mara thought. Wanting them to be okay and doing whatever you needed to make sure they got there.

"I'll never leave you. I promise."

The words were still on her lips as she fell apart, coming so hard that everything turned into light as bright as diamonds.

———

THE NEXT MORNING, Trent woke to the unfamiliar light of the sun streaming through the wide windows. For the past few months, while Avery had been staying here, he'd always slept in the guest room so she could have the biggest bed. It had been a long time since he'd woken up here.

It had been a long time since he'd felt so light and carefree too.

Mara rolled over, and the movement drew his attention. Her hand roamed over the empty space between them, searching. At home, she usually slept half on top of him. She'd always been a snuggler.

He moved to the center of the bed, and once her hand connected with the bare skin of his chest, she let out an indistinct murmur and plastered herself to his side. She'd probably be annoyed to find him in the bed when she finally woke up, but he was going to enjoy having her soft, warm weight against him in the meantime.

After making love to her like a maniac on the floor of her closet, things had gotten awkward. Trent had retreated to the kitchen to give her some space. When he returned to the room, Mara had already fallen asleep or had done an excellent job of pretending to be. She'd gone to sleep all the way on the far right side of the bed so there was no chance that their bodies would touch during the night.

Which was no wonder since he'd probably scared her with his intensity the night before.

After an hour of trying to fall asleep, he'd still been acutely aware of her every move. He'd known the exact moment she'd fallen asleep in truth. He'd lain awake for hours after that contemplating how he was going to get her to trust him again.

Mara moved again and he held still, hoping to hang on to this precious moment before she woke up and he had to see the suspicion and pain enter her dark eyes. She'd gone to bed wearing a nightgown, but the straps had slipped off her shoulders during the night. Her curls were tousled and falling over her bare shoulders.

The sight reminded him that they'd made love last night for the first time in a long time.

After a few minutes, her eyes opened, squinting against the light. When she looked down and realized she was half on top of him, she smiled sheepishly.

"Good morning. I guess I used you as my pillow. As usual."

"That's the way I like it."

At his words, she smiled brightly. Then, as if remembering the prior day, she glanced away and scooted back to the other side of the bed. She sat up and stretched.

"I haven't slept that well in a long time. I guess I was pretty tired." She gave him one last indecipherable look before she slid out of bed and hurried into the adjoining bathroom.

Once the door closed behind her, Trent sat up and pushed the covers back. If they weren't going to stay in bed cuddled up, then he might as well start his day. He'd never been one for staying in bed once he woke up.

He padded over to the closet and pulled out a long black robe. After belting it, he wandered out to the kitchen. The staff had made sure the kitchen was stocked with the basics before their arrival so there should be enough food for him to make a quick breakfast. He could order a grocery delivery for later in the afternoon.

His phone rang while he was in the middle of scrambling eggs. Switching the spatula to his left hand, he reached across the granite counter to grab it. Now that his parents knew he was back in town, his plan to hide out for a few days and show

Mara around was probably shot to hell. When he saw Gina's face on the screen, he knew it.

"What completely unnecessary tasks has my father asked me to do today?"

"Good morning to you too." Gina didn't sound too annoyed with his brusque greeting. She'd worked for his father for years and understood well Trent's frustration with Townsend family theatrics.

"He's scheduled an executive meeting for nine a.m."

Trent pushed the eggs around the pan awkwardly with his left hand. "Nine, huh? I suppose waiting until I've unpacked would have been too reasonable."

"Yes, sir. I've flagged the e-mail and itinerary for you. Should I send a car?"

Trent sighed. He hadn't been back a full twenty-four hours yet, and he was already feeling stressed and over-scheduled.

This trip was supposed to be about Mara. About showing her how committed he was to being with her completely. Instead, his father had found a way to derail things and make it all about him as usual.

"Yes. Send a car. But clear my day starting tomorrow. I want a few days where I can focus without distractions."

"Of course, sir. And if you don't mind me saying so, it's nice to have you back in town for a little while."

He hung up and tossed the phone on the counter. When he looked up, Mara stood in the doorway to the kitchen, the natural light coming through the windows framing her so she looked like an angel.

"Whatever you're making smells like it's done," she commented.

She walked over, the T-shirt she'd slipped on swaying,

showcasing her long legs with every step. She ducked beneath his arm and turned off the gas on the stovetop.

"Well done."

Trent lifted a section of eggs with the spatula to see that the bottoms were completely charred. He sighed and set the spatula down on the counter.

Mara opened the refrigerator, surveying the meager contents. It was such a domestic scene, but one that he'd never imagined happening there. It hit him then how much was riding on this trip.

If anything happened that made her leave him or if she decided she didn't want their life together, nothing else he had could ever compensate for that loss.

A sudden rush of love came over him, so potent he swayed where he was standing.

"Mara?" He waited until she turned around, a bottle of water in her hand. "I'm really glad you're here."

"Me too." A slow, pleased smile spread across her face.

She walked over and kissed him lightly. Then she picked up the pan and dumped the contents in the trash.

"Now, how about I take care of the cooking and you handle everything else?"

nine

ALTHOUGH MARA WAS DISAPPOINTED when Trent told her he had to leave for a meeting, part of her was glad she didn't have to keep her happy face on for much longer.

Things had been moving at warp speed over the past few days, and she needed a little time alone to think and process. She wasn't sure what she was feeling, and a little solitude would probably help her gain some perspective.

"I wasn't planning to have to leave you so soon." Trent yanked at his tie, cursing before he pulled it completely undone and tied it again.

"It's fine, Trent. It's not like there's much trouble for me to get into up here in the ivory tower." She was joking, but she could tell it didn't make him feel better.

Geez, what did he think was going to happen to her while he was gone?

"The housekeeper might come by at some point. She operates like a ghost and tends to be in and out very quickly. She mainly cleans when I'm out of town, but since we'll be here for at least a few weeks, it's inevitable that you'll see her eventually."

"Okay. What does she look like?"

He paused as if he had to really think about the answer. "Um, older lady. Gray hair. A grandmotherly type, I guess you'd say."

"Good." At his quizzical look, she rolled her eyes. "I was imagining some nubile young thing wearing a French maid's uniform."

"Sorry to disappoint." He grinned.

"Is she the one who left the frozen meals?" Mara asked, remembering the neatly stacked containers she'd seen in the freezer.

"Yes. My schedule was always so sporadic when I came into town that she wanted to be sure I'd have something available no matter when I showed up. You'll like her."

"Any other random women in your life I need to be on the lookout for?"

"Funny." He gave her a dark look before going back to messing with his tie.

He'd already dressed, but the cuffs of his shirt were still unbuttoned and the matching jacket to the Tom Ford suit he was wearing was tossed lazily over one of the kitchen barstools. Never a connoisseur of men's clothes, Mara was only sure of the brand because she'd shamelessly snooped while he was getting dressed.

It was at turns fascinating and depressing that the beach bum she'd come to love could coexist inside the same man with a closet full of mouthwateringly sexy men's couture. He finished with his tie and slipped into his suit jacket, the material stretching over his broad shoulders perfectly.

It was so strange to see him like this, but she couldn't deny how incredibly *hot* it was too. Which made her even more confused.

It felt almost like she was cheating on the Trent she'd loved for years by lusting over this new and different version of him. She supposed it would take time for her mind to equate that they were really the same man.

"Did it ever occur to you that I might need some time alone in this huge place to explore? I'll be fine here." She patted his cheek, and when his eyes darkened, she hooked a finger under the knot of his tie. "And maybe when you get back you can show me the rest of this sexy wardrobe that I've never seen before."

His face tightened and his eyes roamed over her face as if he was trying to gauge how serious she was from her tone. She smiled cheekily up at him and he relaxed, pulling her closer until they ended up a tangle of arms and legs.

"I will be more than happy to show you anything you like when I return. In the meantime, explore your new home. Anything you don't like, we'll call the decorator and have it changed." He leaned forward slowly, his eyes on hers the whole time.

It hit her then that he was waiting to see if she'd allow him to kiss her again. Everything was so stilted now between them, like every moment and every interaction carried the risk of blowing up into something else that could shatter them.

She hated feeling this distance between them, especially when she'd always felt that with him, she could be her most authentic self. So she grabbed him by the lapels of his suit jacket and yanked him forward. Then kissed him until they were both squirming and breathing hard.

"Maybe I don't really need to go to work," Trent whispered and then nipped at her bottom lip again.

She shivered as his eyes remained on her mouth, before he ran his tongue over his lips in such a suggestive way that it made her blush. Damn!

"I think you do have to go," she replied breathlessly. "Didn't you say something about board meetings and investors?"

"Not sure I really care about any of that right now."

Since she doubted she'd have the strength to do it if she waited any longer, she stepped away. After a moment, he cleared his throat and then stood back, running his hands through his blond hair.

"Woman, you are dangerous." He gave her a warning look before bussing her cheek with a quick kiss. "I'll be home late afternoon. I'm taking you out to dinner. It's high time I showed you New York. And whatever happens today, just go with it."

With that strange statement, he left.

Despite how things were between them, Mara couldn't suppress a frisson of excitement. She was in the Big Apple. Visions of skipping down Fifth Avenue danced through her head.

She made a brief detour to the bedroom to get her cell phone before settling on the couch. She was used to paying bills in the morning on her cell phone banking app. To her surprise, when she pulled up her account, her mortgage showed a zero balance. Then she noticed that her car note, which she carried through the same bank, had also been paid off.

"Oh Trent, what did you do?" she said.

She hit the button to drill down into her individual accounts, and her mouth fell open. Two hundred fifty thousand dollars had been deposited into her savings account that morning. Fuming, she stared at the numbers on the screen until her eyes swam.

This explained why Trent had been so worried before he left. He knew his money made her uncomfortable. Especially the idea that people would think she was with him so he could take care of her.

This was really pushing her boundaries, which was why he hadn't told her he was going to do it beforehand.

Go with it, indeed.

Determined not to start her day on a bad note, Mara got up to explore her new surroundings. So far the only things she'd seen were the kitchen, that amazing closet, and the bedroom. The living room connected to a hallway on the other side. She pushed open the first door and was immediately hit in the face with the scent of leather and chalk.

She flipped on the light. One wall was dominated by a massive flat-screen television. A pool table took up the center of the room.

Matt would love to play a game before he left town.

She closed the door behind her and poked her head briefly into the other rooms. Trent's home office was outfitted with the usual equipment and looked professionally decorated just like the rest of the house. It was all beautiful but cold.

Unlived in.

With a sudden rush of clarity, she realized it *was* unlived in. Because Trent had been living with her.

Relief flowed through her—sweet, blessed relief. This entire time she'd been terrified that she'd explore and come across more things about Trent that she didn't know. That this was his "real life" and the time he'd spent with her was the sham.

She heard the elevator open again and then the sound of footsteps. With an exasperated sigh, she turned and left the home theater.

"Trent, I told you I don't need a babysitter."

She stopped short when she saw the petite brunette stand up straight from where she'd been rooting around in the couch cushions. Mara recognized her instantly from the pictures Matt had shown her.

She'd spent hours staring at this woman's face, wondering what she had that Mara didn't. Wondering what it was about her that made Trent leave at the drop of a hat and lie to his fiancée.

Mara looked her over, noticing with no small amount of jealousy the designer jeans that fit her slim hips perfectly and the way her long brown hair cascaded over her shoulders in subtle layers. Everything about her was perfectly styled, and suddenly Mara desperately wished she'd gotten dressed and done her hair before exploring the house.

Trent could protest all he wanted that Avery was just a childhood friend, but Mara didn't believe there were too many women who could look at Trent platonically. And the fact that she could come and go in Trent's house whenever she wanted and Mara hadn't even known this place existed until recently just rubbed salt in the still-fresh wound of betrayal.

"You must be Avery," she said finally.

To her surprise, the other woman just stared at her.

After an uncomfortable minute of silence, Mara finally spoke up. "Um, Trent isn't here. He's at work."

That seemed to snap Avery out of her fog. "Right. Of

course. I figured he wouldn't be here." She gestured over her shoulder toward the couch. "I can't find Travis's other inhaler. I figured I must have left it here somewhere."

She got quiet, and when Mara looked at her again, Avery laughed. "Sorry I'm being so weird. You just remind me of someone. That's all."

"Oh?" Mara wasn't sure what to say to that, so she just sat in one of the overstuffed chairs facing the windows, tucking her bare legs beneath her.

"Trent told me he was bringing you home, but things have been so crazy lately. Travis hasn't been feeling well."

She knelt on the floor and peered beneath the couch, thrusting her hand beneath it and sweeping it back and forth.

When she sat back up, she turned in Mara's direction. "So, have you met them yet?"

Completely distracted by how animated and, well, *beautiful* Avery was, Mara could barely keep the thread of the conversation. "Have I met who?"

"The Townsends. Trent's parents."

"Oh yes. They stopped by yesterday." She must have made an involuntary face because Avery grinned.

"Don't worry, they don't like me either. I'm just the slut who drove their son out of town."

It was a strange thing to bond over, but it made Mara feel a little bit better that even Avery, who had been raised in their social circle, hadn't had an easy time fitting in either.

"Well, I haven't met him yet. James. Or Sophia. Trent said I'll probably meet them at his parents' house later this week."

Avery snorted. "Don't rush on that score. There's plenty of time for you to make *Her Majesty's* acquaintance." At Mara's wrinkled brow, Avery waved her off. "That's just what I call her. Sophia was born to rule some small principality. I think fate was just screwing with the rest of us by putting her here."

"I guess you don't get along with Trent's sister then?"

"Sophia is used to being the queen bee. As long as you let her, you'll get along fine." Avery glanced down at the watch on her slim wrist. "Well, I've got to go. Travis is with my mother today. I need to get back. It was so good to *finally* meet you."

Avery waved good-bye and walked back to the elevators. Once she heard the doors close, Mara hopped up and trotted back to the bedroom. In her closet, she stripped quickly and then walked into the bathroom.

This room was just as stunning as the rest of the penthouse, boasting marble floors, honey oak cabinets, and more shower-heads than she knew what to do with. As she stepped under multiple streams of water, she mentally berated herself for not talking to Avery more, pumping her for information. Even though she didn't really feel comfortable with a girl that beautiful being secret friends with her man, Avery was undoubtedly a good source of information about Trent.

She should have at least asked about what he'd been doing all these months when he was visiting.

Although it was amazing to come here and see where Trent came from, it was so easy to get caught up in the way he made her feel. If she wasn't careful, she'd spend the entire time the way she had last night, immersed in him and dazed by passion.

Not that she was complaining. Waking up this morning had been a sensual experience. And not just because she'd been all over Trent. The sheets had been so soft against her skin, and that bed was just made for snuggling.

And other things.

She blushed, remembering how Trent had looked at her. If

she'd given him the signal, any signal at all, he'd likely have given her an entirely different kind of wake-up call. But she wasn't sure she was ready for that. Things had been so raw last night.

She had no idea what had made him go off like that, but he'd seemed so frantic, like he was scared to let her out of his arms. They hadn't even made it to the bed.

Normally that kind of urgency would have made her feel special, but there had been something disturbing about the way Trent reacted. She'd come here to get closer to him, but so far she wasn't any nearer to that goal.

Instead, the real Trent seemed like even more of a puzzle.

And she was terrified that when she finally put all the pieces together, the picture would be something she didn't want to see.

———

HIS YOUNGER SISTER had always been nosy, so Trent wasn't surprised the next day when he received a text message from her inviting them to lunch.

After he showed it to Mara, she said only, "Well, at least she didn't just show up here unannounced."

Trent didn't bother telling her that if she'd known they were in town, she probably would have.

When he'd gotten home last night, Mara had been in a strange mood. He'd wanted to take her out, show her the city, but she had wanted to stay in.

They'd spent their second evening in town cuddled on the couch with some old movies. Now he sat on the bed and watched as Mara changed clothes for the third time. She yanked a blouse over her head and then stared at her reflection critically before making a disgusted sound and pulling it over her head again.

"You look beautiful. This lunch is no big deal. It's just my sister."

Trent had enough experience to know that nothing he said would make a difference since women tended to see a whole host of things men were blind to. All the outfits she'd tried on so far had looked great in his opinion.

She rolled her eyes and looked at him in exasperation. "It's your sister, and everyone else at whatever expensive place she's picked out. I can already see how this entire trip is going to go. I'll be constantly surrounded by people who look at me like I'm an insult to fashion. Did you see your mom's shoes yesterday?"

She'd disappeared into the walk-in closet, so her voice was muffled, but Trent could guess what she was saying. Not that he knew much about women's fashion other than it seemed to matter to a lot of people.

"If you want shoes, I'll buy you shoes." As he'd thought, that made her come out of the closet with a scowl on her face.

"Buying me stuff is not what this is about. But oh, you'd better be glad I'm not a different person, because you don't know the things I'd do for those shoes."

He leaned across the bed, snagging her wrist. "Tell me."

The first tinge of a blush appeared in her cheeks. "Come on. We're going to be late."

She smoothed her hands up and down her outfit and then grabbed her handbag. Trent followed, trying in vain to look at anything other than how damn curvy she was.

They arrived at the restaurant to find that Sophia was already there. To his surprise, his heart gave a little pang to see her. Her eyes sparkled as she looked up at him, a huge smile stretching across her face. She shook her head softly as she rose to greet him.

"Hey, big brother." She raised her arms for a hug, and that's when Trent noticed what had been hidden by the table. The round swell of her belly was unmistakable beneath her fitted jacket.

"You're expecting?"

She laughed prettily and allowed him to kiss her cheek. "I am. You're going to be an uncle again. This time we're hoping for a girl. There's more than enough Townsend testosterone in this family."

Her smile fell slightly when she looked at Mara, but unlike his mother, she at least extended her hand in greeting. "Hello, I'm Sophia."

After they were all seated, Mara asked, "So, this is your second baby?"

Sophia glanced at him in surprise before answering. "No, this is our third. Trent has two nephews that he spoils outrageously already."

The waiter interrupted to bring their water and take their orders. Once he left, Trent picked up Mara's hand and held it on his knee.

"I don't spoil them," he responded to her earlier comment, happy the conversation seemed to be on neutral ground. "I just encourage them in their natural desire to create chaos."

Sophia took a delicate sip from her water goblet. "You give them all the toys parents hate. Basically anything that makes noise or squirts water or leaves permanent stains."

"That's what being a kid should be about."

At that statement, Sophia's eyes softened. She knew how

he felt about their upbringing, and on this one matter, they agreed. Children should be children. Not little robots. Or pawns.

"Well, I'll have ample opportunity to pay you back when you have kids of your own." She looked at Mara finally.

It wasn't the friendliest look, and Trent shifted in his seat, hoping to bring his sister's attention back to him. Sophia wasn't vicious like their mother, but she could be disturbingly blunt.

"We definitely want children, but we have to get through the wedding first."

She turned to face him. "I hope you're back for good. Running away from your problems doesn't solve anything."

"Sophia," he said, hoping she'd change the subject.

She glared at him, her eyes warning him that she knew things about him. Things he didn't want to be public knowledge. Sophia loved him, he didn't doubt it, but she could be incredibly pushy when she thought she was doing something for his own good.

"Not to worry, big brother. I'm just glad you're back."

There was something calculating in her eyes, but before he could dwell on it too long, the waiter stepped between them to put their food down. After he left, Sophia started chatting with Mara about the new charity she was working with and didn't look his way again.

———

MARA WASN'T sure what Trent was hoping to accomplish by sending her out shopping with his sister. There were some people who would simply never be friends, and after Sophia's polite but disinterested treatment of her during lunch, she figured that was their destiny and was surprisingly fine with it.

After she'd come back from the bathroom halfway through the meal, she'd noticed the siblings arguing from across the room. But by the time she slid into her seat, they were both focused on their food. Sophia had made minimal effort to engage her in conversation, and Mara didn't foresee them being best buddies anytime soon.

She thought then of Penny with her warm demeanor and penchant for telling inappropriate jokes. Even though it was partially because they'd known each other since she was a child, there was also a comfort factor there that came simply because Penny didn't view her as a rival.

She didn't get the sense that Sophia shared much of anything well, much less her brother's time and affection.

The doorbell rang, startling her. With a curse, she shoved her feet into a pair of strappy black sandals and grabbed a light cardigan.

Sophia had told them she'd meet them at the penthouse since she needed to check on her kids first. Mara had spent the time going back and forth over whether or not she should change. A dress was fine for lunch, but if she was going to be traipsing around a bunch of stores, it was probably better to keep things somewhat casual.

Her jeans and fitted blouse probably wouldn't win her any style points with Sophia, but she was doubtful anything she did would meet with Sophia's approval. So if that was the case, she might as well be comfortable.

Trent appeared in the doorway to her closet, sipping from a cup of coffee. "Are you ready? I just told the front desk to allow Sophia to come up."

Curious, Mara asked, "Would they really keep her away if you told them she wasn't permitted up here? I mean, what would they do, tackle her?"

Trent threw his head back and laughed, a deep, full-bodied sound that echoed throughout the room. "I adore you, you know that?"

His eyes held hers, and she warmed from the inside out. The awkwardness between them was starting to thaw and it was good, very good, to see the old Trent she knew and loved back again.

"I was just wondering." She smiled sweetly.

Although she had to admit that the mental image of the ever-helpful Walter tackling a wayward visitor was extremely amusing.

"Well, so far none of my family members have been brave enough to test the limits of my security. That's a good thing because I believe Walter probably would tackle someone if he had to. He's very dedicated."

"I noticed. All your... people, or whatever you want to call them, seem very loyal to you. I got an e-mail from Gina. Apparently she'll be handling my calendar as well. She seems really happy to have you here."

Trent was watching her closely. She should have known that her confusion wouldn't escape his notice.

"You didn't like that, did you? Having someone taking over your personal stuff?"

"Um, not really," she admitted. "I'm sorry. I feel like I'm being so ungrateful, but it feels weird to have someone telling me when I'll be going here and there."

"I know it seems strange and invasive, but she's truly just there to make sure that you don't get over-scheduled. In the future we'll have dinners and charity events to attend. It helps to have someone keeping track of all those details and making sure you have a dress for each event. She handles car service too so I don't have to think about it."

"I guess. It's definitely going to take some getting used to. Anyway, I probably won't be gone long. I'm sure your sister was just being polite when she invited me."

Trent paused, the cup halfway to his mouth. "Um, I have to warn you that, knowing Sophia, you'll be gone until this evening. Her shoe fetish rivals yours." He put his mug down on top of her dressing table and pulled out his wallet. "Oh yeah, you'll need this."

A small twinge of unease hit as she accepted the card he held out. It was a black American Express card. In her name.

"This is mine?"

He shrugged absently. "I had you added to my account as soon as you agreed to come."

It was such a small thing to cause these insidious feelings of shame. She'd never been the kept-woman type, and despite knowing that her relationship with Trent wasn't that way, had *never* been that way, it still made her uncomfortable to have him giving her what was essentially a direct line to his bank account.

"I thought these were an urban legend. I didn't think anybody actually had these."

It was a stupid thing to say, but she felt a need to fill the silence. He was still watching her, so she slipped the card into her wallet.

"It'll get easier," he promised quietly.

They both turned at the sound of heels echoing from the living room. Mara stood uncertainly and slipped her arms into the cardigan she'd selected. She stood on tiptoe and kissed Trent's cheek.

"Well, I guess I'd better go. I don't want to keep Sophia waiting. Have a good day, honey."

He grinned at her syrupy-sweet endearment. "You too, *dear*."

She walked out to meet Sophia, who stood in the living room tapping the toe of her Jimmy Choo pump against the hardwood.

"I'm ready," Mara said.

Or not.

ten

TRENT WAS in the middle of answering e-mails when his phone rang. When he heard who was downstairs, he immediately gave his approval. The elevator opened a few minutes later, and his old classmate, David Baxter, walked in.

Six feet of muscle and tattoos, his dark hair cut close and spiked up slightly in the center, Dax was an intimidating sight. He looked like a meathead, but Trent knew from experience that he was as sharp as a razorblade and twice as lethal. He was also a damned good private investigator.

He grinned at Trent when he saw him. "It's good to have you back, man. How have you been?"

"Better now." They clasped hands and Trent gestured at the chair across from him. "Have a seat."

Dax shook his head. "You won't want to shoot the shit when I tell you what's going on. James flew in to LaGuardia last night. He's at the Waldorf."

Anticipation spiked Trent's blood. "He didn't go home?"

There was no change in Dax's expression, but Trent could feel the disapproval palpably. "No, sir."

"Maybe that's a good thing. I don't want Avery to even know he was here unless he's staying."

Trent immediately closed his laptop and strode to the elevators. Without another word, Dax fell into step behind him. They rode the elevator down in silence. Trent took a deep breath. There was no part of him that didn't want to throttle his brother on sight, but he was going to keep his cool for Avery's sake. And for Travis.

In this entire situation, the welfare of the little boy they all loved came first and foremost.

He turned to Dax. "You don't have to come along. You've done your job and found him. Now I just have to make him see reason. Hopefully he'll do the right thing and I can let Avery know what's going on."

"I'm coming with you. Just in case he *doesn't* see reason."

Trent nodded. "He's my brother. He can be an ass, but he wouldn't hurt me."

Dax crossed him arms. "People can do a lot of things when they feel cornered."

The elevator stopped on the garage level and they walked to Dax's black SUV, parked in one of Trent's assigned spaces. As Dax pulled out into traffic, Trent glanced at the time.

Mara would likely be gone most of the evening. His sister was focused about her shopping. Mara was the same way. After a few tense moments at lunch, he'd gotten Sophia's promise that she would be on her best behavior. He would have never agreed for Mara to accompany her otherwise.

It was good that she wasn't around for this. He wasn't going to introduce her to James until he knew where things stood. Also until he knew his brother could keep his mouth shut.

The car pulled up in front of the Waldorf. They walked through the hotel's luxurious lobby and entered the elevators.

Dax hit the button for the thirty-seventh floor. "He has one of the suites. The clerk said he booked the room only for the next few days."

Trent chuckled. "How do you get these people to talk to you?"

A wicked grin crossed Dax's face. "Money. Sex. Or both. Trust me, this girl was so hot, I felt like I owed her *something*."

Trent could only smile. His friend got things done and somehow managed to leave everyone with a smile on their faces. He couldn't quibble with his methods of extracting information.

The elevator stopped and he followed Dax as he approached room 3710. There was a room service cart in the hall and a Privacy Please sign hanging on the door.

"I guess we're about to interrupt his solitude," Dax murmured before knocking on the door. "Room service," he called out in a high voice.

A few minutes later, the door opened slightly. "I didn't order anything else."

Dax stuck his foot in the door before it could close. "Well, I brought you something anyway." He shoved the door open.

James stood in the middle of the entryway in a dressing gown. A cigarette dangled from his teeth. He looked hungover and smelled like vodka. There were clothes and empty bottles all over the room. A lamp lay on its side on the floor, the lampshade bent and ripped.

"Looks like we missed a hell of a party," Trent commented.

James grimaced and covered his ears with his hands. "You did. Come in. Have a drink. How nice of you to stop by."

He walked away, leaving them standing in the entryway.

Trent held up a hand, indicating to Dax that he didn't need to follow. He entered the bedroom his brother had walked into. It looked just as trashed as the rest of the suite.

James fumbled in the pocket of his dressing gown until he found a lighter. With a shaky hand, he attempted to light his cigarette. After the fourth unsuccessful attempt, he gave up and tossed the lighter on the bed next to him.

"As you can see, I'm not really up to entertaining guests right now."

"Everything is a joke to you, isn't it?"

Trent watched with disdain as James flopped back onto the bed, fluffing the pillow under his head. His nephew had been in the hospital wondering where his daddy was, and James was on a drug-fueled bender up and down the East Coast.

"Who's joking?" James smirked.

"It's one thing to screw our father over. He's proven that he only cares about himself. But Avery has done nothing to deserve this."

"You always defend her." The soft tone of James's voice somehow seemed more accusatory than if he'd yelled the statement.

"I don't always defend her. But I do try to consider her point of view and what she needs. Which is what you are supposed to do. She's the mother of your child. Even if you don't love Avery, at least be there for Travis. He's your son."

"Funny thing that is, brother. He looks more like you than me."

Something cold and ugly passed between them. Trent watched wordlessly as James stood and walked over to the small bar in the corner. He struggled to pour two fingers of scotch into a glass, then lifted the drink to his lips, watching Trent over the brim.

"What the hell are you talking about? I've *never* slept with Avery. It's always been you. Ever since we were kids, the only person she's ever been into was you."

James swallowed, his eyes closing briefly as the scotch went down. "I saw the way you used to look at her. And that night at her graduation party the both of you were so wasted. I found you naked in bed together."

Trent's mind raced as he tried to remember all the events of that night. Avery had taken a year off to travel after high school, so by the time she graduated from college, Trent had already been done with school and living full-time in an apartment in Virginia. He'd come up for a rare visit because Avery had begged.

She'd accused him of forgetting about her, treating her just like James did.

He hadn't been dating anyone at the time, so it had been easy to come up for a visit. He'd regretted it almost immediately though because Avery had spent all night telling him the details of her latest fight with his brother.

"I wasn't that wasted. I put Avery to bed and then crashed in another room. She must have come into my room in the middle of the night. But nothing happened."

"Are you sure about that?"

———

WHEN MARA HAD BEEN TOLD they were going shopping, she'd envisioned something like those scenes from the movies where they'd bounce from store to store, trying on clothes and shoes while carrying bags in each hand. The reality of shopping with Sophia Townsend Winbush was entirely different.

They'd come to an exclusive boutique owned by one of Sophia's girlfriends from her days at Yale. As soon as they entered, they'd been shown to a special section in the back and served champagne while they waited.

Mara didn't want to seem completely clueless, so she just sipped her champagne and tried to figure out what they were waiting on. That was when Sophia's old friend Cleo appeared with outfits she'd selected for them to view.

Apparently women like Sophia didn't even do their own shopping. They had someone else pick out the best stuff and bring it to them. Mara tipped back her glass and swallowed the rest of her champagne in a big gulp.

"So, what was Trent like as a little boy?"

Sophia sat, one leg primly folded over the other as Cleo arranged the outfits on the rack in front of them. A second later, an assistant appeared carrying several different pairs of shoes that Cleo snatched before shooing her away.

"He was much like he is now. Focused. Driven." Sophia didn't seem to notice the flurry of activity in the room, but Mara found she could barely concentrate with all the people coming in and out.

"Driven, huh? I guess I just see him differently. I would have said easygoing. Funny, but not in an obvious way. He has a subtle sense of humor, but it's there."

Sophia regarded her with open curiosity. "I suppose so."

Not the most friendly response, but Mara figured this was probably as warm as Sophia was going to get. She decided not to take it personally.

As Sophia nodded to another one of the selections, Mara had to admit that even if the other woman wasn't fond of her, she at least had impeccable taste. Every one of the outfits she'd picked out so far looked like it would complement her skin tone and figure perfectly.

When Cleo finally left them alone to go get more items to show them, Mara glanced over at Sophia.

"What did you mean yesterday when you said that Trent ran away from his problems?"

Sophia picked at the platter of fruit sitting on the table between them.

"You're asking a lot of questions but none of the right ones. Doesn't it seem odd to you that a wealthy young man would suddenly decide to leave it all behind and live like the commoners?"

"I don't think he left it all behind. Hasn't he been traveling here to visit family all along?"

"He's been visiting *Avery*. Not us." Sophia said the name with such disdain that Mara didn't have to wonder what she thought.

It appeared that Avery's dislike of Trent's sister was mutual. Obviously Avery wasn't someone Sophia thought Trent should be spending time with. Although she secretly agreed, she figured Sophia probably felt the same way about her, so that didn't mean much.

"I hadn't realized."

"There's a lot of stuff you don't realize. I'm guessing he didn't tell you about Tia?"

She turned around to face forward as Cleo brought out a selection of handbags and accessories to go with the outfits. Sophia looked over the offerings with a critical eye. Every so often, she'd glance over at Mara and then back to the items as if imagining how they would look on her.

Mara sat quietly, but the whole time, her mind was racing. Who was Tia? And just what the hell did she have to do with Trent's decision to leave home?

What seemed like hours later, Cleo finally packed up the remainder of the outfits, and Mara handed over the black credit card. Once they were alone again, Mara finally broke down.

"Who's Tia?"

Sophia sighed as if greatly put upon, but there was a satisfied gleam in her eye that told Mara she'd been waiting for her to ask.

"Tia was my brother's high school girlfriend. Spicy Latina girl just like you. Her father was some sort of relation to Spanish royalty or something. Anyway, she died. Trent was devastated."

Mara's hand shook so hard that she had to set her champagne glass down after Sophia's callous recitation of events. There had been so many times when she'd recounted stories from her high school days and she'd always wondered why Trent didn't talk about his past more.

He'd mentioned once that he'd been a champion runner and had several medals in track and field. But for some reason he hadn't joined the team in college, which she'd found odd. He also didn't talk about any old friends or seem to keep in contact with any of them. It had seemed off, but she hadn't wanted to push. High school definitely wasn't filled with happy memories for a lot of people.

Was this why? Was he still so devastated over the loss of his high school girlfriend that he couldn't even think about that time?

"When did she die?"

Sophia pursed her lips. "Trent's senior year. It was actually the day after his prom, so it was near the end of the year. Then he disappeared and ended up in some college in Virginia. When did you meet him?"

"Right at the beginning of the term. August," she managed to get out. Trent had met her only three months after his previous girlfriend had died and he'd never mentioned a word to her.

Sophia gave her a pitying look. "Don't feel too bad. Rich men are used to having whatever they want. If one of their toys gets broken, they go out and buy another one."

———

THE ENTIRE DRIVE HOME, Trent turned the conversation with his brother over in his head. Dax seemed to sense his inner turmoil because he didn't ask him any questions about what had been said in the hotel room. He just drove the car, parked, and let him out. Trent rode the elevator back up to the penthouse alone.

Could it be true?

He wasn't sure why James would lie, but then again he didn't understand a lot of things his brother did. But the more he thought about it, the more it made a twisted sort of sense.

All this time he'd wondered how James could leave Travis for months at a time, leaving Avery to deal with everything. And although Avery had told him what they fought about, in way more detail than he actually wanted, the things she'd told him had never seemed like enough to warrant their constant fighting.

Was it because his brother had been carrying this suspicion around ever since Travis was born?

He hadn't had the best relationship with his brother over the years. His father had always focused the brunt of his criticism on James, and nothing his brother had ever done was good enough. Whereas Trent had decided at a young age that he didn't care what his parents thought.

Strangely enough, his indifference and determination to forge his own path had earned a begrudging respect from their father, something that James had never managed despite his many attempts.

But to put that kind of accusation out there, it went way past sibling rivalry. Trent knew what had really happened, but these types of things tended to take on a life of their own regardless of the facts. If James told anyone what he'd seen, then the truth wouldn't even matter. People were always more than happy to believe the worst.

And if Mara ever got wind of it, Trent would have a problem.

A big one.

He entered the penthouse and took a seat on the couch. The purplish hues of dusk painted the sky behind the city with big blotches of color. He wasn't sure how long he sat there, staring out into the night, when he turned his head and saw it.

A picture on the table next to him.

The breath he was about to take got stuck in his lungs. Pressure built as he stared at the familiar image. It had been taken his senior year of high school. He was looking straight at the camera while Avery and Tia both kissed his cheeks.

He snatched the picture so hard the frame bent. With a shaking hand, he traced the faces in the photo. Glancing around frantically, he pried the back of the frame open and pulled the picture out. With trembling fingers, he walked into his office and placed it in the bottom of one of his desk drawers.

Had Walter missed a photo when he'd done the clean sweep the prior day? It had been a tall order, and he'd figured the other man might miss one or two, which was why he'd gone through all the rooms yesterday, looking for any strays. He supposed he couldn't fault him for missing that one since Trent had clearly missed it too.

He walked into the bedroom and stopped short. There were shopping bags all over the bed. "Mara?"

She walked out of her closet. "Hey. Where did you go?"

He glanced over at her bags. "I had errands to run. It looks like your trip was successful. I guess that means you found stuff you liked."

Mara picked up one of the bags and carried it with her into the closet. "It would be hard not to find things you like at the kind of places where your sister shops. She has amazing taste."

Surprised at the compliment, Trent followed, leaning against the door of her closet to observe her as she put the clothes away in the empty drawers of her new dresser.

"Amazing taste. That almost sounds like you like her."

Mara glanced up at him. "I'm not sure I'd go that far, but she did pick out some great stuff for me."

He followed her with his eyes as she went back into the room to grab another bag. Something wasn't right about the way she was moving. Her back was too stiff, and she looked almost mechanical as she tore tags off each item of clothing. It probably would have taken him longer to figure out what was different if he weren't in the same place emotionally.

She wasn't happy. She was miserable and trying very hard not to let on.

As she passed him to go back to the closet, he grabbed her arm. She turned into his embrace and buried her face in his shoulder.

"Hey now, what's wrong?"

Mara let out a soft hiccup and shook her head. The movement sent her long curls tumbling around her shoulders.

"Well, good. I was a little worried there."

"About me?"

He smiled, willing to do anything to erase the miserable look on her face. "Not just about you, but about Sophia too. You're completely capable of taking her on if you want to."

Mara looked down at the clothes in her hands. "At one time I would have agreed with you. Now I'm not so sure."

"I'm sure. You can handle anything. You've never been the type to take crap off anyone."

Suddenly she raised her head, a spark of her usual sass in her eyes. "You're right. I haven't had the luxury of being shy. Especially working in the legal profession, which is such a good old boys' club. So why am I so meek and mild around everyone here?" Then her face twisted and she threw the sweater she held down. "Well, it's actually not that hard to figure out. I feel out of place here. Completely and totally out of place."

"Well, that's not possible since this is your place. You belong here with me."

"No, I really don't. This is your place, Trent. You own this penthouse. You own these clothes. None of this is mine."

He held her cheeks gently between his palms, tracing the sides of her face with his thumbs. She relaxed into the caress and closed her eyes. He nuzzled her cheek, just breathing in her scent.

When she opened her eyes again, he held her gaze as he said, "Well you own me. *I am yours.* So all the rest doesn't matter."

eleven

MARA CLOSED HER EYES, soaking up the warmth of Trent's love. Shivers of sensation radiated from her cheeks where he was caressing her face all the way down to her toes. She'd always felt like she could tell him anything. Her greatest fears and insecurities seemed like obstacles to conquer instead of mountains when he was with her.

"You own me too. I wouldn't be here otherwise."

At her words, his eyes shuttered like he was pleased by her admission. His lashes lowered as he leaned forward. Their lips met and clung, his taste lingering even when he pulled back to kiss the tip of her nose.

"What's really bothering you, baby?"

Mara looked behind her at the massive pile of packages on the bed. Shopping with someone like Sophia made her realize just how empty the activity could be.

Growing up, shopping had been something that she and her mother had done together when they needed a way to reconnect. After she decided she didn't want to compete in any more beauty pageants, it had been harder and harder to find common ground with her mom. Looking through the sale racks and finding the perfect thing to complement an outfit had been a low-pressure activity they could do without arguing. At the end, they'd both be more relaxed and go home with something pretty.

Mara looked at all the clothes and shoes and handbags scattered across the room. It looked like a spread from *Vogue*. Truthfully she'd never owned so much in her life, but it brought her no joy. She didn't look at all the pretty things and attach them to happy memories. And despite her closet being filled to the brim, she had a feeling it would still seem empty.

"This whole day was about changing me. Every time Sophia would look over at me, it was like she was seeing all my flaws and trying to find a way to make me more acceptable. Like I'm not good enough as I am."

One of Trent's hands skimmed up her back and tangled in her hair. Her mouth fell open as her heart beat faster. God, she loved it when he held her like this. One hand in her hair and the other on her hip, like he was never going to let her go. Like he was completely and utterly enthralled with her.

"All those clothes can go back where they came from as far as I'm concerned. You know how you look best?" He rasped the question in her ear, the husky timbre of his voice sending chills down her spine.

"Ask me," he ordered.

Mara shivered, completely turned on by the power and authority in his voice. He was no longer her easygoing, laid-back Trent. His other side, the autocratic, self-assured business scion, was back and slowly kissing his way down the side of her throat.

"How do I look best?" she managed to get out between gulps of air.

Trent pushed her hair out of the way, clearing the path for his tongue to find the curve of her collarbone. "You look best in nothing at all. So you can take all that stuff back to the fucking store if you want."

He spun her around so she was facing the bed. Her head fell back on his shoulder.

"And you see all those shoes? Every time you wear a pair of those sexy-as-hell stilettos, I want you to remember that as soon as you get home they're going to be on my shoulders."

"Oh God," she panted as the imagery his words evoked triggered a deep throb in her belly.

The arrogant statement made her clench her thighs together, desperate to stop the ache in her core that made her feel suddenly, desperately empty.

He must have sensed the movement because he moved, his thigh forcing her legs open. It was ten times as intense this way, when she couldn't close her legs. She could feel how wet she was, and when his hand pushed firmly, inexorably, down the front of her jeans, she knew Trent would feel it too.

"And do you see this ring I bought you?"

He held up her left hand, the diamond on her third finger sparkling in the light.

"I went back and forth for weeks about it. I knew it would cause talk to buy you a diamond this big, but I wanted you to have the best. But it doesn't even matter. *Because no diamond can shine the way you do.* You don't need jewels or any adornment at all. I'm almost blinded every time I look at your perfect naked skin." His voice was gruff, almost angry.

When he curled his hand, his fingers sliding through the

slick lips of her sex, Mara couldn't hold back a scream. He turned her head, and his lips covered hers roughly, swallowing the sound. She'd never thought of herself as the helpless type, but in that moment, she was completely dependent on him.

If he moved or let go, she'd drop to the floor in a quivering puddle of need.

There was nothing to do but allow herself to be swept along as he ravaged her mouth, nipping and biting as she rode his hand. Her entire being was focused on the movement of his finger circling her clit, rubbing slow circles that were driving her closer and closer to losing her mind.

"Now that I have you here, I won't allow anything to hurt you. Do you understand? I exist to protect you. And you exist to make my life worth living."

She opened her eyes, completely caught up in the intensity of the words he'd whispered in her ear and the physical storm caused by his clever fingers. Trent's eyes were fixed on her, his face a mask of obsession and desire.

Then his eyes narrowed and he twisted his fingers, hitting a spot inside her that ignited a firestorm deep within.

"Trent!" His name was all she could manage as the world shifted and splintered.

"That's it," he growled in her ear. "I'd pay any price just to see you like this, coming apart in my arms."

She whimpered, biting her lip so hard she drew blood, her muscles contracting around his fingers. Shards of white-hot pleasure radiated through her as the orgasm washed over her. Her fingers tightened on his arm and her head fell forward, her hair sliding into her face as she shuddered through the final tremors of her release.

All she could do was cling to him for dear life as he lifted her, wrapping her legs around his waist. He came down over her on the bed, burying his face between her breasts. Every inch of her skin tingled from the explosive orgasm that was barely out of her system.

When he nuzzled her breasts through the cotton of her tank top, she knew she would probably be screaming again shortly. But things had been completely one-sided so far. She pushed back and then tugged at his shirt.

"I want to touch you too."

His eyes crinkled at the corners. "I'm definitely down for that."

His shirt disappeared and his hands immediately went to work on his belt buckle. Mara pulled the straps of her top down, exposing the lacy cups of her bra. Trent's gaze stopped there and his hands at his belt moved faster.

"You are so beautiful. It doesn't even seem possible that you're mine."

His words emboldened her to strip out of her top completely, and then she pushed her jeans down her legs with a sexy little shimmy.

She turned, giving him what she knew was a first-class view of her ass in the thong panties she wore, and crawled up the bed. Before she reached the headboard, Trent was there. He draped himself over her back and twisted his hands in her hair to hold her still.

"Stay just like that," he whispered with a soft kiss to her shoulder.

Mara pressed back, arching her back and sticking her bottom higher. His tortured groan made her smile. Then she gasped as he yanked at the sides of her thong, ripping clean through the delicate fabric.

"It's a good thing I wasn't attached to those," she got out just as one of Trent's fingers slid deep before pulling out and spreading her moisture around her clit. Still sensitive, she shivered under the erotic assault.

"I'm supposed to be touching you. Making you feel good."

Even as she said the words, her fingers tightened in the bedsheets. His tongue trailed over her back, tracing down the line of her spine. It took all her self-control to hold still and not squirm under his touch.

"This makes me feel good. Hearing you scream makes me feel good. The only thing I want you to do is come for me. That's all I want."

Everything he said to her and his harsh, dominant demeanor was making her hotter than she'd ever been. When he gently helped her turn over, his every touch reverent, there were no doubts left about his feelings for her. It made Mara feel completely taken over and completely cherished when he focused on her pleasure so totally.

Like all he needed in the world was to satisfy her.

His mouth traveled over the lace of her bra, the contrast between the warm, wet cavern of his mouth and the chill in the air making her gasp aloud. He tugged gently on the straps, drawing them down her arms. Frustrated, Mara reached behind her and unsnapped the band, shrugging the undergarment hurriedly down her arms.

"Touch me. Please."

She tried to reach for him but he held her still, his arms and fingers entwined with hers, pressing her down. Mara sucked in a shaky breath as his head descended, his lips playing over the dent of her navel. She squirmed, her nerves already sensitized and ready for what she knew was coming.

The first wet rasp of his tongue had her coming off the bed. "It's too much. I'm so close," she whispered.

"You're so hot. So ready for me." He pushed his slacks down and his cock bobbed out, hard and ready.

He moved back so he could strip out of the rest of his clothes.

Then he was over her, thrusting deep, and her core contracted, her muscles clenching down on him hard. They both cried out at the exquisite feeling. Trent held still, pressing his forehead against hers. Mara clamped a desperate hand on his ass.

She'd been on the pill for years and they'd long ago ditched condoms, and she'd never been so happy about it. It was an entirely different sensation to have him without anything between them.

He pulled out, teasing her by rocking against her mound.

"You have to move. You have to take me," she pleaded. Her need had risen so high that she was willing to beg if it would get her what she wanted. To be filled. To be consumed by him.

Her whispered words seemed to push him into a frenzy. He positioned himself against her damp opening again, and she moaned as his cock dragged against the sensitive tissue. Her hips lifted of their own accord.

Then he thrust deep, sending her soaring.

"Trent, please." Her cries and passion-fueled noises surrounded them as he filled her completely.

Her orgasm ripped through her, turning her inside out as he pumped through the contractions of her tight inner muscles, forcing himself deeper.

His mouth opened over hers, and she gave herself up to his desperate kiss. She wrapped her legs around him, trying to hold him tighter, press him deeper every time he withdrew. There was nothing like being one with Trent. He'd touched her in ways that no one else had ever managed.

As mind-blowing as the physical sensations were, it was the emotional connection that took their lovemaking to another level.

"Fuck, Mara. You're so tight. So perfect. So mine."

He whispered the words against her neck, tasting her as he thrust furiously in and out of her body. Over and over, until Mara thought she'd die from pleasure. Until she came again, her skin going tight and hot before it exploded into a cascade of tingles all over her body.

Trent groaned too, pushing through her tight muscles one final time before holding himself deep inside, his muscles trembling from exertion as he found his own release.

They lay together for a long time, Trent's head pillowed on her breast. Mara didn't have the energy to move. Finally Trent rolled, tucking her against his side in a protective gesture that brought a small smile to her face.

"Are you okay?" he asked.

"Yeah, just thinking."

His arm tightened against her side. "Tell me. I want to know the things you worry about. I can't give you the perfect world you deserve if I don't know what's bothering you."

She snuggled closer. "I don't know. It's just that there are times when I feel like I can talk to you about anything. But then, other times I feel this wall. Like if I look around the wrong corner, I'll see something that ruins everything."

Trent propped himself up on one arm and stared down at her. "Ask me anything you want."

Mara considered it, watching the play of emotions across his face. All she wanted was to know him. More than anything.

But it seemed that as soon as she peeled back one layer, infinite more were revealed. But perhaps that was just part of the process. Peeling back the layers until she finally knew all there was to know about him. If that was true, then all she could do to hasten the process was keep digging.

"I can ask you anything?" She watched his face carefully, searching for signs that he really didn't want to talk.

But he just regarded her with the same calm, patient expression, so she decided to peel back another layer.

"Who was Tia?"

"TIA PILAR DELGADO was never supposed to be my girlfriend."

Mara shifted against his side, settling her head right over his heart. In that moment, in the warm cocoon that surrounded them, he knew it was finally time to tell her about his past.

"She actually had a crush on my brother, James," he continued.

Mara lifted her head. "If she was interested in your brother, then why…"

Her tousled hair fell over her shoulders in wild disarray. The makeup she'd worn earlier had rubbed off, so her face was almost bare. It was difficult to think of a time when she was more beautiful than when she was like this. Naked and open to him.

And all his.

"Tia was a year below me. James had already turned eighteen by then, and her parents were very strict. If they had known their fifteen-year-old daughter was chasing after an eighteen-year-old senior, they would have freaked out. So she used to tell her parents that she was hanging out with me and Avery."

Mara didn't move, but in the silence, Trent could almost hear the thoughts spinning through her mind. It had all happened so long ago, but sometimes, especially being back in New York, he would see or hear something that brought it all back. Suddenly it was like he was sixteen again, awash with the wonder and discovery of first love and the pain and heartache of first rejection.

"Anyway, she was always at our house and eventually told her parents that we were dating. They weren't happy about it, but at least she was spending time with a family they respected. Not that my parents were home to provide supervision." He laughed softly. "My parents never cared what we were doing, and they were in Europe half the time anyway. We ran completely wild that year."

He stopped, trying to fight the hold of the past. Just talking about it made it all real again, sucking him back into the same twisted emotions he'd experienced the first time.

"Then what happened?" Mara asked.

"We fell in love," he whispered.

Suddenly the room was too hot, the air too close, and the bedsheets tangled around his legs, too confining. He had to get up. When he moved to sit up, Mara leaned back and dragged the sheet up to cover her naked chest.

"You don't have to talk about it." Her eyes were soft, understanding. "I'm honored that you've shared this much. I know this is painful for you."

And just like that, the darkness around his heart lifted. No matter how hard or how painful it was to relive the past, he could do it for her. Because he had her love tethered around him to keep him on solid ground.

"No, it's okay. I want to tell you."

She smiled at him, the sweet smile that always made him feel like he'd found home. It gave him the impetus he needed to think back to what had happened next without fear. The past couldn't hurt him now.

"After spending so much time together, we talked about everything. She knew about my troubles with my father and how much I wanted to break away from this life. I was determined to move away after school and do something, anything, on my own. She felt the same way. Her parents were very religious and had their own ideas about what her future would look like. She didn't want to follow a preapproved plan. Tia wanted to follow her heart and her passion, which was painting. But that wasn't something her parents would have supported. We used to talk about running away together."

"Did you?"

"No. We never got that chance. By that time, I was a senior and we'd been hanging out so long that most people had long accepted us as a couple before we actually were. But we hadn't done anything more than kiss. She wanted to wait. And I wanted her to be happy. But then suddenly, the day after prom, she decided that she wanted me to be her first."

When he stopped talking, Mara scooted across the sheets until she was sitting right behind him. She wrapped her legs around him and rested her head against his shoulder.

"Did you kill her, Trent? Is that the secret? Was it some kind of accident?"

Shocked, he turned slightly. Their eyes met and he was stunned anew at the steady, resolute love in her eyes. There wasn't an ounce of recrimination or fear on her face. Nothing she could have done would have driven home her point more than that.

In that moment, he learned the true meaning of unconditional love. Because he knew without a doubt that even if he said yes, she would love him anyway.

"You are truly the best thing that ever happened to me," he stated before pressing his forehead against hers.

They stayed like that for a few moments, then he tugged her closer for a kiss.

"No, I didn't kill her. She killed herself. Right after we made love for the first time."

Her legs tightened around him. "I am so sorry."

Now that he was telling the story, the words wouldn't stop coming. The emotion that had been corked for so long had finally found release. He couldn't stop until he'd laid it all bare.

"She broke out into tears after we slept together and told me that she'd never loved me. I was just a shadow of the man she truly loved. And then after we argued, she went upstairs to her bathroom and slit her wrists."

He had to stop in earnest then. Images of that awful day came flooding back. All the blood. He'd left the house and walked around to cool off. He'd been so angry. It hurt now to remember that his last moments with her hadn't been happy ones.

When he'd come upstairs and found her in the tub, he'd tried everything to slow the flow of her blood, and he'd been covered in it by the time the paramedics arrived. Even after washing for hours, he could still see the evidence of her heartache all over his hands.

He'd thought he'd live forever, always covered in the stain.

"I was the last person who saw her alive. The police were all over me afterward. They wanted to know everything we'd done. Whether we'd fought. But there was no evidence of a struggle, so my family's lawyers kept them away from me after that. Somehow my father managed to keep things quiet in the press. But then her autopsy revealed she'd been three months pregnant when she died. And suddenly her earlier comments about me being just a shadow of who she really wanted made sense."

"She was pregnant?" Mara's eyes softened as she realized what that meant.

"James eventually admitted it was his."

"How awful. Not just for her family but also for you. She sounds like she was very troubled, and your brother used that to his advantage. How could they both betray you like that?"

"My brother twists people. He leaves heartache and mayhem behind wherever he goes. He screwed with Tia's head, and now he's doing the same thing to Avery. It doesn't even occur to him the damage he's doing. Or he doesn't care. But either way, he hurts people. It's just what he does."

"None of that is your fault. You couldn't have known what would happen that night. There was nothing you could have done."

"I know. But that doesn't stop me from wishing that there had been."

He shifted so he could see her face. She rubbed his chest in slow, supportive circles while he talked.

"As much as I've resented Avery's recent neediness, I made

a promise to always be there for her. We're both victims of loving people who are completely wrong for us. I understand what she's going through because that was once my story too."

"I have to admit, knowing about all this definitely helps me see her differently. I feel a little sorry for her. As long as she's in love with your brother, she'll never know what it's like to be appreciated and cherished. The way you love me."

Trent moved and then pulled her into his lap. She curled up against his chest and let out a soft sigh.

"A lifetime of loving James has twisted her into someone that I barely recognize. But I can't abandon her. After all, a lifetime of loving my brother has done nearly the same to me."

twelve

THE NEXT MORNING, Trent woke feeling lighter than he had in months. They'd talked long into the night, sharing their dreams and fears. It was the first time Trent had told her about what it was like to grow up under his father's thumb. She'd shared the unique insecurities that developed from being raised by an incredibly beautiful mother.

There were so many obstacles they'd have to jump through to be completely open to each other, but he was starting to believe it was possible.

"We're going out," Trent announced as soon as they were done with breakfast.

Mara looked up from her perch on the couch. She still wore one of his T-shirts, and her hair was uncombed. Neither of them had showered yet.

"Out? I thought you said you didn't have to work today?"

"I don't. We are going out so I can show you New York. And not the bullshit ten-dollar tour recommended for tourists. I want to show you all the things about New York that I missed when I moved away. And it definitely wasn't the Statue of Liberty."

Mara stood, her eyes gleaming. "Now you have me intrigued. Give me ten minutes."

When he turned to follow her, she put a hand squarely in the middle of his chest. "Oh no. You have to stay here. If you come with me, we'll get sidetracked and never get out of the shower."

"What?" Disappointed, his mind already on her slick curves covered in suds, he allowed her to push him back a few steps.

"I'll be back." She danced away, disappearing into the room.

Trent used the time to make a list on his cell phone of the places he wanted to take her. When he looked up next, she was standing in front of him in a white tank top and jeans.

He raced through his own shower, yanking on an old faded blue T-shirt and jeans. He met Mara in the living room and offered her his hand. Once the elevator hit the lobby, he pulled her to the front doors. Ernesto waved at them as he opened the doors.

Mara looked at him in confusion when he started walking. "No driver?"

He grinned. "No driver. When I was in high school, I used to ditch my driver all the time and take the subway because we thought it was cool. My father would have had a heart attack back then if he'd known about it."

"Is that what we're going to do today?"

He shook his head. "No, we're going to compromise and take a cab today. I want you to be able to see everything."

He put up his hand and a cab pulled over immediately.

Mara climbed in and then grabbed on to Trent with a squeal as the cabbie pulled out wildly into traffic. He pointed out Fifth Avenue as they passed and the Metropolitan Museum of Art.

"Are we going to the museum?" She twisted in her seat as they passed the entrance.

"Not today."

When the cabbie pulled over at the curb, Trent handed over a few bills and hopped out. Mara followed him, looking around in confusion.

"Where are we?"

"Central Park." He led her across the grass to a bench. He squatted next to the bench and peered at the side of it. "Yeah, this is the right one. Tia, Avery, and I used to hang out in the park all the time. I was sitting here the first time I told Tia I loved her. I was also sitting here when I made the decision to leave New York. I carved my name on the side here."

Mara leaned over to look at the faint scratches. When she looked up at him, he could see that she got it. That he was trying to show her the places that had changed the course of his life.

"I like this bench." She sat back and closed her eyes, tilting her face up to the sun. "I like it more knowing it helped lead you to me."

"Me too." He looked around.

There was always activity in the park. An older man on the next bench read a tattered paperback, his cane resting against his leg. A woman jogged by, the white cords of her earphones dangling down her back. The wind fluttered through the trees.

"It's a good place for thinking. You can be surrounded by people but yet be all alone."

Mara squeezed his hand. "I can see how that could be very comforting when you don't want to be at home."

A group of kids ran by screaming, and the sudden noise broke the tension. "Okay, maybe I take back the part about comfort."

Trent snorted. "Just wait until we have kids. We'll probably have eardrums of steel. According to my mother, I was a screamer."

Mara covered her mouth with her hand. "Great. That's something to look forward to."

"It is. I'm looking forward to all of it." He gestured around the park. "I made the decision to leave New York because I wanted a chance to put everything that happened behind me. But I was just existing. Putting one foot in front of the other, day after day. You were the one who truly brought me back to life."

"I'm glad. That's all I want to do. Because you make me happy too."

A group of fat gray pigeons waddled by, cooing loudly.

"I'm pretty sure these are the same pigeons that were here when we used to come here. Or I guess it must be their grandchildren by now. Damn if that isn't a depressing thought."

"No depressing thoughts allowed today. I want to see more of the places you used to go when you were younger. I want to see it all."

He stood and pulled her up with him, tucking her beneath his arm.

"Trent! Hey, Trent!"

Movement to his left caught his attention. A girl in a long, flowing skirt waved her hands back and forth. She was standing next to a bare-chested man with long, tangled hair who sat in front of an easel. Trent squinted and then whipped around when he recognized her.

Avery had mentioned one time that their old friend Trix was posing for an artist, but she was supposed to be living in Portugal, not here. He tucked his head and walked faster.

"Trent! Wait!"

Mara finally heard the commotion and looked over shoulder. "Is someone calling you?"

Trent increased his pace. "Yeah, it's a girl I knew in high school. She was a bit of a gossip and not the nicest person. I don't really want to get caught and be forced to make conversation with someone I didn't even like, you know?"

Mara walked faster, trying to keep pace. "I get that. There are definitely some people I plan to avoid at my ten-year reunion. If I even go."

A cab was letting out a fare right in front of them as they left the west park entrance, and Trent let out a small huff of relief as Mara climbed in. He glanced over his shoulder one last time. Trix was still staring at him, her head tilted to the side. He waved and then ducked his head and slid in after Mara.

He gave the address for the penthouse since they could easily walk to the other places he wanted to show her. They pulled out into traffic and Mara rested her head on his shoulder.

"I like this kind of sightseeing. If I'd just toured the museums and eaten at some trendy restaurant, it would have been like every other vacation experience I've ever had. But people-watching in Central Park is something I'll never forget. Thank you for sharing that with me."

He turned his head, brushing a kiss over her lips. She

sighed, the soft sound a hum in her chest that speared straight through him.

"Where to now?" she whispered.

He looked out the window at the rush of people and cars flashing by. "Well, I can show you the little boutique where Avery got busted for shoplifting one summer. Then we're going for bagels. *Real bagels*, not those cardboard things you guys eat for breakfast. And then I think I'll take you home and show you a few things you've seen before."

Her eyes heated. "Private tour?" The hand that rested against his thigh inched higher until she cupped him through his jeans.

He sucked in a sudden, sharp breath. "Very private. And I'm thinking bagels are more of a breakfast thing, so we can go straight home."

Her laughter rang out, filling up all the empty holes in his heart.

———

TRENT HAD ORDERED A GROCERY DELIVERY, so Mara spent the majority of the afternoon prepping the artichoke-stuffed chicken breasts she planned to serve for dinner that night.

Matt and Penny were coming over. They'd been on a whirlwind tour of the city the past two days, including an exclusive, invitation-only rehearsal for a new Broadway show. Trent had even arranged for them to meet the actors afterward.

She'd just gotten comfortable on the couch with a magazine when Trent approached, one hand covering the mouthpiece of the cordless handset.

"It's your mom," Trent whispered.

Mara let her head fall back into the cushions. Although she'd sent her parents a message that she was traveling with Trent, she hadn't filled them in on the true nature of the trip.

In her mother's world everything was about finding a husband. It didn't matter how well she'd done in college or whether she liked her job. The only letters attached to her name that would impress Carolina Simmons was the all-important M-R-S in the front.

And Mara had so far proven herself not up to the task of getting her man to commit. At least that was her mother's point of view. Carolina had no idea that the real reason they hadn't gotten married yet was because Mara wasn't ready.

And if she found out that her future son-in-law was a modern-day Midas, there would no forces on earth that would stop her from flying up to visit and badger Mara into planning the wedding.

She held out her hand for the phone. "Hi, Mom."

"I've been calling and calling you all day. Where have you been, *mija?*"

Mara rolled her eyes, but it was in affectionate exasperation. Her mother had called once and she hadn't even left a message.

"I was cooking dinner, Mom. Matt and Penny are coming over tonight so I had a lot to do."

Her mother made a soft harrumphing sound but sounded partially appeased. "That's good. I'm glad you're feeding your brother. Penny is a sweet girl, but I don't know about her cooking."

"Her cooking is fine, Mom. Not every woman needs to cook anyway. Matt is hardly helpless."

It was useless to try to bring her mother around to modern thinking about family life, but for some reason she couldn't stop trying.

"I suppose so. Anyway, I found the perfect wedding dress for you. I tried to join that site online for the pictures, but I can't figure it out. So your cousin, Manuela, is going to put the picture online so you can see it."

"Great," Mara responded, hoping she'd mustered enough enthusiasm in her voice.

It was doubtful she'd like anything her mother had chosen, but she really did appreciate that her mother was trying to help out.

"Have you decided on your colors yet? We really need to think about the bridesmaids' dresses. And how many attendants you are going to have. You have to ask your cousin, Maria."

"I do? Mom, I haven't even seen that side of the family in years. I already have to ask Trent's sister."

"He has a sister? I didn't realize. I'm sure you told me. This is silly that we're trying to do this long distance. Perhaps your father and I should come visit for a while. We still haven't met Trent's family."

"Things are really crazy right now, but maybe we should plan a trip soon. It would be nice to get both families together."

She turned to see Trent motioning to her. "Hold on, Mom."

Trent leaned over and whispered, "Invite them to come visit."

"What, now?"

Trent raised his eyebrows. "No time like the present, right?"

She took her hand off the receiver of the phone. "Um, actually Mom, why don't you and Dad fly up to visit us and meet Trent's parents tomorrow? We'll make all the travel arrangements for you."

"Oh Marina, you don't need to go to such trouble. Your father has so many of those mileage points."

Mara sighed. This was not the kind of conversation that she wanted to have over the phone.

"Actually, Mom, Trent's parents have a company plane. He's going to send it down to pick you up. So don't worry about anything, okay?"

Her mother was quiet for a moment. "Oh my, that's very generous. Tell him thank you so much. I am looking forward to this."

Suddenly overcome with emotion and feeling very homesick, Mara clutched the phone tighter. "I am too. I miss you guys."

"We miss you too, but there is no reason to be sad, Marina. You have a good man who will be a good provider. And to think I was so worried about you. Now your brother, that's who I need to worry about."

Mara tuned out her mom's voice as the woman worried aloud about her brother's relationship with Penny and whether they'd ever start their wedding planning. Even after they hung up and Trent returned, cuddling her against his side as he watched television, her mind was on one thing.

How lucky she was to have found a man who was excited to marry her. They'd come through the hard parts, and now they were safe on the other side. But as she snuggled closer to Trent's side, she had to ignore the nagging feeling that fairy tales didn't last.

"PENNY HAS to know for sure how much I love her now. I sat through the entire show. And they were singing *the entire time.*"

Trent laughed along with the rest of the table as Matt continued telling the story of his first experience at a Broadway show. He glanced over at Mara, who looked completely relaxed and happy for the first time in days.

Even though Matt had come along originally because he didn't trust Trent, he was actually glad he'd been able to come with them. Family was a huge part of what Mara needed to feel happy and secure. Having her brother and Penny there went a long way toward showing her that their way of life didn't have to change because of where he came from.

In fact, they could have all the things they had now and more if she'd allow it.

Penny leaned over and kissed Matt on the cheek. "He's pretending it was awful, but he had fun. I know he did because he went backstage with me."

When he'd asked Gina to set up a tour of the city for his friends, she'd outdone herself by finagling an invitation to a private rehearsal for a show that wouldn't open for weeks. It was a joy to be able to use his influence to make his friends' time in the city memorable and fun.

Matt shoved a piece of artichoke in his mouth. "Whatever. It was people singing for two hours. I would have gone anywhere you wanted after that was over."

Trent took a sip of his beer and leaned closer to Matt, whispering loudly enough for the entire table to hear. "Don't worry, I won't tell anyone that you actually liked it."

Matt scowled. "Hardly. The best part of the day was coming back to that fancy hotel. Thanks for putting us up in such a swank room, by the way."

"It's nothing." Trent took another sip of his beer, suddenly self-conscious.

Normally he would have turned the conversation to another topic, but then he stopped himself. That was exactly what had hurt his friends before, shutting them out of certain areas of his life just because he wasn't sure of their reactions.

If he was asking Matt to trust him not to hurt Mara, then he needed to extend that same trust back. In all areas.

"It's really nothing, and I mean that literally. My family owns that hotel."

Surprise flashed through Matt's eyes. "Oh yeah?"

He peeled at the label on his beer, suddenly awkward since the entire table had grown silent. "Yeah, Castle Towers is one of our flagship properties. It was one of the first hotels my grandfather built."

"It's a beautiful hotel," Penny said.

Matt picked up his fork again. "Cool. Well, if you own it then maybe you can put bigger televisions in those rooms. And free Wi-Fi wouldn't hurt either."

Penny gasped and swatted Matt on the arm. "Matt! He's just joking. Everything in that room is perfect."

Trent laughed, glad they could talk without any lingering awkwardness. It had been one of the things he was most worried about, that he'd lose the easy camaraderie they'd developed over the years and their friendship would devolve into a series of stiff encounters.

But if they could joke about the service at a hotel his family owned, then that bode well for the future.

"I'll be sure to tell my father all your suggestions. Not that he ever listens to me, but for the record, I agree with you completely."

He heard the sound of the elevator opening, and Mara glanced at him in confusion. He pushed back from the table. "Please excuse me, everyone."

Trent held up a hand to Mara so she wouldn't get up. There were only a few people who had clearance to come up, so there was no need to interrupt their dinner while he found out who was there. When he turned the corner, Avery stood in the entryway.

"Hey. I was visiting my parents. They wanted to keep Travis for a sleepover, so I decided to swing by and see what you were up to. I feel like I haven't had a chance to spend any time with you since you've been here."

Laughter rang out from behind him, and she looked quizzically at the sound.

"Oh wow, I'm so sorry. You're having a party. I should have called first." She looked over his shoulder, naked longing and loneliness all over her face. She turned to leave. "I'll just catch up with you later."

Damn it. Trent couldn't let her leave looking like that. To what, go home to her empty place and sit alone? Eat alone?

His hand shot out to stop the elevator doors from closing. "No, you should stay. It's just family. Mara's brother and his fiancée are here. We have plenty of food."

Avery looked up hopefully. "Really? Are you sure Mara won't mind?"

"Of course not." *He hoped not.* "We've got plenty of food, and this will give you two a chance to get to know each other better."

"I'd like that." Avery followed him off the elevator and dropped her coat over one of the stools in the kitchen.

Mara looked up when they entered the dining room. "Avery! Hello." She gestured across the table. "This is my brother, Matt, and his fiancée, Penny. Guys, this is an old childhood friend of Trent's, Avery Maxwell."

Avery waved to everyone as Trent brought her a plate. Mara caught his eye as he passed behind Avery's back and he shrugged. He could only hope she wasn't pissed that he'd invited Avery to stay, but it was getting harder and harder to avoid uninvited guests since word had gotten out that he was back in town.

His place was starting to feel like Grand Central Station.

"So, Avery, how long have you known this guy?" Matt gestured toward Trent.

"It feels like forever," Avery responded. "We were just kids when we met. But there used to be a bigger group of us that hung out. Over the years it seems like everyone has scattered." She turned to Trent. "Did I tell you Trix is back in town? She called me about some new charity she's starting. It provides free art classes or something like that."

Trent froze, then forced himself to continue cutting his chicken. "Not surprised. She was determined to change the world, even when the rest of us were just focused on exams and getting our driver's licenses."

"Well, I'm not sure being a nude model for some guy who calls himself *Drago* is changing the world, but she seems happy. She's back in town for her cousin's wedding."

Matt's head swung back and forth between them. Having known him so long, he could interpret his buddy's facial expressions perfectly. He was watching Avery, or more accurately, watching his interaction with Avery.

It seemed his friend still hadn't let go of his suspicions that he was cheating on Mara. Trent sighed.

"This is absolutely delicious. Trent, I know you didn't cook this."

The comment drew laughter from the rest of the table. Even he had to smile a bit. "No, this is definitely not my doing. Mara is a magician with food. Every dinner tastes like it comes out of a five-star restaurant."

Mara shrugged, but her cheeks tinged pink at the compliment. "It's nothing, really. There's a little trick to how you layer the spices when you stuff the artichokes in, that's all."

Avery turned the full force of her smile on Mara. "Would you teach me sometime? I'm okay in the kitchen, but I would kill to be able to make something that tastes like this."

"Of course. That would be fun." Mara glanced over at him, her eyes shining with pleasure.

For years, she'd lamented her lack of time to spend on her recipes. Once he convinced her to quit that job she hated, she could spend as much time as she wanted working on her recipe book.

Hell, he'd buy a publishing company for her to distribute it if that would make her happy. Although knowing her damn independent streak, she wouldn't want him to do that. She'd want to make it on her own.

Not that it would stop him from doing it anyway.

He was finding there wasn't a whole lot that could stop him from doing things to see her smile.

thirteen

FLUSH with the warmth of good wine and even better conversation, Mara carefully stacked the plates on the counter next to the dishwasher. If Trent caught her doing it, he'd fuss at her to leave it for the housekeeper, but it was too deeply ingrained in her to clean up immediately.

She looked up when someone entered the kitchen. Avery stood behind her, holding several wineglasses.

"Here you go. I figured I'd grab the ones left on the table. Trent is showing off his game room."

Surprised, Mara accepted the glasses and set them on the counter next to the plates. "You didn't have to do that. You're a guest."

Right at home, Avery opened the dishwasher and pulled out the bottom rack. "I know we've only met twice, but I already feel like we're friends. Besides, I wouldn't want to be stuck cleaning up all this by myself!"

Mara rinsed the wineglasses and set them on the counter next to the plates. "Trent is going to tell me to leave it for Bianca, but I just can't do that. It'll annoy me every time I walk by the kitchen to see a mess on the counter. Plus, I'm still not entirely certain Bianca even exists. I've never seen her."

"When we were staying here, she started coming by more often. Little boys tend to create messes. I think she was happy when I moved back into James's place."

Mara's hand paused around the stem of one of the wineglasses. "Trent told me you had stayed here for a while."

Avery continued loading, occasionally scooting around Mara to wash things off in the sink.

"Yeah. I'm not sure if he told you that James and I haven't been getting along so well. It was probably a mistake for me to move in with him. But it's just we have a child together, and I really thought that this time he'd do the right thing."

All this time she'd been feeling jealous of the time Trent had spent with Avery only to find out that she really was a nice person. It made her feel a little guilty for all the bad things she'd thought about her.

Uncomfortable with the turn the conversation had taken, Mara rinsed off a handful of silverware and then dumped it into the front slots of the machine.

"Hopefully that will change. At least you guys have a history together. His parents know your parents. That has to help, right?"

"It does help some. Like I told you, I'm not much of a cook, but I'd really like to change that. Mr. Townsend, Trent's father, he's so conservative. The type of guy who likes women who can cook and are quiet and polite. As you can imagine, I am not his idea of daughter-in-law material. Being a great cook would really impress him. Maybe you can teach me how to spice things up a bit. He really likes spicy food." Avery smiled. "I'm more of a boring, plain chicken breast kind of girl."

"My mom taught me how to make plenty of spicy dishes. Colombian food definitely doesn't lack heat." Mara grinned, already thinking of what dishes she could prepare when they had Trent's parents over for dinner.

"See, you'll be fine then." Avery smiled and went back to loading the dishwasher.

Even though Avery was trying to be helpful, it made Mara feel even worse to be reminded of all the things she didn't know about Trent's family. Avery had been friends with him for years and probably had tons of inside knowledge. Yet she was still struggling to find acceptance.

What chance did Mara have of getting the Townsends to like her if Avery couldn't even pull it off?

———

TRENT HUNG up the phone and leaned back in his office chair. His father was still technically on medical leave, but as usual, he was ignoring most of his doctor's advice and was back in the office part-time. Trent had long ago given up on the idea of changing his father's ways, but all that mattered was that his short tenure as interim CEO was over.

He was officially off the hook.

He closed his laptop and glanced at the clock on the wall. Mara's parents were due to fly in that afternoon, so he'd been trying to finish up as much work as possible before then. As if on cue, the door opened and Mara stuck her head in.

"Are you almost ready? We should probably get going. If they arrive and we aren't there, Mom will be frantic."

He stood and rounded the desk. "Definitely. Gina has a car

coming for us in about ten minutes, and she got confirmation that their flight is still on schedule. Don't worry."

She nodded quickly. "I know. I just don't want anything to go wrong."

"Even if something happens to delay us, it's not the end of the world. I'll just have a car meet them there. They won't be stranded."

"They aren't used to all of this, Trent. If we send a car, my mom will be offended. She'll think that we aren't really happy that she's here if we don't pick her up ourselves."

"Well, I definitely don't want them to think that. I'm really happy they're coming. Maybe it'll put a smile back on your face."

She'd been down ever since the prior night, which made no sense to him because they'd been having such a great time with Matt and Penny. Even though Avery had been unexpected, she'd been relatively well-behaved during dinner.

Avery's personality was a bit grating for some people, but she hadn't done anything too outrageous at dinner and Mara hadn't seemed like she'd minded.

Unless she'd just been pretending to keep the peace.

"I'm not sad, just a little homesick," Mara finally admitted. "Things are so different now, and since my days aren't filled with work anymore, I'm at loose ends. It's a little lonely being home all day. I wasn't expecting that."

Inwardly, Trent cursed his shortsightedness and inattention. Of course she would be feeling a little strange going from working a full-time job to being on her own in this big place all day.

"Come on. Let's go get your parents and then we'll talk more tonight."

They rode the elevator down to the lobby, and Mara followed him outside to where a limousine waited at the curb.

"Wow. This is really nice." Mara turned to him, her eyes huge when she realized the big car was for them.

"It's honestly just easier so we can all ride in the same car on the way back. Traffic can be crazy at this time of day, so we might have a bit of a wait. I know you'll want to sit and talk with them."

He nodded at the driver, one of the regulars from the car service. If they were going to be in town on a semipermanent basis, he'd need to look into getting their own driver. And he'd definitely want to get some protection for Mara. There was no way he'd be comfortable letting her roam the city on her own.

On the ride to the airport, Mara squirmed in her seat. By the time they drove onto the tarmac, her face was practically mashed against the window.

He chuckled at her excitement. "We're almost there, baby."

She turned to him, a bright smile on her face. It warmed him through to see her so happy.

They waited as the crew led her parents off the plane. Mara opened the door of the limousine before the driver could open it for her.

"Mom! Dad! I'm so glad you're here." Mara's words were cut off as her mother enveloped her into a big hug.

Carolina Simmons was an older version of Mara, slim and breathtakingly beautiful. Trent realized that if Mara took after her mother, he had no hope of his obsession with her lessening as time passed.

Mara's father, George Simmons, stuck out his hand as the two women embraced behind them.

"It's wonderful to see you again, Trent. Thank you so much

for bringing us up on such short notice. My wife has been talking of nothing else since you suggested it."

Carolina stood on tiptoe to kiss Trent's cheek. "Thank you so much for flying us here. Your plane is wonderful. I've never flown so comfortably."

"Anytime. We're thrilled you're here to spend some time with us."

Mara squealed when her father ruffled her hair. She grabbed him around the waist. "Looking good, Daddy. Have you lost weight?"

He groaned and looked over at Carolina. "Your mother has put me on a diet."

"Your *doctor* has put you on a diet. You have high blood pressure."

George looked at Trent wryly. "I can't imagine why."

"Oh hush." Carolina laughed. "I am just looking out for you. What will I do if you aren't here to take care of me?"

For some reason the words seemed to make Mara sad. Trent wouldn't have noticed if he hadn't been looking at her right then because she immediately squared her shoulders and pasted on a bright smile.

What was that about?

He made a mental note to ask her about it later. But they had to get on the road if they wanted to beat the traffic.

"The driver has already transferred your luggage from the plane so we can head back. My parents are meeting us at our place tonight for dinner."

Carolina nodded. "Excellent. Then we can talk about the most important thing."

"What's that?" he asked.

"Your wedding, of course. I'm thinking perhaps we need to think a little *bigger*."

As Carolina ducked into the limo, Mara sent him a look of abject horror before she got in too.

———

MARA SCRUTINIZED the neat row of julienned carrots before her and the ingredients she'd lined up on the counter. She preferred to keep things simple with vegetables, so she was planning to do a quick sauté in an onion and butter reduction.

"Mom, is the grated orange peel ready?"

A little citrus would add just a hint of spring to the vegetables without overpowering their natural sweetness. The julienned carrot salad would go well with the spicy beef flanks she was preparing for dinner.

Carolina handed over the bowl of orange zest she'd just finished grating. "What are you planning for the main course? I should have probably warned you that your father is supposed to be watching his salt."

"I already made some plain marinated chicken breasts for Dad since I know he has to watch what he eats."

"I'm so glad you remembered. Your father will probably wish you had forgotten though. The bland food has been difficult for him to adjust to."

Mara laughed. "I bet it has. It was no trouble. I can use the leftovers for salad toppings tomorrow. Besides, I'll sneak him a little bit of the beef flank. A little won't hurt, right?"

"I don't think so. His problem is mainly stress. I thought

when he retired things would be better, but now he has started taking consulting jobs. I think he's bored."

"I can understand. Even though I'm enjoying having this time to cook and do things I normally don't get to do, I also feel a little lost. Before I was so busy, but I felt like I had a purpose. Now I don't know."

Her mom wiped her hands on the dish towel next to her and then put her arm around Mara. "You have a purpose now. You are taking good care of your future husband. This is a good thing. I worried about you working so many hours and then driving home alone at night. Before long you will have children, and then you will have no time to worry about these things."

Mara put the knife down carefully on the cutting board before turning to her mother. The last thing she wanted was another bloody mishap.

Now that she understood about Trent's past, the incident with the knife made so much sense. His shock and panic at the sight of her blood must have taken him straight back to that horrible night. The last thing she ever wanted to do was cause him to relive the worst day of his life.

"Mom? Is it possible to ever really know a man? I mean, even after all these years, do you feel like you really know everything about Dad?"

If her mother wondered what caused her to ask the question, she didn't let on. She just pulled Mara over to sit on one of the barstools.

"Tell me what is going on, Marina. First you're avoiding planning the wedding and then the next thing we hear, you're with Trent in this big, fancy place. Flying in private planes. What is really going on?"

That was all it took for Mara to lose her tenuous hold on her emotions. "Oh Mom," she sobbed.

She sank into her mother's hold, sniffling softly as all the feelings she'd tried to bury came rushing forth. Confusion, fear, inadequacy, and hurt.

A lot of hurt.

"Things are so messed up. I didn't know about Trent's family being so wealthy. He said he doesn't like talking about it because then all people see is the money."

Carolina made a soft sound of agreement. "I can understand that. People do crazy things for money. But this is not the biggest issue. I am more concerned about why your eyes look so sad."

Mara wiped her face with the back of her hand. "I felt so confused when I found out. Like maybe he didn't trust me enough to tell me before. Now that I'm here, I understand a lot better. His family isn't close. Not like we are."

"Then that will be your gift to him. To bring a sense of family and comfort to his life. Just like I did for your father. That is my purpose, and I feel great pride in it. There's no shame in making love and family a priority in your life."

"Then you didn't just marry Daddy to get away from your village?" she asked quietly.

Carolina pulled back abruptly, her dark eyes searching Mara's face. She steeled herself for her mother's censure. Instead, her mother squeezed her shoulders very gently, like she was afraid to hold her too tight.

"Oh sweetheart, is that what you thought?"

Mara nodded, suddenly feeling very small. "You always told me that I was so lucky to be beautiful so I could marry a rich husband. That's all you've ever seemed to care about, that I get married and be taken care of. When I turned fifteen—"

"At your quinceañera party," Carolina finished with a sad smile. She pulled Mara into another embrace. "My baby, I haven't been the best mother, I know. I was too caught up in being the perfect wife. From the moment I saw your father, I knew I'd never want anyone else. It wasn't the money. It was him. The way he looked at me. I think you know what I mean."

"Yeah. I definitely do." Mara thought of the way Trent watched her. Sometimes it felt like she'd dissolve under the intensity of that stare.

"But when I was growing up, girls didn't have many choices to get ahead in life. If your father hadn't been a handsome American who could afford to support me, my mother would have never allowed us to get married. She would have probably pushed me to marry one of the wealthy men in a nearby village. Much older, wealthy men. I was always so grateful that your father had money because it meant I could be with the man I loved instead of just the man who could afford me."

Mara hugged her mother back. Despite the fact that she was no longer a child and it shouldn't have mattered, a part of her was pitifully relieved to know that her parents really were happy together.

"Your young man loves you and can give you a wonderful life, yes. But that is not why you're here. You're here because you love him. You're lucky to have found each other for that reason alone."

Carolina stood. "Now, let's get this dinner together. The Townsends will be here soon. You said their family isn't close, but I think tonight perhaps we can start to change that."

fourteen

SOMETIMES WHEN YOU EXPECT CALAMITY, karma decides to screw with you and give you harmony instead.

As he looked down the dinner table that had never before been used, Trent marveled over the changes Mara had made in just a few short hours. He wasn't sure where the centerpiece in the middle of the table had even come from, but somehow she'd made things look elegant and inviting.

At the other end of the table, his mother and Carolina were engaged in conversation. Next to him Mara caught his eye and gave him a tentative smile. They were both completely surprised and pleased at the turn of events. They'd been expecting a repeat of the awkwardness when he'd first introduced Mara to them.

However, his mother and Carolina seemed to be getting along well. They were both shrewd women who knew exactly what they wanted for their children. Although their interests might not be perfectly aligned, they seemed to recognize and respect the quality in each other.

Mara got up to put the finishing touches on dinner.

"Pretty fancy setup," Matt commented.

Since Matt and Penny were still in town, they had come over to lend their support. His friend had made an effort to dress up, which Trent knew was a major concession for him. After years of wearing fatigues and combat boots, Matt didn't do formal well. But he'd put on a collared shirt and khakis for the occasion.

Penny sat on his left side, making a valiant effort to include his father in the conversation. Carolina had been especially pleased to have the whole family together since she could now start wedding planning in earnest with them all in attendance.

Matt and Penny were especially behind according to her, and Trent had witnessed Matt rolling his eyes more than once at his mother's badgering. Trent had tuned out after a certain point, but he assumed that was what she and his mother had been talking about so animatedly.

"This is all your sister's doing. If it were me, we'd be eating fast food from paper plates."

Matt snorted. "You're a long way from paper plates now." He glanced over at Trent. "But yeah, that does sound more your style."

While Mara was bringing out the food, Trent uncorked the red wine his mother had brought, a South African Bordeaux blend. He circled the table, filling glasses for those who wanted it. When he got to his father, he stopped. Were you allowed to drink after having a heart attack?

"Dad, can you have wine now? Dad?"

His father was staring at Mara puttering around in the kitchen. His brow furrowed. "She looks so *familiar*," he muttered.

Trent followed his father's gaze. Mara stood in the kitchen, her hair bundled up high on her head as she arranged food on another plate. The hairstyle made her look younger.

Much younger.

Oh no.

Trent sucked in a sudden sharp breath. His grip on the wine bottle tightened as he turned back to his father.

"Wine?" he asked loudly.

James turned around and looked up at him, startled. "What was that?"

He held up the bottle in question, and at his father's nod of assent, filled it halfway.

Mara brought the last plate and put it down in front of her father. Then she sat down to his right and squeezed his hand on top of the table. The bun on top of her head wasn't secured with a band, so he tugged at it until her long hair unwound and cascaded over her shoulders. As he ran his fingers through the long strands, her cheeks pinkened.

"You always have a thing for my hair. Behave yourself," she whispered indulgently. Then she turned to the rest of the table. "Dinner is served, everyone. Please enjoy."

"This looks fabulous, *mija*. You've truly outdone yourself this time." Carolina cut into her steak and took a delicate bite.

"It really does look amazing, baby. Thank you." Trent cut into his own food, but before he could take a bite, his father dropped his fork and started coughing.

"Dad, are you okay?"

His father was slowly turning red, his cheeks distending slightly as he coughed. He took a long drink from his wineglass. "It's just a little spicier than I expected." He promptly dissolved into another choking fit.

"James! Are you having another heart attack?" His mother jumped up from her seat and stood at his father's elbow.

Trent took a tentative bite of his own food. It was definitely a little spicier than usual, but nothing he couldn't handle.

James cleared his throat and took another sip of wine. "No, it's fine. I was just taken off guard."

Mara looked horrified. "I'm so sorry. I should have made something more bland. I have more of the plain chicken breast."

Antonia sat down again and took a bite of her own steak. "Oh dear. Perhaps you shouldn't eat this, James. You just got out of the hospital. This might be a bit much for you so soon."

Mara leaned over to Trent. "*This is awful*. And things were going so well."

Suddenly Carolina spoke up. "Spicy food is good for a man. It's an aphrodisiac."

The entire table went still. Matt snickered. Trent had to take another bite of food to smother his own grin. Mara was constantly lamenting her mother's blunt ways, but Trent found it funny more often than not.

Mara just covered her face with her hands. "Mom!"

"Don't look so shocked," Carolina chided. "These children think they know everything about love. They forget our generation did it all first. And still does. They should take advice from their elders as we were taught to do. Isn't that right, Antonia? You have a strong, virile man too. I'm sure you know about what it takes to keep a man happy."

"Oh God, *make it stop*," Mara moaned from behind her hands. "Mom, I'm sure Mrs. Townsend doesn't want to talk about her private life!" To Trent's father, she said, "I'll just go to the kitchen to get you another plate, sir."

To everyone at the table's surprise, Antonia picked up her own wineglass and said, "Actually, I agree. We *definitely* know what it takes to keep a man happy. Young girls these days have no idea."

Trent's mouth fell open. Then he turned to Mara. "If you're going to the kitchen, I'm coming too. Or maybe we should just leave the penthouse completely. I can always buy another one."

At his comment, Penny giggled before clamping a hand over her mouth. Her blue eyes sparkled as she looked across the table at Matt, who shrugged.

"Family dinners, Simmons-style. Trust me, this isn't as bad as they can get." Matt looked at his mother sitting next to him, who was busy blowing George a kiss.

Mara laughed, a high-pitched nervous sound. "I beg to differ. This is pretty bad, I think."

Carolina made a rude sound. "Nonsense, Marina. I'm simply stating the facts. Not everyone knows that spicy food builds a man's animal instincts."

James looked across the table at Carolina. Then he looked down at his plate again. "It does?"

"Oh yes." Carolina looked over at her husband, who raised his wineglass in a mock toast.

Mara slid down slightly in her seat. "This has to be a nightmare."

With one last hesitant glance, James cut into another piece of steak and raised it to his mouth. After chewing for a few minutes, he declared, "You know, this is really quite good."

He looked over at Antonia and smiled, a private, slightly lecherous smile that made Trent very glad he didn't have a full stomach.

After a moment of mental gagging, he glanced over at Mara. "I feel like I'm watching a horror movie. My parents are flirting with each other."

"Well, my mother is talking about *keeping a man happy* and *animal instincts* in the middle of dinner. I am beyond mortified. What are your parents going to think?" Mara whispered back.

Trent looked over at his father, who was happily chewing his food. "I think they'll probably go home and do things that will make me want to claw my eyes out if I imagine them. So I'm not going to worry about it."

Mara looked over at him, her eyes huge. He was sure he looked just as disturbed.

Trent was in the middle of cutting his own steak when he got his second shock of the night.

"Mara, where did you learn to cook?" James asked, looking very much like he actually wanted to know the answer.

Mara looked just as surprised as he did at his father's sudden interest. Surprised and delighted. The rest of the table went completely silent. Even his mother looked astonished.

Mara recovered quickly, glancing at Trent before answering. "From my mother. She was always the best cook in her family, and she started teaching me at a young age." She smiled over at Carolina, who preened under the attention.

"Mara used to bake with this plastic pink kiddie oven. Even then everything she made was great." Matt grinned at his sister, who relaxed slightly.

"I had so much fun with that stove," Mara said wistfully. "Although I'm sure that thing was a fire hazard!"

"Well, everything is delicious." James looked over at Trent. "My son is a very lucky man."

George took Carolina's hand and kissed it. "My baby girl

definitely took after her mother in more than just her beauty. We did good, huh?"

Mara blushed. "Dad! Well, I'm having a wonderful time here. I've been spending a lot of time cooking, and I'm even thinking about doing a cookbook."

"You are? That's exciting," Penny said.

Even Matt looked over at her. "I didn't know you were considering that."

Mara speared one of her carrots. "It's just something I've been thinking about lately."

Carolina clapped her hands together in delight. "Oh, how wonderful! That would be perfect for you."

"Make sure you put your mother's *arroz con pollo* in there," George suggested. "The way Carolina makes it is slightly different than the way I'd had it here in the States. It's a little spicier than what I was used to."

Carolina was nodding along as he spoke. "Oh yes. Where I'm from, that's just the way we season things."

Antonia took another delicate bite of her steak. "What part of Colombia are you from?"

"A little town near Barranquilla. It's on the northern coast. We like things with a little more spice." Carolina winked across the table at her husband.

"More than this? This is about all I can handle." James chortled. "I've never been able to handle spicy foods too well."

Mara suddenly went still. "You don't like spicy food? At all? That's... well, I'll have to remember that." She blinked several times and then took a long sip from her wineglass.

She hadn't eaten much, Trent noticed. She'd been nervous about everything being perfect for this dinner, but all things considered, he thought it was going well. As well as could be expected, anyway.

Trent leaned over and whispered, "Are you okay?"

She didn't meet his eyes as she said, "Perfect. I just learned a lesson, that's all."

He looked at her strangely, but before he could ask what she meant, he heard his father ask Carolina how much spice was recommended for "vigor" and decided he hadn't had nearly enough alcohol to deal with this dinner.

"Does anyone want more wine?" he asked, looking down the table. "Or perhaps something stronger?"

OVER THE NEXT FEW WEEKS, things slowly approached some kind of normal. Matt and Penny had flown back home the day after their dinner.

Mara's parents had stayed on a few more days, and he had taken them on a tour of the city, showing them the Statue of Liberty and the Empire State Building one day and then the next having a driver drop them off in the middle of Times Square. Carolina had been thrilled.

At one point Mara had leaned over and whispered, "I preferred your private tour," and it had taken all his willpower not to rush them along so he could take her back home and get her under him.

Once her parents returned home, she and Trent quickly settled into their new routines. Mara had finally agreed to resign from her job and was beginning to treat the penthouse like it was her home too.

He spent time during the day checking on his investments and considering several new ventures while Mara perfected a few recipes she'd always wanted to work on. The phenomenal smells coming from the kitchen usually tempted him to quit work by late afternoon, and then he'd spend the next few hours watching Mara make magic in his kitchen.

His place had never seemed more alive.

It was a Thursday afternoon and he was going through all the mail he'd been ignoring for weeks when he came across a heavy envelope stamped with his family crest. He ripped it open, reading the time and date on the front of the invitation inside.

"What is that?"

He looked up, surprised. Mara was on the other side of the kitchen counter stirring something that smelled like heaven.

"Oh, it's nothing. Another one of my mom's charity things."

Mara paused, her hand on the big, wooden spoon. "What kind of charity thing?"

He read from the invitation. "It's a benefit for the hospital. All proceeds go to funding the Townsend Grant for asthma research."

She made a small sound. "Sounds like a great cause. Shouldn't we go? It would probably mean a lot to your mom to have the whole family there, right?"

"I usually just send a check. I don't think she's actually expecting me to show up."

Mara resumed stirring. Then she pulled out a cake pan and poured in the mixture. She angled the pan to get the mixture to settle just so. It was oddly relaxing to watch.

"Is Avery going to be there?"

Trent paused, something about her tone of voice triggering

his internal alarms. Then he dismissed the feeling. Mara had never been the jealous type.

"Probably. Why?"

She shrugged, but the way she didn't look up when she did it made him think it mattered. A lot.

"Just that she seems to be at all the family events. She's there and I'm not. Shouldn't it be the other way around?"

"Whoa. Where is this coming from? You've never seemed bothered by Avery being around before."

She pushed the pan back and forth and then dropped it on the counter several times. He thought she might have dropped it a little harder than was strictly necessary.

"Did you know before our dinner that your father doesn't like spicy food?"

Trent shrugged. "Not exactly, but he's a conservative kind of guy. My father is pretty white bread as far as... well, everything."

"See, I figured you would say that. Because Avery told me that he liked spicy food. She made it a point to say that I was lucky I could cook interesting cuisine because that would really impress your father. So, like an idiot, I chose to listen because I wanted to make a good impression. Instead, I almost ended up giving him another heart attack!"

Trent's fingers clenched around the envelope in his hand. "She said he liked spicy food? Did she say 'James likes spicy food' or did she specifically say my father? Maybe she meant my brother?"

Mara shook her head. "I knew you would do this. Come up with some way that I must have misinterpreted her. It has to be my fault, not hers, right? Why are you defending her?"

The accusation was dangerously close to what James had said to him a few weeks ago. He held up his hands.

"I'm not defending her. I was just saying…"

At her death glare, he decided it was time to change tactics. Mara had been incredibly good-natured about his friendship with Avery so far, but he had to expect that there would be some areas where they clashed. It was inevitable.

And Mara was incredibly territorial about stuff like this. Keeping her away from family events when Avery was free to attend sent the wrong message, and he could easily see how she'd be offended by that.

"If you really want to go, then we'll go, but I have to warn you that these things are boring. I didn't think you'd be interested in another night of hanging out with my parents."

Mara crossed her arms. "You know, your parents actually seem like they've loosened up a bit. If they can deal with my mother and her inappropriate sex talk at the dinner table, I'm starting to think they aren't the reason you don't want us to go anywhere. We can't just hide away up here forever. I feel like I haven't met any of your friends."

"You're my friend," he responded automatically, then sighed since he knew that wasn't what she meant. "Maybe my friends are assholes?"

She turned to put the cake pan in the oven and set the timer. Then she came around the counter and looped her arms over his head.

"Am I such a hick that you don't want to introduce me to anybody?"

"*What?* Mara, that is not the reason. If anything, I don't want to see how many of my old friends will hit on you the second my back is turned."

"Nice. Some friends you have."

She might have thought he was making excuses, but Trent knew all too well that his friends hitting on her was a virtual certainty. His brother usually didn't go to these events either, but if he did, Trent would be keeping her away from him too.

"Well, for most Upper East Siders, morality is a fluid concept."

"Charming. I can't wait to meet the gang."

"Fine. Let's do it. Maybe it won't be that bad. It's probably going to be mainly my mother's friends and whoever else has nothing better to do than drop two thousand dollars a plate for dinner on a Saturday night."

Mara nodded along with his diatribe. "Apparently I fall into the third category, so don't knock it."

"You do not fall into the third category. We have *way* better things to do on a Saturday night, but I'm willing to humor you. I guess I have been hogging you all to myself. I want you to be happy here. Or back in Virginia. Wherever you want to be, I'm there."

"Good. Because I think I want all of the above. I really want both of our families to be involved in our lives."

Over the past few weeks, he'd been really surprised at the changes he'd noticed in his father's demeanor. They weren't a warm and fuzzy sitcom family by any means, but he felt like when he said something his father was making an effort to at least listen.

"I'll call them now and let them know we're coming."

Mara beamed at him before going back into the kitchen. He picked up the invitation and took it with him to his office. He pulled out his cell phone. He wasn't sure if his parents were staying at their place in the city or at the house in Montauk, so he just dialed his father's cell phone number.

His father answered on the first ring.

"Dad, it's Trent. I wanted to let Mom know that we'll be at the charity gala on Saturday night."

"She'll be glad to hear it. Your sister will be in attendance. I'm not sure about your brother. He's probably still avoiding me." It was the first time he'd heard his father voice any regret over that situation.

"Well, Mara wants to go. I wasn't expecting to be in town this long, so I'll need to hire a permanent driver. If you have anyone you can spare, I'd be grateful."

"Why don't I just send over Shane?"

"He still works for you?" Trent sat down in his office chair and leaned back.

Shane Morrow had been his driver when he was in high school. He figured the older man had retired by now.

"No, he's still here. He keeps making noises about retiring, but he'll never do it. He's like me. Needs the job to survive. He's been driving me the past couple of years, but I'll shift a few things around. He was always fond of you."

"I'm not sure about that. I was a little jerk. I used to ditch him all the time."

"You were a teenager." James seemed to think that statement explained everything. "Speaking of which, I finally realized why Mara seemed so familiar."

He'd been expecting it ever since that dinner. He'd braced himself every time the phone rang for this very conversation. But now that it was here, Trent found that he was just tired. Too tired to explain or worry about what his father was going to do.

His father must have interpreted his silence as anger. "I shouldn't have brought it up. That was a nasty business. For all of us. I tried to clean things up as best as I could, but I never really asked if you were okay through it all. If you needed anything."

"Dad, I'm fine. It's all... fine."

"Good. I'm glad you're back, son."

Trent had to fight the urge to hang up. Tender concern just wasn't the way his father communicated, and as many times as he'd wished his father gave a shit growing up, he had no idea what to do with that concern coming at him now.

Now that it couldn't help him.

"Look, I have to go. Give my message to Mom, will you?" He hit the button to end the call and closed his eyes.

Mara was still in the kitchen making something that looked like chocolate pudding. He winked as he passed her and entered their bedroom. His closet wasn't nearly as opulent as hers, but it was a similar setup, just slightly smaller in size. He closed the door behind him and pulled out one of the lower drawers of the dresser.

After the day he'd asked Walter to remove all the personal pictures in the house, he'd never gone looking for them. He hadn't cared.

But they had to be in this room somewhere.

He stood on tiptoe and ran his hand over the top shelf. A box of shoes shifted and fell, narrowly missing the side of his face. With a curse, he moved to the side, his foot catching on something. He barely managed to grab the dresser in time to keep himself from falling on his ass.

The box had been pushed underneath the far right section of the closet beneath his winter coats. He pulled it out and ran his hand over the top. It was secured with a single piece of duct tape. After only a moment of hesitation, he pulled the tape off and spread the flaps open.

The picture on top was a companion to the one he'd found in the living room that day. In this shot, Tia looked directly at the camera, a bright smile on her face. Her dark hair was bundled up on top of her head in that messy bun, the way she'd always worn it. Avery had her arms thrown around Trent's neck like she was trying to get his attention, but his head was turned to the side, looking down at Tia.

His expression was like someone seeing fireworks for the very first time.

Time passed and he had no idea how long he knelt there, holding that picture frame, his mind immersed in memories. It wasn't until he heard the ding of a timer and Mara's voice singing a low tune that he came back to where he was. In his closet, looking at a picture that could rip the very fabric of his world right down the center.

He put the picture back in the box and closed the flaps, then shoved it back under the coats where he'd found it, his fingers trembling as he arranged the long coats to hide the box again.

It couldn't stay hidden forever though. There would always be certain things he couldn't say or do without fear. The truth would hurt her. As it hurt him. But as things stood, she was hurt anyway by the distance she sensed between them.

Until she knew the whole story of how they'd met, that distance would just grow wider and wider.

At some point he would have to take that final leap and trust her to listen without judgment. They could never move forward otherwise. But how could he do it when there was such a high chance that she would leave him? That this was the one thing she wouldn't be able to forgive?

He would show her after the gala and hope that love was strong enough to overcome his greatest shame.

fifteen

MARA STARED at herself in the mirror, feeling like she was looking at an image of someone else. After she'd convinced Trent that she wanted to come to his mother's charity ball, she'd realized eventually that she'd committed to a black-tie event and had no idea how to prepare for it. The past few days, she'd been in a whirlwind of details, trying to make sure she had everything she needed.

Although she wouldn't admit it to Trent, having a personal assistant as efficient as Gina had made the entire process as painless as it could be. Although she already had a dress, she hadn't had a formal purse that matched the dress or known of any local salons where she could get her hair done before the event.

Gina, the miracle worker, after seeing a picture of the dress, had ordered a new bag for her. Then she'd arranged for a hairstylist and manicurist to come to the penthouse in the afternoon to get her dolled up before the event. They hadn't met in person yet, but she knew Gina would be in attendance tonight.

As she looked at her reflection, Mara decided she owed the other woman one big, grateful hug.

Her long, dark curls were swept up off her shoulders in an intricate twist that had taken the hairdresser more than an hour to create. She ran her hands over the bodice of her dress. The lavender strapless evening gown was one of the designs Sophia had chosen for her. It hugged her bosom perfectly and then flared slightly over her hips.

Even her shoes were exquisite, she thought as she gazed down at the silver Christian Louboutin stilettos on her feet. From head to toe she felt and looked like a princess.

She'd also had a massage. She let out a happy sigh. Her muscles were still humming after that rubdown. Mara had been buffed and polished like a precious stone, and now it was time to go.

"Baby, are you ready?"

Trent stopped in the doorway, his eyes going hooded and dark when he saw her standing in front of the mirror. He walked behind her, and she watched in the reflection as he moved closer. He was a masculine vision in his black tuxedo, the edges crisp and perfect, the stark formality of it a contrast to his blond hair.

One hand came around her waist, pulling her back against his chest. Her ass snugged up against him and he pressed forward, imprinting the length of his hard cock against her back.

"I see *you're* ready," she breathed.

"That's an involuntary response whenever I see you," Trent replied. His fingers trailed up her arm, leaving a line of goose bumps behind. "You are breathtaking."

"Thank you. I'm kind of nervous."

"You have nothing to be nervous about. The other women who have to stand next to you are the ones who should be nervous."

Mara smiled, relieved that she looked okay. She'd never had low self-esteem, but being around women like Trent's mother and sister brought out insecurities she hadn't even known she had. It made her constantly self-conscious, worried that she'd do something stupid or make some social misstep that would embarrass Trent.

His lips descended and she closed her eyes, already anticipating the press against her skin. The dragging sensation over the side of her neck didn't disappoint, awakening a whole host of sensations, the tingles created by his touch warring with the butterflies caused by her nerves.

"My father sent over my old driver. I wonder if he'll tell on me if I put the privacy screen up and do dirty things to you in the backseat."

Mara gasped out a sigh as his teeth clamped down on her earlobe. A rush of desire made her clench her thighs together. The tiny thong she was wearing was already saturated.

"Trent, we haven't even left the house yet." Although she was admonishing him, she couldn't hold back a soft laugh at his eagerness.

"I know. It makes more sense to take the edge off before we're bored to death talking to a bunch of my parents' friends."

The reminder that she was going to an event where his parents would be present cooled her down instantly. She stood up straight.

"I'm not going to be able to talk to your mother with a straight face if I know I just seduced her son in the limo."

Trent grinned. "Okay, I'll wait to debauch you in a dark

corner once we're there. It'll be more fun to see if I can do it without anyone catching us." He tucked her hand into his arm and led her to the elevator.

"You're just joking about that, right?"

Her only answer was another one of those maddening little smiles.

Trent introduced her to his old driver, Shane Morrow, who turned out to be an extremely fit fifty-something older man with a no-nonsense demeanor. He held the door for them and Mara ducked inside, tucking the small train of her dress under her legs. Trent slid in next and the door closed, sealing them inside.

The sensual atmosphere of before was back, and she was reminded of his earlier comment about doing dirty things in the backseat.

She was glad it was so dark that he couldn't see her blush. Or how desperately she actually wanted him to do those things.

The ride to the event was relatively quick, and other than a few heated glances, Trent behaved himself on the way. She wasn't sure if the threat of his mother's displeasure or the presence of their new driver was responsible for keeping him in his seat on the other side of the car. But before she could think about it too long, they pulled over to the curb outside a fancy building lit with what looked like a million spotlights.

"Where are we?"

Trent looked over at her. "The Metropolitan Museum of Art."

Excited at the prospect of finally seeing the famed museum, Mara leaned over and peered out the window. A woman in a long black dress passed by their car and then stopped right before the grand steps leading up to the building to pose for pictures.

Mara gulped and ran a nervous hand over her hair again.

"You look beautiful. Now let's do this." Trent shoved the door open and held out his hand to assist her out of the car.

Mara slid across the seat and allowed him to help her up. To her relief, the photographers took pictures of them as they passed but didn't ask them to stop. They ascended the steps, Mara trying hard not to gape at the massive white columns as they entered. A man at the door nodded knowingly at Trent.

"You know him?" she asked.

"He knows me," Trent responded with a small, wry smile. "I have no doubt he's aware of all my family members. We're all on the board of my mother's charitable foundation. She insists on it. This is a fundraiser for the Townsend Grant for asthma research. Mom set it up after Travis was diagnosed."

The inside of the building was just as imposing as the outside. And it was *crowded*. She looked around in astonishment at the crowds of impeccably dressed people holding champagne flutes and plucking hors d'oeuvres off the trays of the tuxedo-clad waiters roaming the room.

She hadn't expected there to be so many people. The price tag alone for entrance had made her imagine a much smaller, more intimate affair.

There are this many people with thousands to blow on a charity dinner?

She thought back to what Trent had told her about the Upper East Side. Most of these people were just as wealthy as his family. It was like an invitation into an exclusive club, but one that she hadn't even known existed. When yet another woman strolled past her with a completely ostentatious set of diamonds dripping from her neck, Mara had to forcibly close her mouth. There was enough pressurized carbon in this room to buy a small country.

They approached a small group of people, and when they turned, she recognized Trent's parents and his sister. When they saw them, his mother held out her arms for Trent and to Mara's surprise, Antonia air-kissed her cheeks. His father nodded at them both.

Sophia turned, her arm entwined with a handsome older man with dark hair. She tilted her cheek up for Trent's kiss of greeting.

Trent put his hand at the small of her back. "Mara, this is Sophia's husband, Thomas Winbush."

"Pleased to meet you." Mara extended her hand, and the other man shook it jauntily.

"We were sorry to miss your dinner a few weeks ago. One of the boys was sick. We heard from Dad later that it was quite a night," Thomas said.

Heat rushed to Mara's cheeks. "It was something all right. My parents are always interesting dinner companions."

Sophia chuckled. "I definitely won't miss the next one." She turned to Trent. "And Mom said that Mara convinced you to come tonight. I'm happy to see you here. You don't come out nearly enough."

She looked at Mara, and for once her smile didn't appear forced. Was Trent's sister actually warming up to her? Mara was doubly glad she'd pushed him to come out tonight.

"Well, that'll be changing." Trent looked down at her, a warm, private smile on his face.

Sophia looked between them, and then a teasing smile lit

her face. She walked forward and entwined her arm with Mara's free one.

"I'm going to introduce Mara around. My friends are dying to meet the woman who enticed you to come out of hiding."

"No." A brief look of panic flashed across Trent's face, and he clamped his arm down, trapping Mara at his side.

She looked at him in alarm. He'd never been the shy type, so she couldn't imagine that he really needed her to stay close and help him socialize.

Sophia wouldn't be denied. She tugged at Mara's arm. "Trent, you can't monopolize her all night. She needs to mingle. Meet people."

Trent glared at his sister, the kind of look that would have intimidated anyone else. "She can meet people with me."

Sophia simply sniffed. "Neanderthal."

"Shrew."

The two siblings grinned at each other in a way that told Mara the exchange must be a familiar one.

"I'll bring her back. Eventually." Sophia hooked her arm with Mara's and tugged slightly.

As she led her away, Mara glanced back at the last minute. Trent's eyes stayed on hers until they were separated by the crowd.

———

TRENT LOOKED over his father's shoulder and out at the crowd. He'd already greeted most of the people his mother wanted him to meet. It was important to her that members of the entire family were visible and seen as publicly supporting all their charity work. He'd been ducking that particular obligation for too long.

If it hadn't been for Mara's insistence, he probably would have continued avoiding all public appearances the way he'd been doing for years. But if seeing him at a charity dinner encouraged some of the donors to open their wallets a little wider to help other kids like Travis, then he could certainly put in some face time.

Avery appeared at his elbow. She nodded hello to his father. "I need to talk to you." She looked around him. "Are you alone?"

"Mara's with my sister and her friends. What did you need to talk to me about?"

"Not here. Let's go up to the roof garden. I want you to see something."

Trent followed her, nodding hello to several people he knew on the way. The roof garden was one of his favorite spaces in the city. It was actually so visually stunning that he found it difficult to concentrate on whatever art exhibit was currently on display.

There wasn't much that could compete with the Manhattan skyline in his opinion.

When they reached the roof, Avery spread her hands. "Isn't it magnificent?"

Trent followed her gesture to the huge metal sculptures covering the entire roof. Each sculpture was entwined with live ivy, giving the appearance of a labyrinth.

"It's a maze?" he asked, moving forward to peer at one of the metal sculptures. He wasn't into art the way Avery was, but he could appreciate pieces that made you think.

"In a way. But more than that, part of the display is sculpture and the other part is glass. It's a really unique effect when you walk through it. You're never quite sure if you're coming or going. It's the work of a Danish artist. Your mother convinced him to exhibit here early just for the gala."

Trent followed her into the beginning of the small maze, noting how the glass sections provided a warped view of the people on the other side. Once they were far enough in that no one was behind him, Avery looked over at him.

"James told me. About what he saw at my graduation party."

"What are you talking about?" Trent suddenly remembered his brother's wild accusations a few weeks ago. "He didn't? I told him that nothing happened. He shouldn't have said anything to you."

She trailed her hand over one of the glass partitions. "When I woke up next to you, I couldn't remember how I got there. I was freaked out, so I got up and went back to my room. You don't think we could have..."

"No. I mean, I don't think so."

"But you don't actually remember what happened either, do you?"

Trent's heart rate sped up. The sound was loud in his own head. Feeling completely cornered and strangely defensive, he tried to make a joke.

"Not exactly. But we were both hammered. I'm not sure I could have even performed under those conditions."

Avery didn't laugh.

"Haven't you ever wondered? About what things could have been like if you and I..." She gestured between them.

His heart rate kicked up another notch. The way she was looking at him, he'd never seen that particular look on her face before. She was eyeing him the way you sized up someone you were imagining naked.

It was wrong and just one shade too close to incestuous for Trent's comfort.

Before he could formulate a response, Avery leaned against him, and then her lips were on his. Her hands wrapped around his neck so tightly they were strangling him.

Trent backed up a step, breaking the contact. When she stepped forward as if to kiss him again, he moved back again, bumping into one of the glass panels in the exhibit.

"Avery. *Stop.* Things were never like that with us. We were friends. We *are* friends."

"But we could have been more. I've always cared about you, Trent. You were the only one who was always there for me."

She reached out for him, latching on to his wrist. Trent gently pried her fingers open, trying not to be too rough. He wasn't sure what was going on. Maybe she'd had too much to drink?

"Avery, of course I've always been there for you. We've always been there for each other. Ever since we were kids. That's what friends do."

Her eyes never left his face. If she'd heard what he said, she gave no indication of it. Instead, she just kept gazing at him with that lovesick expression that he'd never thought would be aimed at him instead of his brother.

"I don't know how I would have gotten through the past few years without you. *I love you.* Travis loves you. You've been more of a father figure to him than your brother ever has. Doesn't that mean anything?"

"It means I love my nephew." Trent looked away, at a complete loss as to what to say.

"But what if he's not your nephew? What if he's your son? Our son."

This conversation wasn't one he'd ever thought about having. All the memories he had of his teenage years included Avery, but she seemed to have recast them in a different light. One where he was the hero who had saved her from all her problems.

He hung his head. Mara had been right the whole time. She'd seen something in Avery he hadn't been able to discern. And now he was going to have to try to explain this to her on top of everything else.

How would he feel if one of her male friends had plastered his hands, and lips, all over her?

The word homicidal came to mind.

He wasn't rational when it came to Mara. Anything or anyone that threatened her or their life together affected him like a mortal threat. But he would have to hope that Mara had a better grip on her emotions than he did on his own.

"Avery, I'm going to ask Sophia and her husband to take you home."

She yanked her hand away, stumbling into one of the sculptures. He grabbed at her, trying to keep her from falling.

"You're not sending me anywhere with that bitch. Sophia hates me. She always knew the way I felt about you. She never thought I was good enough. Bitch." She knocked his hand away when he reached for her again. "Just leave me alone."

He watched as she walked across the garden to reenter the building. He pulled out his phone and texted his sister, asking her to keep an eye out for Avery. Sophia wouldn't be happy about it, but she would do it.

Despite Avery's behavior tonight, he couldn't just let her wander off without knowing if she had a way to get home safely. She'd obviously had a few drinks and said things she would regret tomorrow. But he would have to deal with that later.

First, he had to find Mara.

He needed to get her out of there before anything else went wrong.

―――――

MARA HAD NEVER MET SO many fake people at once.

She'd allowed Sophia to squire her from group to group until they eventually ended up with her friends, a bubbly group of women just as posh and perfect as Sophia. They had been nice enough, but they'd quickly turned the conversation to people she didn't know and events she hadn't attended.

As her mind wandered, she noticed a pretty, middle-aged brunette standing near Trent's father. Leaning over to Sophia, she asked who it was.

"Oh, that's just Gina. She works for my father."

"Would you excuse me?"

Sophia's mouth moved, but Mara walked away before she could even answer. After ducking around a waiter, she made her way across the floor to where Mr. Townsend stood.

"Hello again, Mara. Are you looking for Trent?" he asked pleasantly. "I think he's around here somewhere."

She looked over at Gina. "Actually, I was hoping I could steal your assistant."

James looked surprised but nodded affably. He glanced behind him at Gina. "Certainly."

She held out her hand to Gina and then, on the spur of the moment, pulled the other woman into a hug. "I wanted to thank you in person for everything you've done to help me. I would have been lost without you this past week."

Her cheeks rosy with pleasure, Gina clapped her hands in front of her. "Of course. I was happy to do it. I'm so fond of Trent. Well, we all are."

"I can tell. Well, I won't keep you. I just wanted to make sure I said hello." She let out a little sigh as Gina walked over to rejoin Mr. Townsend.

Someone bumped into her elbow. She turned at the contact.

A young woman about her age wearing an absolutely divine pale cream ball gown smiled brightly. "Oh, hello. I saw you with the Townsends. We haven't met yet. I'm Nancy Callahan."

Mara extended her hand to shake. "Hi, it's nice to meet you. Mara Simmons."

"So, you're the future Mrs. Trent. You're the hot topic tonight."

"I am?" Mara glanced around warily.

Nancy took a sip of her drink. "Don't worry about it. Before long someone else will be getting a divorce or going into rehab. Then people will have something else to talk about. So, what committees are you on?"

Mara had to resist the urge to rub her temples. People here

had a way of talking in circles. "Committees. What do you mean?"

"Well, I work with the Garden Society and the Children's Hospital. I assume you've been working with Antonia on some of the Townsend charity initiatives."

"No, I'm not. I'm not on any committees."

The other woman looked at her strangely. "Really? None at all?"

Mara finally started to lose her patience. "Well, I've never had time. Until recently I had a full-time job."

At the other woman's blank look, Mara just shook her head. "*A job.* Where you work all week and then you get a paycheck at the end."

While the girl was digesting that, Mara grabbed a champagne glass from the tray of a passing waiter.

"It was *lovely* to have met you," she said before walking away.

The drink cooled her off slightly but she didn't stop moving, fearful that she'd get pulled into another inane conversation. When she finally saw Trent walking toward her, she could have cried with relief. He headed straight for her, ignoring several people who tried to stop him on the way.

When he reached her side, the first thing he said was, "You look upset. What did Sophia do?"

She gulped down the rest of the champagne in her glass. "It wasn't Sophia. She was actually nice and introduced me to her friends. It's these people."

Trent looked around them and then back at her. "I told you these parties were boring."

"I just met a woman who asked me what committees I'm on. When I told her none, that I used to work a job, she looked at me like I was an alien. I guess she assumed that I should spend my days the way she apparently does, flitting from luncheon to luncheon, gossiping about people, and writing checks instead of actually getting my hands dirty."

Trent cupped her elbow and led her to the side of the room, angling his body to block out some of the crowd.

She expelled a breath and rested her head on his shoulder. "I'm sorry I'm complaining. I wanted to come; it's just so far from the world I'm used to. I think it's culture shock."

"This was part of my fear," he admitted in a low voice.

"What?"

"Your ability to have a normal life will be curtailed if you're with me. If you're my wife, it'll be nearly impossible for you to work a normal job with people who actually need their paychecks. You saw the way your friend at work reacted. Imagine if everyone there knew. You could stay home, but eventually it'll feel like I'm keeping you prisoner."

She looked up to see Trent watching her with sad eyes. "Welcome to the gilded cage," he whispered.

Mara wanted to deny that what he said was true, but then she tried to imagine going to work every day, having lunch with her coworkers while they complained about bills and how to make each paycheck last, and she just couldn't envision it.

She looked down at the gorgeous lavender evening gown Sophia had chosen for her. Even though Trent's sister hadn't given her the warmest reception when they'd first met, she hadn't allowed that to prevent her from choosing well. The dress was perfection. It also cost almost as much as the new gutters she'd had installed on the town house last summer.

That bill had made her cry, and now look at her. Walking

around with several thousand dollars on her back like it was nothing.

As much as she would like to tell herself that money wouldn't change her, it was impossible. She'd already changed, and there was no pretending.

Trent entwined their fingers, rubbing a slow circle over the back of her hand. "Do you regret coming here?"

She put her other arm around his waist, pulling him closer. "No. I don't regret anything. I love you. All this other stuff will take some adjusting to, but I can do it."

She looked up at him, feeling like her heart was in her throat.

"I can live in a cage if you're in there with me."

part three

"But we loved with a love
that was more than love—"
— *Annabel Lee, Edgar Allan Poe*

sixteen

NOTHING IN TRENT'S life to date could compare to hearing Mara say that she was in it for the long haul.

She leaned up and whispered in his ear. "I remember some rash promises about being debauched in the limo."

Her arm around his waist moved slightly lower and she stepped closer, sliding up against him in one sinuous movement. Just like that, with one move, he was hard. His breath hissed out between his teeth as she rubbed against the length of his now painfully throbbing cock.

Only she had ever had the power to do this to him, turn him into a barely civilized caveman who thought of nothing but getting her naked.

"Can you call the car?" she whispered.

"I don't think I can wait that long." Grabbing her hand, he pulled her along.

She stumbled after him, trying to keep up with his long strides in her ridiculously high heels. It had been a while since he'd been in the museum, so he just headed for the first roped-off area he saw.

A guard stepped in front of them. Behind him, Mara let out a small squeak of surprise as she bumped into his back.

"Sir, this area is off-limits."

Trent reached into his pocket. "Can I convince you to develop a case of temporary amnesia for the next thirty minutes?" He handed over several hundred dollars.

The guard pocketed the money and then turned in the other direction, deliberately not looking their way. Trent tugged Mara's hand, pulling her along the corridor and then turning out of sight.

"Where are we?"

"One of the medieval exhibits."

"Really?" She looked around excitedly.

"Yes, I plan to have you naked while the knights of the Round Table watch." He kissed the skin on the back of her neck, which peeked out from beneath the loose tendrils of her hair. "You are so beautiful. And all night I've had to watch other men drooling over you. Coveting you."

She spun in his arms, her hands resting on his chest. "They can covet all they want, because I'm with you."

"I know." He said the words and meant them.

No matter what else was happening in his life, the one thing he had for absolute certain was Mara's loyalty.

There was no amount of money or prestige that would entice her to betray him. It wouldn't matter if the man hitting on her was a CEO or the sheik of some small country; she was with him in every sense of the word.

He cupped the base of her neck, wishing her hair was loose and free so he could tangle his hands in it. It was an action borne of desperation. He wanted to erase the memory of Avery's kiss and her touch.

At the thought, he lifted Mara and put one hand behind her on the wall to steady them. She had to hike up her dress to get her legs around him. Just the sound of the material sliding over her skin was erotic as hell. He reached between them, searching for the damp cotton between her legs.

"You should never even bother with panties," he grumbled as he pulled the flimsy material to the side.

Mara panted as his finger slid deep. "Well, normally I'm not flashing my naughty bits around."

"You'd better not be flashing anyone but me."

She whimpered as he bit her neck playfully. Her ears and neck had always been sensitive, and he loved teasing her that way, making her so hot for him that she sometimes came before he even got inside her. Their connection had been explosive since the first time they'd been together.

He'd stayed away from her for years, knowing that their chemistry was potent. Dangerous. He'd tried to do the right thing and leave her alone, but he was far too selfish for that.

He needed her.

Angling his palm, he rubbed circles directly on her clit. As he worked her, she bucked her hips. Her eagerness just spurred him on. It was an honor to know her body so intimately, to know exactly how much pressure would get her off and have her screaming his name. He watched, loving the play of emotions on her face as she succumbed to desire.

Finally her mouth fell open and he kissed her, swallowing her cry.

"Always so wet for me," he mumbled against her neck.

He thrust two fingers in, testing her readiness, and they both moaned. She reached down and unzipped him herself, carefully pulling his cock out. Mara apparently was tired of waiting. He jerked into her hold, cursing at the intense pleasure as she gripped him, rubbing her thumb over the tip.

"I want you now." She didn't give him the option of waiting.

With a firm hold on him, she was in the driver's seat and she knew it. The situation wasn't unlike every other area of their lives. Although he could be arrogant and demanding at times, he knew that truly Mara was the one in control.

Because if she ever left him, he would be shattered. She held the key to his entire existence in the palm of her hand.

He wondered if she even knew.

"Don't you know I'd give you anything? Anything at all."

"You don't have to give me anything other than you." She guided him into position and her eyes closed as he pressed forward. "I love the way you feel. You're the only one who's ever made me feel this way. Like I can't even wait to take my clothes off."

A primal rush of satisfaction flowed through him at being the only man who could give her this. Who could satisfy her.

Trent lost all sense of time and place as his instincts took over. There was only her arms around his neck and the rolling motion of his hips. Mara kept her eyes on his as he thrust into her wildly, unable to slow himself down. Looking down at where their bodies connected just made every sensation more intense.

She squeezed her eyes shut as her muscles clamped down on him, the flutters of her orgasm throwing him headfirst into his own release. He kissed her again, his tongue invading her mouth, and all thought fled. His legs locked, trying to keep them upright as he came.

"Oh my God, that was intense," she whispered. Her fingers tightened on his shoulders as she struggled to stand up.

As his reason returned, shame washed over him. Mara deserved so much better than being fucked in a random corner. Like it was some illicit encounter.

It only made what had happened with Avery earlier seem even worse. Mara should be spread on a bed of roses, pampered and protected. Not stealing embraces in a public place where only one morally ambiguous security guard stood between her and being publicly humiliated.

"We have to leave now. I'm taking you home."

If she was shocked at his sudden change in demeanor, she didn't say anything. She just did a sexy little wiggle to get her dress to fall back into place and then ran her hands over her hair.

"I need to stop by the bathroom. You know, to clean up." She gave him a meaningful look.

Trent nodded. He led them past the security guard at the entrance and down another corridor to the restrooms. She pushed the door open, but before she entered, looked back at him.

"I'll be just a minute. Hold these for me."

After she was gone, Trent looked down at what she'd pressed into his hand.

Her panties.

———

TRENT CHECKED his watch for the second time. Mara was taking a long time, and he was starting to get some strange looks just hanging out in the hallway outside a women's restroom. He was ready to get the hell out of there.

The more time he had to think about the situation with Avery, the more he realized that he had to come clean with Mara immediately. He couldn't predict what Avery would do. She wasn't herself lately, and the knowledge made him nervous. He definitely needed to get them home, away from prying eyes.

He still wasn't ready to think about the implications of whether his memory was faulty. Just because he didn't remember if anything had happened that night didn't mean it was impossible. He groaned.

What if he was Travis's father?

He'd have lost years of time with his son that they could never get back. Not to mention how it would affect his relationship with Mara going forward.

It wasn't that he thought she couldn't accept and care for a child who wasn't her own. But in light of the things she'd told him about Avery, he knew the situation had the potential to go nuclear. His thoughts turned to Mara's accusations about Avery tricking her, deliberately trying to sabotage their family dinner.

It brought up some truly troubling possibilities, because if that was true, then Avery's behavior tonight wasn't born of insecurity and alcohol.

It was something she'd been thinking about for a long time.

The bathroom door opened and Mara finally appeared. Her hair was now in a low ponytail, and she'd wiped the rest of her lipstick off completely.

"I'm ready to go. There's only so much I can fix in a public bathroom." She smiled up at him warmly, almost like she didn't mind that he'd just mauled her in public.

Trent put his arm around her shoulders and ushered her forward. Just before they got to the main entrance, he heard someone call out his name. He turned to see Sophia rushing after them.

She looked between them. "Where have you been?"

Mara flushed red and looked down at her shoes. Trent pulled her against his side and answered before his sister could read too much into that. "We were just on our way out. Did you need something?"

"I just wanted to tell you James was here. He was looking for you."

Trent stood up straighter. Coupled with Avery's earlier revelation, his brother's sudden appearance was not a good thing.

"When was this?"

Sophia spoke to several people who passed by, her smile never faltering. "About half an hour ago. He was arguing with Avery, and then he asked me if I'd seen you. Then he just marched off."

"Okay. Thanks for letting me know."

She put her hand on his arm. "He looked really upset. What is going on between the two of you?"

Sophia had always hated to see them fight. It wasn't fair to put her in the middle of their dispute. There was nothing that she could do to help, nothing anyone could do.

"Nothing for you to worry about. Thanks for the warning though."

With a worried smile, she headed back into the party. Trent scanned the crowd, wondering if his brother was still roaming around. Hopefully he could get outside and leave without an altercation.

"What was that about?" Mara asked.

He sighed. "I have something to tell you. But not here. There are too many people around."

She didn't speak again, just allowed him to lead her outside, docile as a child. When he glanced at her, she was hunched over, her shoulders rounded like she was bracing for something to hit her.

And it killed Trent to realize she was right to be scared.

———

THE RIDE back to the penthouse wasn't filled with sexual tension like the ride to the gala had been. Trent had been moody and quiet ever since they'd left, and nothing Mara said seemed to draw him out.

All he would say was "not here" and then go back to brooding and staring out the window. Eventually she gave up and just rested her head on the seat.

It was perplexing that he was in such a bad mood when she felt so loose and satisfied.

Was he angry with her for teasing him in the middle of the party?

The thought worried her, that her bold proposition had somehow embarrassed him. Then she threw that idea out completely. Trent had been with her one hundred percent, and he'd been the one to take her to the roped-off area of the exhibit. If he'd been embarrassed by the idea of getting caught, he would have just taken her to the limo.

He definitely wouldn't have hiked her dress up amongst a roomful of medieval weaponry.

They pulled up to the front of their building, and when Shane opened the door, Mara followed Trent out. The cool night air brushed over her skin and she clutched her wrap around her shoulders.

As they rode the elevator up, Mara was already planning what she would do to relax after she took off her dress and shoes. It was fun to wear such fancy clothes, but the strapless bra she had to wear with the dress was starting to pinch, and the soles of her feet hurt from the high arch of the heels.

"I can't wait to take these shoes off. And take a hot bath."

Trent smiled down at her indulgently. "I hope you don't mind if I join you."

When the doors opened, they walked hand in hand through the entryway. Mara draped her wrap over one of the kitchen barstools and set her purse down on the counter. She took out her cell phone to check if she had gotten any messages.

"Oh, my brother called. I wonder what he wanted." She was about to call him back when she looked up and noticed the figure standing in the living room.

"Avery? What are you doing here?"

Trent looked up sharply at the words, his gaze moving around the room wildly. Avery didn't move, just stood there, still wearing the formal gown she'd worn to the gala.

Trent stepped forward. "Mara, I'll take care of this. I think she had too much to drink tonight. You can go ahead and get ready for bed. I'll just call her a cab."

But Mara couldn't move her feet. There was something... proprietary about the way Avery was looking at Trent. Then she raised her hand and Mara could see that she was holding a piece of paper. Trent stalked forward and snatched it.

"Avery, I don't have time for this right now. I already said everything I wanted to say earlier. You have to leave."

"Look at it, Trent. James just gave it to me tonight," she rasped.

Mara moved forward, her feet moving of their own accord. Trent finally looked at the sheet of paper in his hand and then paled.

He placed one hand over his heart. "Holy shit."

Mara walked over and looked over his shoulder. When she realized what she was looking at, she backed up until she bumped into the couch. When her knees hit the furniture, she sank down.

"That's a DNA test. Who is it for?" she asked, even though she already knew the answer.

Avery was the one who answered. "Travis. My son. And Trent's son. James had the test done, and he's not the father." She looked over at Trent. "It has to be you."

Mara squeezed her eyes closed. "I can't believe I trusted you all those times you swore that she was just a friend."

She cursed her own stupidity. He'd lied to her so many times, and yet she'd believed him when he said he thought of Avery like a sister. If Travis was their child, he'd clearly not been telling her the truth.

Trent still stood in the same position. "I wasn't lying. I honestly didn't know. When my brother told me he thought Travis was mine—"

"When?" Mara demanded. "When did James tell you this?"

Trent looked pained. "A few weeks ago."

"Weeks! You knew about this for weeks and didn't say anything?"

"I only knew that my brother thought it was true, and I didn't say anything because I thought it was bullshit. I didn't think anything happened that night other than the both of us nearly having alcohol poisoning. I figured James misinterpreted something he saw."

"You don't *think* anything happened. Think? You don't *know*?"

His mouth opened and his jaw worked, but no sound came out.

White-hot rage rushed through her. "You don't, do you? You knew all along that this could be true, and you didn't say anything."

"I should have. I know that now. But I was just trying to prevent this from being blown out of proportion."

"We're right back to where we were before. With you keeping things from me and hoping that I don't find out. With you managing me! I'm not one of your companies. We're supposed to be partners."

Avery spoke up. "I'm so sorry, Mara. I didn't know."

Mara spun toward her, her rage shifting focus instantly. "I'm sure you are. Sorry that your last little stunt didn't work out the way you hoped. You may have Trent fooled, but that victim persona you've got going on doesn't fool me."

She was far too disgusted to deal with Avery right then. Because despite her words, she seemed a little too pleased with the way things were going. Every time there was a problem in her relationship with Trent, somehow Avery seemed to be right in the middle of it.

"Why are you yelling at me? It's not my fault." Avery looked over at Trent helplessly.

Trent stepped between them. "Look Avery, maybe you should go. We're all saying things we don't mean right now."

"Why are you protecting her?" Mara wanted to throw something.

Avery stood to the side with that innocent and wounded look on her face, and of course, Trent jumped to defend her. As if Mara was a danger to Avery's delicate sensibilities.

"I know you feel bad for her, but it's not your fault that she and James have a fucked-up love life. We have our own problems to deal with. She's a liar, and she's just doing what she always does—make up stuff to get between us."

Avery held up the piece of paper in her hand. "I'm not making this up. James had the DNA test done, not me."

Mara ignored her and walked back toward the kitchen. Trent seemed to suddenly wake from his trancelike state, because he rushed after her, catching her arm.

"Please don't leave. Let me explain."

"Oh, I'm not leaving."

"You aren't?" Trent and Avery spoke in unison.

"No. I live here. *You* are the one who is going to leave," she said, looking at Avery meaningfully. "Trent and I have a lot to talk about, and we need privacy for that."

The stunned look on Avery's face told Mara that she'd made the right decision. Avery was counting on Mara running at the first sign of trouble so she could have Trent by default. Well, Mara wasn't going to make it that easy. Avery clearly didn't know what real love was like.

She was in this thing with Trent until the finish line, even when things got hard.

Avery's breath came faster and her hands clenched into fists. "But you have to leave! You aren't right for him. You're just like her. God, *you died and I still can't get rid of you.*"

A chill went down her spine at the words. "What are you talking about?"

Suddenly Avery grabbed her by the arm and pulled her down the hall to the master bedroom, slamming the door behind them. When she turned the lock, Mara's heart skipped a beat.

"What are you doing?"

On the other side, she could hear Trent yelling. Avery didn't stop, just started looking around the room. Then when her eyes landed on Trent's closet, she pushed Mara in that direction. Mara stumbled in and fell. Avery pulled the door closed after them and then pushed the dresser in front of the closet door to block it just as there was a thunderous crash on the other side.

"Now, where would he hide them? This is the only room I haven't checked." Avery peered in each of the dresser drawers, leaving them hanging open when she moved on.

She ran her hands over the suits and coats hanging on the rack. Mara was about to yell at her to stop touching Trent's stuff when there was a bang on the door. The knob turned back and forth and then jiggled wildly.

"Avery, *open the damned door!*"

Mara shivered. She'd never heard him act like this. He sounded different. Violent. Then there was another loud bang and she realized he was trying to force the door open. Avery was now down on her hands and knees, looking for... something.

The closet door vibrated again as Trent rammed it. Mara

whimpered as the sound reverberated through the room. If he hadn't been acting so crazy, she would have just opened the door and let him in but at the moment she was actually scared to do that.

"Trent, please calm down. You're scaring me!"

The banging on the door stopped instantly, but she could still hear his frantic breathing on the other side of the wood.

"Mara, please come out. Come out now so we can talk about this."

She glanced over at Avery. "What are you looking for?"

"Pictures. Didn't you notice there are no pictures in this place? I left one for you to find, but he must have taken it. You need to see so you can understand. Aha!"

She'd found a brown cardboard box pushed into the corner. After rooting around inside, Avery turned around, a picture frame held triumphantly over her head.

Mara took the frame, her arm shaking slightly before she even turned it over. Maybe a part of her knew what she would see. Or maybe it was just a reaction to Avery's sadistic smile or the sound of Trent ramming his shoulder against the door again.

But when she turned the picture over, only a small gasp escaped.

"Now you see," Avery spat. "You're not the love of Trent's life. *She is.*"

Mara clutched at the wooden frame until her fingers turned white. In the picture, a much younger Trent grinned back at the camera, a look of carefree joy on his face. The girl in the picture had her arms wrapped around him and a beautiful, open smile on her face.

Even her smile looked identical to Mara's own.

"She looks like me," Mara whispered. "This isn't possible. We met at college. It was totally random."

It seemed so long ago now, that first day on campus when they'd met. Matt didn't even know that she'd met Trent on campus before she'd seen him in Matt's room. They'd bumped into each other in the registrar's office. She'd been there clearing up an error on her class schedule. He'd seemed so interested in her, and she'd been flattered.

All the emotions she'd expected to feel when she first saw the picture suddenly slammed into her like a tsunami. A soft sob escaped before she could hold it back.

What she'd assumed was interest must have been shock. The way he'd stared at her... Then he'd shown up in Matt's room as his new roommate. Their friendship had been a foregone conclusion at that point.

But had he really been interested in her, or was she just a stand-in for the girl he'd lost?

seventeen

TRENT SLID to the ground on the floor outside the closet. As soon as he'd heard Mara's broken cry, all the fight had drained from his body.

His shoulder ached from where he'd been ramming it into the door, but he didn't even care. The pain was just one of many aches at this point, and the majority weren't even physical.

How had things gotten to this point? He stared blankly into the room. When he'd seen Mara in her evening gown, it had signaled a turning point in his mind. She'd embraced his world with warmth and a willing enthusiasm to adapt. Galas and socializing weren't important to him, and he would have gladly continued to ignore all those things, but they were important to his parents. His sister. His world.

Mara had seen all that before he did. She'd made the effort to be a part of things and had functioned as a bridge, pulling him from his solitude and back into the light. Watching her work the room at his sister's side earlier that night had seemed so right. Like the kind of thing he could imagine doing for the next ten, twenty, or even fifty years.

For the first time, he'd been able to see a future completely unencumbered by the past, and that future had been bright.

But now the joy he'd experienced earlier was only a distant memory.

When the door finally opened, Avery stepped out. The yellow-hued light from the closet spilled out into the room, and her shadow loomed on the floor. She didn't say anything, just stood next him, waiting. He could feel all the questions she wasn't asking and the comments she wasn't making swirling through the air between them. When she knelt beside him, he turned his head away.

A few minutes later, he heard the soft pads of her footsteps as she walked away.

He didn't look at her as she left. The next time he looked up, Mara stood in the doorway.

She stepped over his legs, the small train of her gown swishing around her legs. Bracing one hand against the wall, she carefully sat next to him. Her cell phone was still clutched in her hand, and a picture frame rested in her lap.

When she spoke, her voice sounded rusty. "Sophia told me that day when we went shopping that you'd had a girlfriend who died. She mentioned that she looked like me. But the way she said it, I thought she was just being bitchy. Everyone has a type. I've always had a thing for blond guys. I figured you have a thing for naturally tanned brunettes. No big deal."

Trent wanted to reach out for her so badly, to just pull her into his lap and kiss the tortured look off her face. But even though she was sitting next to him, talking to him, her body language screamed *stand back*. He had to respect her space.

Especially when he hadn't been giving her the respect she deserved in any other aspect.

"Sophia was upset that day when she met you. We argued over lunch. I made her promise she wouldn't say a word about Tia. That was something I needed to tell you myself. Then when you came home and asked about her, it was an opportunity. I've never told anyone exactly what happened before."

He chanced a glance over at her. She was watching him with the kind of care you give a person who could go off the deep end at any minute.

"No one? What about your parents? The police?"

He shook his head. "My family's lawyer told me to answer the questions posed to me and offer nothing additional. I told them the facts. Tia and I had gone on a date and then I'd taken her home. I had to tell them that we were intimate, which was humiliating enough, but no one knew what we argued about. It wasn't just myself that I was protecting."

"James. You were protecting your brother." She let out a soft sigh.

"If they'd known that she was heartbroken over James, it would have just thrown fire on the rumor mill, and for what? It wasn't going to bring her back. It didn't matter."

"But it does matter. All of this matters. Because it's still affecting you now. It's affecting you, your brother, and Avery. I think that's why Sophia told me. She wasn't trying to be mean; she was trying to protect both of us. Because this—" She held up the picture frame. "You have to see how *incredibly disturbing* this is."

"I was going to tell you tonight. That's why I wanted to come straight home. I knew that it was just a matter of time before someone said something to you. Or until another picture surfaced. I just needed to make you understand first."

Mara closed her eyes. "This whole time I've been trying to understand. Even after you told me about Tia, there was this distance between us that I could never cross. And I knew that she was at the heart of it. Her death was a defining moment in your life."

Her hand shook as she picked up the picture frame again. She stared down at the image. Trent knew exactly which one it was too. The one he'd stared at for so long that day.

"And I kept wondering what was the big deal about Tia? He already told me how she died, so what else is there? We looked something alike, but if it was just a coincidence, then why would you go to such lengths to hide it?" Tears slid down her cheeks as she looked at him directly for the first time. "But it wasn't just coincidence, was it?"

"Mara, please..." He could hear the pleading in his own voice. Begging wasn't like him, but he'd do anything not to have to tell her this.

"*Oh God*," she managed to get out over her choked sobs. "That's it, isn't it? Meeting you wasn't a coincidence at all."

"No, it wasn't."

Her face fell, and it hit him then that she'd been hoping he would deny it so they could go back to pretending things were fine. But he couldn't lie to her anymore.

"Tell me. Tell me what you did," she demanded.

"I saw you and it was like a dream." He thought back to that day on campus that seemed so long ago now.

He'd been touring the campuses of several colleges in Virginia. He'd only stopped in Norfolk because of the campus's proximity to the beach. He'd been young enough to think that his college experience should be filled with days surfing and nights with beach bunnies.

Then he'd seen her walking across the pavilion.

"I followed you that day. Watched you go into the registrar's office. I couldn't take my eyes off you."

She closed her eyes. "I remember. I was so flattered. You seemed so different from the other guys who hit on me. It was like you were listening to every word I said and savoring them for later."

He had been, he thought. Every word, every breath she'd taken had been like a miracle. He'd wanted to absorb everything about her.

"It was like seeing a ghost. I thought I was being punished." Trent's head fell forward, and his hands massaged the side of his temples.

Mara shifted, turning so she could see his face. "Why would you think you were being punished?"

"Because of the way things ended. She killed herself right after we fought, and I couldn't help but ask myself if her state of mind at the end somehow led to what she did. I'd been dreaming about her for months, about the way she looked at the end, all bloody and cold."

"So you followed me?"

"I did. I followed you for the rest of the day. I saw you go into Matt's dormitory, and when I saw you together, I was overcome. I thought he was your boyfriend. I went back to the registrar and paid the woman behind the counter a thousand dollars in cash to let me peek at the file of the boy in room 27B. Then when I saw his name and realized that you were related, I paid her again to arrange a clerical error that would put me in that same room."

"And then you showed up in Matt's room the next day and we met again. Matt never knew that we'd met already. I never told him," she admitted quietly.

"I never did either. I wasn't planning to do anything other than watch over you. I used to follow you when you went out on dates to make sure you got home safely. I left money in your room for you to find when I knew you were short before payday. I just wanted to take care of you."

"No, Trent. You were trying to take care *of her*." Mara put a shaky hand over her heart, crying in earnest now. "You were imagining that I *was her*. Were you thinking of her every time you held me? When you kissed me for the first time?"

Trent reached out for her, but she moved away. "No, that's not how it was at all. I wish I could just explain."

"There's no way to explain this, Trent. This whole thing is sick. You were imagining someone else when you were with me. Tell me the truth. All those times when you were following me and helping me, it was because *you were pretending I was her*, wasn't it?"

He wanted so badly to deny it. But he could tell she knew by the look of disgust on her face. His secret shame was revealed, the one thing he'd never wanted her to know.

"Yes," he whispered.

Even though she'd demanded to know the answer, she crumpled over like she'd been punched. She breathed in and out through her mouth, so fast he worried she was hyperventilating.

"You were thinking about her when you were with me. Were you thinking about her when you made love to me?"

It was twisting him up, telling her these things that he knew would hurt her. Especially having her look at him like this, like he was someone she didn't even know. Although he deserved it, it still hurt like hell.

"Mara, that's not how it was. I've known you for years. By the time we... By that time, I hadn't thought about Tia in a long time. After that, all I saw was you. You are the one I'm in love with. I blocked out that part of my life completely."

"But you didn't. It's still a part of you. She's still a part of you."

He stood, his muscles protesting. It felt like he'd been through a war. "Please, let's just go and talk about things. You can take your bath."

Mara shook her head violently. "No, I can't talk to you right now. I need some space. I can't even look at you."

He backed away. "I'll leave. I'll sleep in my office tonight." He turned back to where she still sat on the floor. "I am so incredibly sorry."

"The worst thing..." She looked up him.

Even the mascara trails running down her cheeks didn't diminish her beauty. It made her look precious and fragile, like a priceless object with a crack right down the middle.

"What's the worst thing, baby?" He couldn't hold back the endearment.

Because even though she was so angry with him and probably hated him right now, she was and always would be the thing he cherished most in the world.

"The worst thing is I'll never know whether we really fell in love. Every moment with you, all those memories we made, they weren't real. I'll never know if you really saw *me*. How could you when the whole time you were looking for someone else?"

———

MARA RODE THE ELEVATOR DOWN, her arms wrapped around herself. She wasn't sure if she was doing it to keep people away or to hold herself together.

She passed the doorman and several well-dressed people in the lobby, but she could barely see them. She stumbled out into the cool night air and turned left, then right. The ding of the elevator car across the lobby propelled her forward. Trent would be coming after her.

She had to move.

A group of young women passed by, chatting happily. Mara tucked her head and followed behind them, matching her gait to theirs.

"Mara! Mara!"

At the sound of her name, she almost turned but caught herself at the last minute. Tears burned the backs of her eyelids and it took all her willpower not to look back. It would be so easy to turn around, go to Trent, and let him make the hurt go away. To let him reassure her that everything was fine and that he loved her. But the one thing she couldn't do was lie to herself.

Ignoring the instinct to turn around and run to him, she surged forward, allowing herself to blend with the flow of the pedestrian traffic.

She hadn't brought a coat, and she stood out in her evening gown and sparkly heels. In that moment, she wanted to rip off the offending garments and run naked through the streets. It was just more evidence of how foolish she'd been. Trying to change herself to fit into Trent's world when the reality was she'd never fit in. She'd always been nothing more than a stand-in for the one thing money couldn't buy.

The love he'd lost.

When they reached the corner, the chattering group of girls turned and she stopped.

"Where am I?"

A man walking next to her gave her a strange look, so she tucked her head and went the opposite direction.

The closest sign said Park Avenue. Wasn't there a subway line somewhere nearby? Then she bit her lip to hold in a sob. Even if she could figure out which subway line was closest, it wouldn't matter since she didn't have her purse. All she had was the phone in her hand.

After walking to the other side of the street, she stood next to one of the buildings and scrolled through the contacts on her phone. She couldn't call her brother yet. He'd dropped every-thing to follow her out here the first time, and she knew he wouldn't hesitate to do it again.

But right now, she didn't really need a lot of questions and outrage. As she scrolled past all the familiar names, she consid-ered and discarded each one. They'd all want to help, but they'd want answers.

She needed someone who would just get straight to the point and ask her what she needed. Then her thumb scrolled over a name that made her pause.

Ethan Westbrooke.

Her hands shook slightly as she pushed the button to make the call. If she thought about it too long, she'd talk herself out of it. Right now, she needed the extra boost of courage that came with feeling desperate.

"This is Ethan."

The deep, familiar baritone was so reminiscent of home and her old life that tears sprang to her eyes.

"Ethan? It's Mara Simmons."

"Mara? This is a surprise. Didn't you move to New York?"

She glanced around her, at the people, the cars honking, and the unfamiliar buildings. It was a horrible feeling to realize that her "home" was a place where she no longer felt safe.

"Yeah, I did. I know it's really late and I'm so sorry to do this to you, but I need some help."

There was a pause before he answered, "Of course. What do you need?"

"This is really embarrassing, but I need a way to get out of the city. I just... need to get out of here."

Her voice broke on the last part, and her shame was complete. She was shivering on a street corner while crying to her former boss.

"He fucked up already, didn't he?"

"Yeah. I don't have my wallet. I don't have anything," she admitted.

The words echoed through her mind, and she thought strangely that they applied to way more than just the current situation she found herself in. All the things she'd learned about Trent over the past few weeks and all the dreams she'd envisioned for their future were gone. And she was left with nothing.

"Just hold on. I'm going to get you a hotel room and ask them to hold a key for you at the front desk."

After she told him the address of the building behind her, she listened as he talked to someone in the background. She got a sudden visual of him scowling the way he often did.

"Ethan?"

"Hmm?"

"Thank you. Seriously. I haven't talked to you in so long and you're doing all this for me. I just... really appreciate it."

He paused and she could sense that he was surprised. "You're very welcome. Just tell me that you're okay."

"I'm not. Not at all actually. But I will be."

———

TRENT STALKED DOWN THE STREET, scrutinizing the faces of every woman he passed. He saw a woman with long dark hair and he reached out in recognition.

"Mara!"

She turned and her face came into full view. "Get your hands off me!" The older woman yanked her arm out of his grip and hurried away, throwing worried glances back at him.

Trent stopped in the middle of the sidewalk, ignoring the disgruntled comments and curses from the people who flowed around him.

Where was she?

She couldn't have gone far with no coat and no money. Her purse was still in the penthouse along with all her clothes. Her things. But after going up and down the street twice, there was no sign of her. He'd thought she was walking off to get some distance. He hadn't actually thought she'd disappear into thin air. Out there alone, with no way to even get back home.

As he approached his building, Ernesto opened the door, a concerned look on his face. "You didn't find her?"

Well, that answered his question of whether or not Mara had come back in his absence. "No. Let me know immediately if she walks back this way, would you?"

"Of course, sir."

Back in the penthouse, he crossed to the bar and poured a drink, his hand shaking so badly that he spilled almost as much as he got in the glass. He took the shot of whiskey straight, relishing the burn as it traveled down his throat and landed square in the middle of his gut. He needed that burn to make him feel alive.

Because part of him felt like he was living in the middle of a very bad dream.

I have a son.

He hung his head. No wonder his brother felt like Trent was trying to take his place. Their father was trying to replace him at work, and even his girlfriend wasn't loyal to him. He wasn't blind to his brother's faults in the slightest, but he was starting to get a broader view of where some of his brother's behavior stemmed from.

The sound of the elevator opening stopped him in his tracks. He rushed back over to the doors. "Mara?"

Avery stood in the entryway, watching him warily. For several long moments, neither of them spoke. Trent went through a gamut of emotions—surprise, disgust, rage, and finally sadness.

Because he knew that their friendship had been broken today in a way that could never be repaired.

"I know you're mad at me."

Trent just stood looking at his oldest friend in the world and was suddenly completely deflated. "Mara's gone."

A brief expression of joy crossed her face before she quelled it. "I shouldn't have showed her that picture. I'm sorry."

"You're not sorry."

Her head jerked up at his harsh tone. "Trent, I know—"

"I want you to go, Avery. And not come back."

She took a hesitant step backward. Then she swallowed before nodding. "What about Travis?"

"I'll make arrangements to see him. We can coordinate through my mother. But I can't see you right now. Probably not for a long time."

She looked like she wanted to say something else, but then she looked at his face again, at his rigid stance, and turned to leave. Just before she reached the elevators, she looked back and said, "She wasn't right for you. Maybe I'm not either, but I just had to make you see."

He stood in the same spot for a long time, even after the elevator doors closed.

eighteen

WITH A SIGH, Mara sat on the edge of the bed and kicked off her shoes. Ethan had come through, providing her with a reservation number for a suite at the closest hotel he could find, The Carlyle. She didn't even want to think about how she'd looked coming into the elegant lobby, shivering and wild-eyed, clutching her cell phone to her ear like a lifeline.

But now that she was here, she realized how silly she had been running off without her things. There was no way she could sleep in her evening gown and makeup. She walked into the bathroom and peered at herself in the mirror. Her mascara had smudged beneath her eyes since she'd been crying the whole way here.

With a little sigh, she walked back out into the room and picked up the phone next to the bed. The man who had checked her in downstairs had been so nice, and she thought that perhaps they might have some complimentary supplies she could use. At least a toothbrush.

"Hello. I just checked in and I forgot, well, everything.

There's soap here, but I don't suppose you guys have extra toothbrushes, do you?"

The voice on the other end of the line was steady and soothing. "Of course. We pride ourselves on providing everything our guests need. Would you like a toiletry kit?"

"Yes, that would be great. Thank you so much."

"We'll send someone up with your items shortly."

Mara had just drawn a bath when she heard the knock on the door. After a quick glance through the peephole, she opened the door to a bubbly maid who brought in not only the toiletries she'd requested but also champagne and strawberries, compliments of the hotel.

She wondered what had prompted this level of service and then realized that Ethan must have laid down a huge deposit on the room in order for her to be getting this treatment. It seemed her debt to him was just growing bigger and bigger.

She bit into one of the large, juicy strawberries and decided that if she ever had to get stranded in the city, this hotel was the place to do it.

She stepped out of her evening gown and hung it in the closet. Then she walked back into the bathroom. The toiletry kit contained the usual items: toothpaste, a small travel-sized toothbrush, floss, and a small tube of body lotion.

She pulled out a small packet and then gave a mental cheer. The facial towelettes would be perfect to sponge off the rest of her heavy makeup. Wetting one slightly, she attacked the heavy mascara first, sighing with relief when she finally looked like herself again.

Once she'd brushed her teeth and washed her face, she climbed into the huge soaker tub. Steam rose from the water and she let out a bone-deep sigh of appreciation. Resting her head against the side of the tub, she told herself that she was going to take a little time not to think or obsess or cry. Just a break from it all to soak and relax. After a half hour, she finally felt warm again.

At least in body if not in spirit.

After wrapping herself in one of the huge fluffy towels, she poked around the room until she found a large white bathrobe hanging in the closet. Slipping it on was like wrapping herself in a cloud. Tucking the collar beneath her chin, she climbed onto the big bed and wondered what she was supposed to do now.

For the first time, she allowed herself to really appreciate the grandeur of the room. The king-sized bed was swathed in the softest linen and piled with mounds of fluffy pillows. The room also contained a cherrywood writing desk and had a small balcony. It boasted a modern decor that screamed sophistication. Ethan had really put her up in style.

She wondered if this was what Trent had meant when he said that money changes how people see you. She could see how this kind of pampering could attract the wrong kind of girl. The kind who just wanted a caretaker instead of a partner.

But she'd never been like that with Trent. They'd always been in it together, supporting each other. Or at least, she'd thought so until finding out that she actually didn't know anything about him.

Or that he didn't really know her.

How could he when all he was seeing every time he looked at her was a dead girl's face?

Suddenly cold, she pulled back the comforter and snuggled underneath. Across the room, her cell phone sat on the desk, tempting her. Part of her wanted to call him, let him explain everything away with pretty words and kisses.

She'd give anything to go back to that moment at the museum when she'd believed that they were going to take on the world together, two birds in their gilded cage. She buried her face in her pillow, trying to smother the memories.

Would she ever be able to forget the way he'd looked at her tonight? In a room full of the most beautiful, sophisticated people she'd ever seen, Trent had only had eyes for her.

But then her heart broke anew as she thought that maybe he wasn't seeing her at all.

That was the crux of their problem. At the heart of it, Mara could never be sure of what he saw when he looked at her.

Was he seeing her or the ghost of the woman he really wanted?

She'd given up her job, moved to a new state, and had completely changed her way of life. There was almost no limit to what she was willing to do for him.

But the one thing she couldn't do was be someone else.

DARKNESS GAVE WAY TO LIGHT, and for the first time in years, Trent was awake to experience sunrise over the city.

His cell phone chirped, so he tilted it up to see the screen. It was almost out of power again. That was no surprise. He'd been on the damn thing all night. He'd called everyone Mara might contact. Dax had combed the city, looking for hotel reservations in her name.

They'd checked all the public parks and all the places he'd

taken her on their tour. Nothing. It was as if she'd vanished into thin air.

Panic clawed at the edges of his mind, and he wondered if this was her intention. She wanted him to suffer not knowing where she was. If so, she'd achieved her goal.

When his phone dinged again, he looked down at the display and then answered immediately.

"Matt? Have you heard anything?"

"She's safe. And that's all I'm going to tell you."

The repressed rage in his friend's voice shouldn't have been comforting. But clearly Matt knew where Mara was and had spoken to her or he wouldn't be mad. When Trent had left a message, he hadn't included many details. Obviously Mara had filled him in herself.

"Is she okay?" How could she be okay when her purse and money were at the penthouse?

Unless Matt had gotten her a hotel room and just wasn't mentioning that part. He couldn't blame his buddy. He knew that if Trent had that information, he'd use it to try to track her down.

"I don't know. Are you?"

"No."

Matt grunted on the other end of the line. "I warned you before this all went down not to hurt her. But in a way, I blame myself. I knew I shouldn't have let her talk to you. I knew you would just spin more lies, the way you've been doing all along. But hear me now—stay away from her. I don't know exactly what happened just yet, but once I know she's okay, I'll be coming for you."

"I never meant to hurt her. You have to believe that. Of all the things I've ever told you, I've never lied about that. I'm going crazy over here worrying about her. Please tell me if she's coming home."

"Like I said, she's safe. You really don't want to ask me any more questions right now." There was a soft click as his friend hung up.

He set the phone down beside him. Then he picked it up and threw it across the room. It hit the wall and shattered. He clenched his fingers, wishing there was something, *anything*, else he could throw.

He needed to hit something. Needed something to hit him back.

The elevator doors slid open and he chuckled mirthlessly. "I have to revoke everyone's security privileges."

"I didn't realize I had any."

Trent turned at the sound of his brother's voice. Then he turned back to face the dawn. "What do you want?"

He felt his brother come closer. When he finally gathered the energy to look over again, James stood next to his chair. He looked over at the shattered remnants of Trent's phone on the floor across the room and then back at him.

"I heard about what Avery did."

"How long have you been carrying this around?" Trent asked.

"What? You mean wondering if Travis was mine?" James moved past him and took a seat on the couch.

This close he could see that his brother didn't look any better than he felt. He had dark circles under his eyes and his hair looked like it hadn't been combed for days. He was still wearing his tuxedo from the prior night. Trent looked down in consternation at his own clothes. He hadn't changed either.

"It didn't occur to me until he got a little older. He looked so much like you. And it made me think about that night."

"I really don't remember anything happening." Trent clenched his fists, wanting to smash something. "But I should have taken you seriously when you first told me. I should have done a lot of things. Everything I've been doing for the past few years has been a mistake."

James let out a sigh. "You're not the only one." He looked around the room, seeming to take stock of how quiet it was. "Your girl, she's not here. You lost her over this, didn't you?"

Trent didn't answer. Then he said, "I never had her. Not really."

———

MARA ROLLED over and hugged her pillow against her. Caught in the space between dreams and wakefulness, for a moment she wasn't sure where she was. Just that she was warm and her eyelids felt very heavy. She smiled, wondering what new adventures she and Trent would have that day.

Then she came fully awake and realized she was in a hotel room and that her adventures with Trent were over.

She turned her head, and the rest of the room came into view. Sunlight peeked around the edges of the heavy drapes. With one hand, she pushed back the comforter and with the other she massaged her throat, which was suddenly scratchy and dry.

When she sat up, her head started pounding. Raiding the minibar last night probably hadn't been the best idea she'd ever had, but at least it had given her a break from crying her eyes out.

What the hell was she going to do?

The time for crying was over, and it was time to take action. She needed to get her stuff and go home. But she wasn't sure she could face Trent without breaking down again.

An idea occurred to her, and she grabbed her cell phone from the nightstand. Before going to bed, she'd sent her brother a message and then turned it off to save the power. She turned it back on and instantly several messages showed up. All from Matt.

She dialed her brother's number. His sleep-gruff voice answered after several rings. "Hello."

"Hey, sorry if I woke you."

Matt cleared his throat, and when he answered her, he sounded like he'd come wide awake. "No, it's fine. How are you?"

Guilt creeped in. She'd been so distraught the prior night that she hadn't been thinking straight. She'd left her brother a message that she was safe and where she was but had turned her phone off before going to sleep. Knowing his overprotective streak, he'd probably been up late worried about her.

"I'm sorry. Things were so crazy yesterday, and I just needed some time to get my head on straight."

"I talked to Trent this morning. He was looking for you."

"You didn't tell him where I am, did you?"

"No. I don't want him anywhere near you. I can come up there and get you. You'll come back here and stay with me and Penny for a while. You won't have to be alone."

Her heart swelled with love and appreciation. She'd always had him to rely on, and knowing that he was there for her made it easier to go forward with what she had to do. But she couldn't allow him to disrupt his life any more than he already had.

Once upon a time, she'd been a bold and confident woman. She'd allowed herself to forget that, but it was time to take that back.

"I don't want you to do anything but give Penny a hug for me. And to get me a phone number out of that file you have on Trent."

"A phone number?" Matt sounded confused, but she could tell from the rustling sounds on the phone line that he was moving; probably searching through the junk pile he called his desk to find the file.

"Yes. I need the number for Sophia Townsend Winbush. She's Trent's sister. There's something I need to ask her."

Matt read the number, and she jotted it down on the pad of hotel stationery.

"Thank you. I promise everything is going to be fine. I'll call you when I'm back in town."

Matt grunted but then said, "Will you at least let me know your flight number and when you're arriving? Give me that much at least."

She smiled to herself. "I'll send it to you once I book the ticket. I love you."

"I love you too, sis. And I'm still going to kick his ass when I see him."

She shook her head, smiling at his grumbling as he hung up the phone. Looking down at the pad of paper, she typed out Sophia's number.

Although not the warmest soul she'd ever met, Sophia had known all along that Avery was a snake. She also seemed to want the best for her brother. It was a long shot, but maybe she'd be willing to help Mara now. When she heard a clipped voice answer on the other end of the line, she launched into the whole story, not giving Sophia a chance to hang up before she understood everything.

When she finally paused, Mara took a breath. "Sophia, are you still there?"

"Yes, I'm here. I can't say that I'm surprised by any of this. This is exactly what I feared would happen."

"You saw through Avery before I did. I should have listened to you. But I figured that you didn't like me either, so maybe you were just down on any girl who was close to your brother."

Sophia's sigh came over the line. "I'm sure it seems that way, but I have good reason. Honestly, I have nothing against you personally, Mara. I just didn't think it was a good thing for my brother to have a permanent reminder of what happened with Tia. When you two showed up to the gala, I thought that perhaps I'd been wrong. Trent looked so happy. I haven't seen him look like that in years."

"I think he *was* happy that day. Before Avery came and dropped her bombshell into the middle of it all."

"What did she do now?"

Mara hesitated. She wasn't sure Trent wanted anyone to know about the situation. Then she decided she didn't care. He'd kept so many things from her, including the truth about how they'd met.

Sophia was the only person in this screwed-up world who had been straight with her. Despite her cold demeanor, she was at least trying to help, and Mara knew she was only acting out of concern for her brother.

"She was waving around a DNA test that James had done on Travis. It was negative, so James is not his father. Apparently she and Trent had too much to drink one night and..."

"Oh God. No wonder Trent looked so frantic last night."

"After that, Avery showed me a picture of Tia. Finding out that Trent was a father wasn't enough to drive me away, so she used her final trump card."

Sophia's voice softened when she said, "I'm sorry. When I told you about Tia, I knew you'd go home and ask him. I figured that he'd be forced to tell you then. When you didn't leave after that, I assumed you knew and understood."

"He told me about her death. Not about her life. I wonder now how I could have missed that. He was very deliberate with the things he told me."

"My brother isn't a bad guy, Mara. He was never like this. Lying and keeping secrets. He needs to heal and move on. Seeing you every day can't have been helping him. He's been isolated from his family and his real life ever since, and he needs to stop that and face reality. Tia's gone and she's not coming back."

"I agree. And that's why I'm going to leave. Trent needs to figure things out, and he can't do that while I'm here. But I need your help to do it. Can you get him out of the house for a while? Ask him to meet you somewhere?"

"I can do that. I'll have to think of a way to get him to show up, but yeah, I'll do it." Sophia sounded shocked but happy.

Mara tried not to think about the fact that she was happy because Mara would be gone and out of Trent's life.

"Tell him that I called you. Tell him you know where I am but that you'll only tell him if he meets with you. That'll give me time to go back to the penthouse and retrieve my stuff. Then I'll be out of your hair for good."

The thought made her want to start sobbing again, so she focused on the mechanics. The only way she could go through with this was if she thought of it like a mental checklist. Bullet points that would carry her from point A to point B.

"Mara?"

"Yes?"

"I wish you all the best. I really do."

"Thank you, Sophia. I really hope this is the right thing. For all of us."

nineteen

AFTER JAMES LEFT, Trent finally got up. He'd been sitting in the same chair, in the same clothes, for almost twelve hours straight. He called his parents and then checked in with Dax, who still had no idea where Mara was. After a brief moment of hesitation, he called him off.

Mara was safe and didn't want to be found. If he found her and tried to see her against her will, it would just be one more time that he'd ignored her wishes. She would think he was still pursuing her for the wrong reasons, and that was a major point of contention between them.

She didn't believe he'd really fallen in love *with her*.

He stripped, leaving his tuxedo in the middle of the floor. In the bathroom, he scrubbed his skin, anxious to get dressed and start figuring out a plan. He had to convince Mara to talk to him, and then maybe they might have a chance to work things out. The longer he left her alone, the longer she'd persist in her thoughts that he didn't really care about her.

He had to explain everything.

He could not lose her over this. Not when they'd come this far.

When he stepped out of the shower, his phone was ringing. Sophia's picture flashed across the screen. His first instinct was to ignore it. He could check in with his sister after he'd fixed things with Mara. But when she called back again, he answered. It wasn't like Sophia to call more than once.

"Sophia, I really can't talk right now."

"You'll want to talk to me. I know where Mara is."

Trent paused in the act of pulling on a pair of jeans. "What? How do you know that? Where is she?"

"She called me. She told me what happened and asked me to let you know she's okay. She's thinking about everything."

"Where is she?" he repeated.

Sophia sighed. "I can't tell you that. Come meet me for lunch. I need to see that you're okay with my own eyes."

"I don't have time to play games, Soph. This is too important. *Tell me where she is.*"

"No. I need to know that you're okay. If blackmailing you to get you here is the only way to do that, then that's what I'll do."

"Fuck!" He yanked a shirt over his head and then stuck his feet in the first pair of shoes he saw. "Tell me where to meet you."

"Just come to my place. I'll see you soon."

It was just like Sophia to put him through some kind of test before she'd give up the information. He grabbed his wallet off the kitchen counter and stuffed it in his back pocket. As he was leaving, he nodded at Ernesto. The older man gave him a sad smile.

Great. Now he was an object of pity to everyone from his family members to his doorman.

He hung his head and headed east toward the condo Sophia shared with her husband and two children. Like his parents, they maintained two residences, one in the city and the other in the Hamptons. He realized with a start that he didn't even remember what Sophia's place looked like. For years he'd been ignoring invitations and taking every opportunity to avoid his family, and he'd missed out on so many things.

He hadn't gotten far when he bumped into someone. He started to move around them when a hand clamped on his forearm. He looked up in surprise.

"Avery? What are you doing here?" It seemed strange that she would just happen to run into him on the street. "Are you following me?"

"Trent. Please don't walk away."

"I have nothing to say to you." He pushed past her, intent on walking on and leaving her behind. She could follow him if she wanted to. Sophia sure as hell wasn't going to let her in.

"You can talk to me here or I'll make a scene. All I want is for you to listen to me." Her loud voice carried and several people walking by glanced their way.

Trent cursed under his breath and then turned back. "Fine. Come upstairs. I'm not talking about this on the street."

They walked back in the direction of the penthouse, and Trent ignored Ernesto's shocked look as they entered the building.

Once they got upstairs, he walked to the living room, trying to keep distance between them. Avery followed, standing a few feet behind him.

"I know you don't believe me, but I'm so sorry. I shouldn't

have come here after the gala. Not like that." She reached out for him and Trent backed up a step.

"Don't touch me. Ever again."

Her face changed, the soft vulnerable look replaced by a manipulative, sly look he'd never seen before. How long had he been blind to her true character? Had she always been this way, or was the stress of loving and hating his brother what had driven her to this level?

"It's over, you know. She's not going to forgive you."

"Don't talk to me about Mara. In fact, don't talk to me at all." He moved to walk past her. Avery grabbed his arm.

"I understand why you wanted her. As a memento. You couldn't help yourself. But I'm trying to help you move past that. To move on."

He stared at her, wondering how she could have missed the point so completely. She still thought this was about what had happened when they were teenagers. It seemed she was the one who hadn't moved on.

"It wasn't like that. Yes, I was shocked when I first saw her. I was curious. But after I spent time with her, I realized she was nothing like Tia. And after that, she was all I could see. Just her."

"But you don't need her anymore. James is out of the picture, and we can be a family with our son now."

Her casual disregard for his brother, and even her own son, sickened him. Didn't she realize that playing musical chairs with his father figure wasn't in Travis's best interest? His brother hadn't been around a lot lately, but that little boy adored him. It wasn't a matter of just telling him he had a new daddy.

Avery seemed completely oblivious to the emotional consequences for everyone involved.

"I can't believe how long my family has been a victim of your manipulations. No more." He walked back to the elevators, waiting until she followed him. "My mom was babysitting Travis last week. I know she has a lot of his stuff at her place, so I called her this morning and asked her to do something for me."

"What?" Her brow crinkled in confusion.

"Send me his hairbrush." Trent shouldn't have found it so satisfying to watch her face as she figured it out. But it was. Immensely.

"Why would you do that?" she asked in a shaky voice.

"Because I'm tired of being manipulated. James told me that you provided the sample from Travis for the DNA test. I don't trust you. Not anymore. If he's my son then I'll deal with that, but until we know for sure, stay away from me. Stay away from my family."

"You can't force me to stay away from anyone. They're my family too."

"Your connection to this family is through James. James isn't here. And after the way you've behaved, you'll be lucky if he ever comes back."

He crossed the room and picked up the phone on the counter. When he dialed the front desk, Walter answered immediately.

"Miss Maxwell is no longer welcome on my property. The next time she shows up without prior authorization from me, have her removed. Forcibly if necessary."

Walter's voice didn't betray any surprise at the request. "Of course, sir."

He hung up and turned around. Avery watched him in stony silence. He walked to the elevator, not caring if she followed at this point. He had somewhere to be, and getting to Sophia's was more important than dealing with Avery right now. But when he turned around and saw her behind him, he was compelled to add one last thing.

"Oh, and Mara was never a memento. Mara is unique, unlike anyone else I've ever met. I didn't keep the secret because I was still harboring some obsession for Tia. I did it because I was afraid she wouldn't understand. She is the best thing that ever happened to me, and I was afraid of losing her. It turns out I had every reason to be."

When he got to the ground floor, he waved Walter over. "If she doesn't come down in five minutes, go get her please." Then he walked off and didn't look back.

———

ACROSS THE STREET from the penthouse, Mara took a moment just to stare at the weathered gray facade of the building. It was odd to think that she hadn't ever done that. They'd always been so busy, rushing here and there, and she hadn't taken time to really look at the place.

But now that she knew it unlikely that she'd ever be back, she was assailed with a crippling desire to remember everything. She wanted to have every minuscule detail embedded in her memory for the days when she looked back on the fairy-tale life that had almost been hers.

She kept her eyes on the front entrance, fiddling with the cuff of her long-sleeved *I love NYC* T-shirt she'd charged to her room at the hotel. She hated to prevail on Ethan's kindness any more than necessary, but that had been a requirement to prevent herself from having to do the walk of shame at this time of day wearing an evening gown.

Although if she was honest, she looked just as ridiculous in the campy T-shirt, a pair of drawstring exercise shorts, and her sparkly stilettos. Her look was a cross between tourist and red-light-district hooker. Not that anyone cared. At home she would have drawn stares in this crazy outfit, but she hadn't gotten more than a few curious glances here.

Sophia had promised to call at exactly noon. She'd come early so she could go in as soon as Trent left. Ten minutes later, Trent exited the building. She almost missed him because his head was down and he was walking so fast. After he disappeared into the crowd, she crossed the street. Ernesto opened the door for her with a pleased look on his face.

"Miss! You are back!"

She smiled at his enthusiasm. Although she made it a point to speak to him whenever he held the door, he usually just tipped his hat in her direction. He'd never gone out of his way to talk to her.

"Mr. Townsend has been looking for you."

When she saw him pull out his phone, she put a hand on his arm to stop him. "Wait, you aren't calling him, are you?" She needed time to grab her stuff and get out of there. That wouldn't work if Ernesto gave away the plan.

"I'm about to go see him. But I forgot something upstairs. I don't want him to know I'm coming." He looked unsure, so she added, "We had a fight last night. I want to surprise him."

Ernesto chuckled and winked at her. "Young love. The fighting. The making up."

Mara nodded along, thinking that he had no idea.

"I don't have my keycard. Can you let me up?" For a moment, she worried that her plan would fail just because she didn't have that stupid security card for the elevator.

Ernesto motioned to the concierge. Walter whispered something to the young man behind the desk with him and then walked toward them.

"Miss, you forgot your card? It's okay. For residents, I can let you up."

He got in the elevator, slid in his card, and then hit the button for the penthouse. Once the doors closed between them, she pressed her hands to her face. It had been one of the hardest things she'd ever done to watch Trent walk away. She'd wanted to run after him. To just look at him. But it wasn't the right time for that. They'd have to talk eventually, but not when she was like this. Not when she was so raw and felt like her every emotion had been slit open for the world to see.

When the elevator doors opened, she walked through the kitchen and directly to the bedroom. There was no time for her to do anything but pack her clothes because she wasn't sure how long Sophia could hold him off. As soon as she entered the bedroom, she was hit with his scent. Stopping in the middle of the room, she closed her eyes and inhaled.

His crumpled tuxedo was in the middle of the floor at her feet. Feeling like a complete weirdo, she picked it up and buried her face in the fabric. Without questioning why she did it, she slipped the bow tie in her pocket.

She flipped on the light in her closet and grabbed her suitcase. Operating on autopilot, she didn't even stop to think about what she was taking. She just threw in the stuff in the dresser drawers and grabbed the few dresses she'd brought along. She looked at all the clothes Trent had bought her and hesitated.

Should she take them? They represented a life that she wouldn't have now. Why would she need them in New Haven?

At the thought of New Haven, she wondered briefly why she was even going back. With no mortgage or car payment, she didn't need to rush back into getting another job. Maybe she should travel or visit friends out of state? A change of pace might be exactly what she needed. But the thought of being somewhere new made her feel desperately lonely. Her family was what she yearned for, and there was no shame in that.

She froze in place at the sound of the elevator doors opening up front. Voices drifted from the living room. With a shock, she recognized Trent's voice and then... Avery's? What were they doing together? She slipped off her shoes and walked into the hallway, trying to be as quiet as possible.

"Stay away from my family."

"You can't force me to stay away from anyone. They're my family too."

Avery turned slightly and Mara shrank back out of sight. Her heart was beating so fast that she couldn't hear what they were saying anymore. By the time she gathered the nerve to creep forward again, it was quiet. She was about to stand up, thinking they must have left when she heard Trent's voice.

"Oh, and Mara was never a memento. Mara is unique, unlike anyone else I've ever met. I didn't keep the secret because I was still harboring some obsession for Tia. I did it because I was afraid she wouldn't understand. She is the best thing that ever happened to me, and I was afraid of losing her. It turns out I had every reason to be."

Tears slid down Mara's face as she took in every word and held it in her heart.

The sound of the elevator doors closing gave her the

courage to peek her head around the corner. Avery stood in the middle of the entryway, her hands clenched at her sides. Mara sank back down, holding her breath. What would Avery do? What if she started looking around the penthouse and found her there?

Suddenly Avery let out a scream of frustration. "It didn't work. He's still going back to her."

Mara pulled out her cell phone and activated the recording app. Trent needed to see that Avery was manipulative and mean. She peered around the kitchen island. She couldn't see the other woman, just her feet. Avery was facing in the other direction, so she took a chance and darted out to hide behind the sectional sofa.

"He's getting another test done. What am I going to do? I just wanted him to see me. Why doesn't anybody see me?"

Mara wanted to jump up and choke the shit out of her. The only reason Avery would be upset about another DNA test being done was if she'd somehow tampered with the results the first time.

How could she be so reckless, not only with a man's life and reputation, but with her son? To put him in the middle of a scandal, and all for what? Money? Did she actually think Trent was going to marry her after what she had done?

There was a rustling sound and Mara's heart sped up. She was coming closer. What if she turned the corner and saw her? Avery had already proven herself to be a passenger on the crazy train, but what if she was violent? Mara clutched her phone tighter, ready to use it like a weapon if need be.

But Avery's footsteps went in the other direction. She heard the click-click of her heels on the floor, and then the elevator doors closed again.

Mara scrambled up and then raced back to the bedroom. All the stuff she'd been contemplating taking with her? She ignored it and just zipped up her case. She'd asked Ernesto not to tell Trent that she was there, but what if he mentioned something to Avery? She had to get the hell out of there now.

She turned around, and the figure in the doorway was so unexpected that she let out a startled shriek. The other woman dropped the towels she was holding and screamed too. After a harrowing few moments when Mara wasn't sure if her heart would ever leave her throat, she got control of herself and peered closely at the other woman.

Older. Graying. Grandmotherly.

"*Bianca?*" she asked in disbelief.

The other woman nodded quickly, clearly terrified.

"I'm so sorry! I didn't know you were here."

Bianca answered her back in a small voice. She had an accent that sounded faintly Slavic. "I change the linens. Then I hear that one. I don't like that one."

Mara realized she must be talking about Avery. Bianca had been doing the same thing she had been, hiding out somewhere in the house while Trent and Avery were fighting.

"No, I don't like that one either." She knelt and picked up the towels on the floor. "I'm very sorry I scared you. I'm on my way out."

"Be careful, miss. That one is not so nice." Bianca backed away, the towels clutched to her chest.

When she disappeared into the bathroom, Mara walked to the kitchen and called down to the front desk. "Walter, I need a cab waiting for me out front."

She rode down on the elevator, wrestling with her two suitcases, her carry-on, and her handbag. As soon as the elevator doors opened, Ernesto appeared and helped her wheel the suit-cases to the curb.

"Enjoy your trip, miss."

"Thank you. For everything." On impulse, she hugged him and then ducked into the cab. As she pulled away from the curb, she pulled up the recording app. When she pressed play-back, Avery's voice came out loud and clear.

Mara was mad at Trent, yes. But she still loved him, and there was no way she was going to allow Avery to spread lies about him or trick him. She forwarded the voice file to Sophia and then decided it was out of her hands.

From now on, she was on her own.

twenty

SOPHIA OPENED THE DOOR, flanked by his two nephews. Despite how crappy his day had been so far, Trent couldn't help but smile when he found his arms full of laughing boys.

"Come on in. They've really missed you." Sophia moved aside so he could enter.

Trent was bombarded anew with shame as he realized that in all his visits to help out Avery, he hadn't made more of an effort to see Sophia and hang out with his other nephews. It was almost impossible to believe how much they'd grown while he hadn't been paying attention.

Tommy, the oldest, was so big it was hard to lift him now. At five, he took after his father and was tall, thin, and dark-haired. The youngest, Chase, watched him from Sophia's arms while chewing on his pacifier. His small tuft of blond hair stood straight up on his head.

"What are you feeding these kids? I swear he shouldn't be this big already."

Sophia smiled down at her son, wiping his chin with his

bib. Trent held out his arms and she transferred the baby to him.

"They eat everything in sight. This one doesn't even have all his teeth, but that doesn't seem to matter."

He followed her to the interior of the house, setting Chase down in his playpen. When he stood, Sophia hugged him. It took him off guard, and then he had to blink to ward off the burning sensation at the back of his eyelids.

"I'm so sorry for how I've been acting. And you shouldn't have to be in the middle of any of this. James came by this morning. We talked. It's all going to be okay."

"Good. That's really good." She wiped her own eyes and knelt to move a baby toy before he stepped on it.

"How did Mara sound to you? Did she sound okay?"

"She did. We talked about everything. She told me what Avery did. God, I should have done more to warn you away from her." Sophia made a face. "Hindsight, I suppose."

"Where is Mara? Her brother called, but he wouldn't tell me where she was."

"She was staying at the Carlyle."

"I need to go there. I need to talk to her."

Sophia opened her mouth and then looked away, a faintly guilty look on her face.

"What?"

"Mara is the one who asked me to set up this lunch meeting. She asked me to keep you busy for an hour. I think she wanted that time to get her stuff from the penthouse."

"*What?* You're helping her leave me?" Trent was stunned by the betrayal, especially since he'd thought she was on his side.

"Don't look at me like that," Sophia pleaded.

"I know we haven't had the best relationship over the years. Mom and Dad are insane, I know that. And you've had to deal with their shit a lot more than I have. That can't have been easy. But I feel like I don't even know you anymore, Soph. I always thought no matter how different we were that I could count on you."

"You can count on me. I'm only doing what I think is best for you. You think it makes me happy to see you in so much pain? It's just like when Tia died all over again. You never got over that, and this girl is just prolonging the pain. She's not Tia. Being with her won't bring back the love of your life."

Trent sat down, defeated. "Tia wasn't the love of my life. She was a spoiled, selfish bitch who wanted to use me to get to James."

He glanced around, then relaxed when he saw that Tommy wasn't close enough to overhear.

"What?"

Trent held his head in his hands. Sophia disappeared and then came back with a glass.

"It's scotch. You look like you could use it."

With a soft laugh, Trent took a sip of the drink. They sat in silence for a few moments. When he raised his head again, Sophia was watching him.

"Why haven't you said anything before? Everyone assumed that you were in love with Tia. You were devastated when she died."

"I was, but it was because she told me right beforehand that she'd never loved me. That I was just a shadow of the Townsend she really wanted. She'd slept with me hoping to make James jealous. When it didn't work, she was so upset she slit her wrists."

Sophia placed a delicate hand on his arm. "Trent, I never knew. I'm so sorry."

"No one knew. That was how I wanted it. I figured maybe I wasn't enough for her while she was alive but at least I could protect her memory after she was gone."

"But who is going to protect you, Trent?"

He finished his drink in silence, her question hanging in the air between them.

———

MARA STRUGGLED THROUGH THE AIRPORT, trying to keep track of her two suitcases and her carry-on bag. Part of her wanted to laugh at herself. She'd completely rebuffed all her brother's attempts to help. She'd asked him not to fly out to New York or even to pick her up at the airport.

She had forgotten how much stuff she'd brought with her. It was a little easier to over pack when you were traveling by private plane and had people to help you.

She emerged from the terminal into the humid air and closed her eyes, inhaling the familiar smell and feel of home. When she opened them again, the dark-haired man in front of her took one of her bags and held out his hand for the other one. She handed it over and had to resist the urge to cry with gratitude at having a brother who loved her so much.

Because even though she'd forbidden him to come, it hadn't stopped him from sending someone else.

"Hi, Tank. Thanks for coming."

"No problem."

She fell into step beside him and had to control her urge to just stare at him. Tank Marshall, a giant of a man, worked with her brother for Alexander Security. He wasn't her type at all, but she had to admit there was something compelling about him. Something solid and dependable and real.

She also felt completely safe since he was built like a tank just as his name suggested.

Tank lifted her luggage into the back of a shiny black Escalade. It looked brand-new and way too nice to be one of the company vehicles that she'd seen Matt drive. She remembered then that Matt had said the man had recently come into an inheritance.

"Don't let the money change you," she blurted out suddenly and then flushed. "Sorry. I shouldn't have said that."

Tank didn't seem bothered. He opened her door for her and then waited while she got herself situated. Then he rounded the vehicle to the driver's side and swung his big body up into the seat.

"It's okay. Matt told me what's been going on. So I under-stand what you're saying. And I won't. I'm lucky that I have someone to keep me grounded. My brother on the other hand, he doesn't."

Mara grinned. Big, bad Tank Marshall had a girlfriend? "I didn't know you were seeing someone. Good for you."

"Yeah, she is good for me." He looked down at his hands, flexing them, and she noticed then the scars on his knuckles, the thin white slashes standing out against his tanned skin. "She's the best thing for me there is."

They were both quiet on the way home, and she didn't speak again until he pulled into the driveway of her town house. Trent had driven them to the airport last time, and she'd left her car at home.

It felt weird to think of driving herself around town after taking cabs and being driven places for so long, but she was actually looking forward to it. She wanted to get on with the business of picking up her life.

Because being where she was now, this hollowed-out shell of herself, was the worst thing she'd ever experienced.

Tank had already exited the truck and carried her bags up to the porch. She opened the door with her key and he carried them inside. She stood in her living room, feeling oddly out of place. Then she turned and noticed that her small dining table was set for dinner.

"How... what?"

A second later, her friend Ridley Alexander came out of her kitchen carrying a small bowl. She placed it on the table. When she turned and saw Mara standing in the doorway, she let out a soft cry of surprise and moved to hug her. Mara sank into the embrace, stunned by how much she needed it.

"Ridley, what are you doing here?"

Her friend gestured around the house. "You've been gone so long that the girls and I thought we'd come spruce things up before your arrival."

Kaylee appeared in the doorway. "Hi, Mara. I just finished with dinner. Mrs. Alexander helped me make enough food to last you for a while."

At the sound of her name, Julia Alexander came bustling out of the kitchen. She walked over to Mara with her arms outstretched. Her dark hair was pinned up into her usual style that made Mara think of the screen sirens in her favorite old movies.

"Welcome home, honey. I heard you've been put through

the wringer these past few days. But you don't have to worry about a thing now. Come on in and put your feet up."

Penny appeared from the hallway leading to the bedrooms. She had a blue kerchief tied around her head and was holding a spray bottle and a sponge.

When she saw Mara, she grinned. "Bathroom is clean. No more dust bunnies."

"Penny! You're here too?"

Her future sister-in-law gave her a strange look. "Of course I'm here. You didn't think I wanted to stay home with your sourpuss of a brother, did you? He's so grumpy that you ordered him to stay away. I didn't even tell him where I was going because he would have decided to come along anyway. You need time to relax and settle in before he comes at you with a bunch of questions."

Mara nodded, not surprised at all that Penny knew her brother so well. "I do. I can't believe you all did this for me. I don't know what to say."

Julia took her carry-on bag off her shoulder and ushered her forward. "No need to say anything, honey. We're your family. And family takes care of its own."

Mara sat down on the couch in her nice clean living room and inhaled the mouthwatering smells of whatever fabulous things Kaylee and Mrs. Alexander had whipped up for her. Overwhelmed by the show of friendship and generosity, she opened her mouth to thank them all.

And just burst into tears.

———

BACK AT THE PENTHOUSE, Trent stood in the center of Mara's closet staring at the empty drawers and shelves. It looked like she'd packed by taking her arm and sweeping everything off each shelf one at a time. There were belts and jewelry littering the floor. The shoes hadn't been touched and neither had the rest of the formal evening gowns she'd purchased when she'd gone shopping with his sister.

She'd only taken the things she'd had before she'd come here. Considering how much Mara loved pretty things, especially shoes, he understood what a sacrifice that must have been. It also sent him a message that he'd been trying to ignore until now. She wasn't coming back.

Mara had gone home and she hadn't wanted to take anything that tied her to him.

It was over.

Up front, he paced the room. His instinct was to have the jet readied so he could fly back to New Haven. He could wait for Mara at her house. She'd have to come back there eventually. He had a beatdown coming from Matt, and he was ready to take it. He'd let Mara rage at him. She could yell at him, scream at him, call him names, and kick him while he was down.

He didn't even care. He'd volunteer for her anger because at least her anger was part of her. Instead of what he had now.

This nothingness.

Frustrated, he kicked the side table over. The wood splintered and cracked as it fell. The sounds of destruction just spurred him on, so he kicked it again. Then he picked up one of the small sculptures the designer had placed artfully on the other side table and threw that against the wall too. The sound of it fracturing and then dropping to the ground in pieces fueled his emotions.

There was nothing else for him to throw in the living room, so he stalked back to the bedroom again. When he saw the dents in his closet door from when he'd tried to ram it open, his anger deflated. This kind of violent emotion wasn't something he was used to, and expressing it didn't even help, it just drove everyone away.

Driving people away was something he was good at. Or at least something he understood. He'd spent years trying to keep people out until one beautiful, vibrant, loving girl had made her way into his heart and showed him how to feel again.

And now she was gone.

He collapsed on the bed, his shoulders hunched forward as he let despair wash over him. She was gone.

Gone. Gone. Gone.

The words flowed through his mind on a loop until he squeezed his eyes shut, trying to block it out.

If he'd trusted Mara enough to tell her the truth, there was a chance that over time she might have understood. He could have shown her over the years with every glance, touch, and conversation that he saw her as her own unique individual.

Now he just had to look back on it all and remember what could have been.

twenty-one

Two months later...

LOOKING out over the city that he both loved and hated, Trent ignored the beeping sound coming from his pocket. Without even looking at it, he already knew what it was for. It was an alarm set to go off at the same time each week.

He was about to be late for an appointment.

Resting his head on the cool glass, he closed his eyes and tried to absorb the energy of the city below him. He had a busy day planned, and if he missed his appointment it would throw off the rest of his schedule. He couldn't afford any deviations from schedule.

It was part of his new system of life. Everything had a place. Everything had an appointed time. It kept him focused so he wouldn't miss out on the things that mattered. He spent time with his family, on work, and quiet time in meditation.

His favorite bench in Central Park seemed happy to have his company again.

A few minutes later, he was in the elevators going down to

the lobby. When he approached the front door, Ernesto tipped his hat. "Have a good day, Mr. Townsend."

"You too. I won't be home for a while, so I'll say good-bye now."

The older man looked a little sad at that news but not altogether surprised. Trent had surprised himself by staying in town as long as he had. A multimillion-dollar penthouse was just as lonely as any other place when the person you loved wasn't there.

Ernesto hailed him a cab and then held the door for him. "Take care of yourself, Mr. Townsend."

When he shut the door, Trent waved to him. He gave the cabbie his destination and then closed his eyes

They pulled up to a high-rise in Midtown. He gave the cab driver a handful of bills and then climbed out. He'd long ago sent Shane home. It wasn't fair to the other man to keep him on call when Trent was spending the majority of his time holed up in his office. This was the only recurring appointment he had. And even these were coming to an end.

He took the elevator to the eleventh floor and then entered the spacious office suite. The pert blonde behind the counter acknowledged him with a smile as he signed in. He sat in the waiting room but didn't bother with a magazine.

He looked up a few minutes later when the blonde called his name.

"Mr. Townsend? Dr. Winston will see you now."

He stood and buttoned his suit jacket. "Thanks, Donna."

He entered the cool interior of the office. It was always slightly dark in the room. He wasn't sure if that was done on purpose or not. It gave the instant impression of entering some kind of cocoon, away from the outside world. It was cheesy, but it did make him feel like he was in a safe place.

Dr. Winston was already seated behind his desk. His gray hair looked slightly darker, almost as if he'd colored it, and it amused Trent to think that even his psychiatrist was prone to insecurities.

"I'm glad to see you back here, Trent."

Trent sat in one of the leather chairs facing the desk. "You didn't think I would come back?"

The doctor's expression didn't reveal anything when he replied, "Our last session was quite intense."

Trent looked away. "It was. But I'm here. I want to talk about this. I need to talk about it."

The doctor nodded approvingly. "That's good. Talking about what drove you to leave New York last time can only help you. We cannot understand what you were feeling without the context."

Trent was finally able to admit that was true. He'd been running away from more than just his father when he'd left the city seven years ago. More than just his family and more than just the pain of losing Tia.

Her death hadn't been the only thing that had hurt him. It had also been the humiliation of knowing that she hadn't loved him back. The shame of realizing that their fight had likely contributed to her death.

Because even when you were angry with someone you loved, it didn't negate the pain of the loss.

Dr. Winston wrote something on his notepad, the pen making a soft scratching sound as it moved over the paper.

"We've been over your childhood and your rivalry with

your brother. But last time you started to tell me more about the day after your prom. About your friend Tia."

His hands suddenly clammy, Trent wiped his palms on his slacks and tried to push down the vague sense of panic clawing at his insides. For years, he hadn't talked about any of this and now he was going through every phase of that time in his life, detail by detail.

An image of Mara's tear-ravaged face gave him the strength to sit up straighter. The only thing she'd ever asked of him was to know him. Completely. It was the one thing he'd been unable to give her because he hadn't been ready to face certain things about himself. Even though he couldn't have her, it was the last thing she'd asked of him.

His love for her drove him to try to be the man she'd been in love with, even if it was too little too late.

"I'm ready now. I'm ready to talk about Tia's death."

———

MARA PUT the finishing touches on her spinach quiche and put it in the oven. She was proud of the way it had turned out, even though it had taken several tries to get there.

She made a notation on the pad of paper on the counter, crossing out something and adding the new amounts of the ingredients she'd changed. She was working on the recipe that would introduce the savory section of her cookbook and wanted to get it just right.

Matt had been more than happy to test each iteration of the recipe. He wouldn't admit it, but he would have eaten mud pies if it made her feel better. He was just happy that she was getting back to normal.

Well, as close to normal as she would ever be.

For the first week after she'd come home, her friends had kept a close eye on her. Despite being heavily pregnant, Ridley had come over each morning and coaxed her out of bed.

At first, she had barely been able to manage that without falling to pieces, but Ridley was persistent in her own sweet way. Mara had broken down one day, sobbing on her friend's shoulder, and Ridley had just put her to bed and stroked her hair. She vaguely remembered mumbling something about what a good mother Ridley was going to be.

Her friend had just laughed and told her to sleep.

After that, the girls came over as a group to entertain her on the next Friday night so she wouldn't have to be alone. They pretended it was just their usual girls' night out, but Mara knew it was mainly their way of checking up on her. The guys hadn't crashed their party this time.

Mara suspected they'd been threatened by Ridley, who could be surprisingly forceful when she wanted to be.

The next week, she'd taken her first trip outside her house. She hadn't gone far, just to visit her brother and Penny. She knew it had taken a lot of effort for Matt to stand back and let her work things out on her own. He was used to being her protector. It was just part of who he was.

But this time Mara didn't need a protector, she just needed the comfort of knowing that he was there. A big hug and a quiet movie night at their place had gone a long way to helping her feel like she was on the path to being okay again.

On her way but not there yet.

Mara sat on her couch and tucked her feet under her. She flipped aimlessly through the channels until she found a home decorating marathon. After watching her second episode, the timer went off, and she got up to take her quiche out of the oven.

While it was cooling, she quickly wiped down the counters and rinsed the towel in the sink. She didn't have much time to taste the quiche before she had to get dressed. It was strange to have an appointment. To have to be somewhere at a certain time.

Not that she thought Ethan would be angry if she was late, but she didn't want to keep him waiting. He'd come through for her, and now she was ready to return the favor. He needed her to train his new assistant for him, and she was more than happy to help out.

It would give her something to do besides sit in the house. It would be good to have a purpose again. To be needed.

She sat down a few minutes later with a plate. The quiche was perfectly seasoned, and the crust finally had the right consistency. She pressed her fork against the flaky, buttery crust and sighed in appreciation. When she looked at the clock on the wall, she ate the last few bites and then put the plate in the dishwasher.

As she passed back through the living room, she turned the television off. She'd never watched much TV before, but over the past few weeks it had been a lifeline. It brought noise into a house that had never seemed so quiet and empty before.

Even before Trent had proposed and subsequently moved in, she didn't remember ever feeling lonely or scared in the house. But ever since she'd gotten home, she was acutely aware of how solitary she was.

Living alone.

Eating alone.

Sleeping alone.

Her stomach cramped as she thought of how Trent had always slept right next to her, no matter how big the bed was. She'd wake up right on top of him more often than not, feeling like she was sleeping on a furnace due to all the body heat he generated. But despite the fact she must have been heavy, he'd never complained.

God, she missed him.

Nights alone had been the hardest thing to adapt to. She missed him so much it was a physical ache sometimes. He'd seemed to love it, being her pillow. Keeping her warm. He'd loved it and he'd loved her.

Although that was up for debate because it had been months and there had been no contact. She'd been so upset when she first arrived home but it hadn't truly occurred to her that she would just never hear from Trent again. For years he'd been as much a part of her life as the air she breathed, but he hadn't called and he hadn't come back to see her. He hadn't even made an attempt.

Obviously he hadn't loved her enough.

———

TRENT CLIMBED the steps to Matt's house and hesitated before he rang the doorbell. The last time he'd come to see his old friend, he'd gotten away without any broken bones. It was either extremely optimistic or extremely foolish to assume he could do it twice. So when the door swung open, he braced himself for impact.

But Matt just stood in the doorway watching him. Finally he moved aside. "Come on in. If I'm going to knock you on your ass, it won't be in front of the neighbors."

Trent stepped into the front hallway, grateful for the respite from the summer heat. Being away from the humidity, even just for a few months, had lowered his tolerance to it. He'd changed into casual clothes on the plane, so at least Matt couldn't make fun of his suit.

"I'm not sure whether to be impressed that you won't give up or just wonder what the hell is wrong with you. Why are you here?"

"Did you get the journal entries I sent you?"

Matt's face changed. He glanced down and then back at Trent. "Yeah, I got them."

Trent understood the discomfort. Part of his therapy had been writing down his feelings about Tia and her death. His feelings about himself and his part in it. It had proven so helpful that he'd continued writing about his college years, his friends, and his new life.

It hadn't been easy to write, and he imagined it wasn't the easiest thing to read either. But he'd wanted his friend to understand the things he'd done hadn't been done lightly.

Taking responsibility for his mistakes meant owning up to not only his actions but also what had led to them. It had been cathartic to get all that stuff on paper. He couldn't imagine letting anyone else but Matt read his private thoughts.

Except for Mara.

"I wanted you to understand."

Matt clenched his fists. "You didn't see her when she came back here. You didn't see what this did to her."

"No, but I saw what it did to me. I wouldn't wish it on anyone. I'm not asking for forgiveness for that. There's nothing I can ever do that would make up for it."

"She's finally doing better." Matt said it like it was a challenge.

Trent understood what he was really saying. *She's doing better and you being here could screw that up.*

"I just need to see her. One last time. But for once, I want it to be right. I want it to be somewhere she feels comfortable. A place where she can walk away if she wants to."

"If she walks away, are you going to let her?" Matt demanded. "Or are you going to try to convince her to come back? Because I think she's had enough of people trying to push her into doing things their way."

"The only thing I want to do is introduce myself to her. The new me. I'd like to think this is the new and improved version. Anything that happens after that is up to her."

Matt's face relaxed. "As usual, I don't agree with any of this, but you two are going to do whatever the hell you want anyway."

"So you'll help me?"

Matt grunted and gestured toward the living room. "Come on. If you're going to see her today, then we don't have much time."

twenty-two

SOME THINGS CHANGED but there were some things that never would, Mara thought as she entered the office to hear Ethan yelling. A few seconds later, a young girl with glasses and long, platinum-blond hair came marching out. She wiped tears away as she ran past Mara.

"That bastard," she mumbled under her breath as she passed.

Mara sighed and entered Ethan's office. He looked up when she entered, his face set in the same disgruntled expression she remembered.

"Stop scaring them off. I agreed to help you train the new girl, not to help you hire a new one. Is being nice really that hard?"

His grumpy expression softened slightly. "Yes. I need someone who can take a few harsh words without falling apart. This is a rough world."

"Believe me, I know. But I also know that you are not nearly as gruff as you'd like everyone to believe."

"You're mistaken," he insisted.

"I'm not. You've been found out. Now if we can just get you to admit it."

There was a knock on the door. They both turned. The young man in the doorway looked at Ethan. "I'm sorry to interrupt, sir, but I need to borrow your former assistant for a moment. Urgent legal matter."

She thought she saw Ethan's lips twitch. "Get out of here, both of you. Some of us have work to do."

Mara walked out of the office and grinned at her friend. "Danny! I'm so glad you're here."

He pulled her into a hug. When she'd started at the firm, Danny had been one of the first people to welcome her aboard and show her around. Even though his father was one of the partners, he'd started as a junior associate just like anyone else and worked his way up.

Luckily he'd inherited his father's brilliant legal mind, so he was advancing quickly. It gave her a small pang to think that she might not be around to see him get the promotion he so richly deserved.

"I just wanted to say hello."

"I'm glad you did. I've missed talking to you."

"Everyone around here has missed you too. Don't be a stranger, okay?" He tapped her nose and walked off.

When she turned around, Lanie stood next to her old desk. She raised her hand in an awkward wave. "Hey, Mara. I heard you were back."

"Yeah, just on a temporary basis. Until I can train Ethan to talk like a human being instead of grunting and shouting."

"I heard that!" Ethan yelled from his office.

Lanie paled and backed away.

Mara closed Ethan's office door and rolled her eyes. "He's getting better at least."

"If you say so." Lanie smiled. "It's good to see you back. It's been so boring here without you. I wanted to say that I'm sorry about last time. I didn't mean…"

"It's okay. Really. We're not together anymore, so it doesn't even matter."

Mara really didn't want to talk about it. It seemed like a lifetime ago when Trent had picked her up at work. Or a past life that she could only remember through dreams. It didn't even seem real when she looked back on it.

Probably because so much of it hadn't been real.

And wasn't that the biggest shame of all, she thought.

She was going to have to live the rest of her life with this sick sense of heartbreak, and she didn't even have the comfort of knowing that her love had been real while it lasted.

Lanie winced. "I'm sorry. Maybe I shouldn't have even brought it up."

"No, it's okay. It's just one of those things. So, what have you been up to?"

They chatted amiably until the blonde returned. Lanie promised to come back and see her over the course of the week.

It turned out that the blonde, a recent graduate named Erin, was way more adept and organized than she'd expected from Ethan's description. The morning flew by, and it was lunchtime before long.

"Do you want to get some food? I was going to try that new falafel place." Erin stood and stretched her arms overhead.

Mara glanced at the time and then grabbed her handbag. "Actually, I'm supposed to meet my brother. We're just going to take a walk and look at the water. I'll see you back here in an hour."

Mara exited the building and walked to the bridge. It was comforting to see the view that used to be a part of her daily routine. She pulled out the sandwich she'd brought from home and took an absentminded bite.

Matt had wanted to be supportive of her first day back. She'd told him it wasn't necessary. After all, she was only back temporarily. With her savings, she could afford to really think about what she wanted to do.

After she finished her cookbook, she wasn't sure if she wanted to pursue a publishing deal or if she wanted to apply to culinary institutes. Training to be a chef had been one of those dreams that had always seemed out of the realm of possibility, but if she'd learned anything over the past few months, it was that anything was possible.

Nothing was truly out of reach.

After ten minutes of standing on the bridge, she started to get a little hot. Where was Matt? It wasn't like him to be late.

She pulled out her cell phone and then sighed when she saw that she had several messages. He'd probably gotten caught in traffic. The bridge tunnel that connected Norfolk to the peninsula, where New Haven was located, could be unpredictable even during the middle of the day.

But when she pulled up her messages, she didn't see anything about traffic.

—*Hear him out.*

—*I hope you're not mad at me for butting in.*

—*Are you there?*

Mara's heart thumped in her chest. She looked up, squinting against the bright sun overhead. The wind whipped her hair around her face, and she pushed it back frantically as she turned in a circle, her eyes scanning all the people walking by. A crowd of teenagers passed by, two boys and two girls, obviously on a double date.

Once they were out of her line of sight, her eyes settled on the tall, blond man in khaki shorts and a blue golf shirt who stood a few feet away.

She covered her mouth with her hand, hoping he didn't notice it was shaking. He came toward her then, and he was so beautiful it made her head hurt. She could only stare up at him, brown eyes meeting blue, taking in every line of his face. Within minutes, she had catalogued everything that had changed over the past few months.

His eyes had faint shadows underneath like he wasn't sleeping. Under her makeup, she had them too. Even though his shirt stretched over shoulders that were as broad as she remembered, he looked like he'd lost a little weight.

Unfortunately, that hadn't been true in her case. If anything, all the baking she'd been doing had added another inch to her hips.

"What are you doing here?" she asked finally.

"Just having a walk. What about you?" Then, to her astonishment, he held out his hand. "I'm sorry, I haven't introduced myself. Trent Townsend. It's lovely to meet you."

He had her hand in his before she could yank it back. "What are you doing, Trent?"

"I'm introducing myself to the most beautiful woman I've ever seen. You know, this is weird, but you look a lot like someone I once knew. But after talking with you even just these few moments, I can tell you're nothing like her."

Mara bit her lip to keep herself from crying. "Is that so? How can you be so sure?"

"Because I've spent the past few months in therapy talking about my old friend. I'm completely clear on how I feel about her. I loved her then, but I've moved on."

"I wish I had that certainty," she admitted.

He kissed the back of her hand. "Will you walk with me?"

———

TRENT HOOKED his arm through Mara's, ignoring her look of surprise. It was a beautiful summer day. The water sparkled in the distance, and boats glided over the surface, their white sails snapping jauntily in the breeze.

A perfect day to fall in love.

"You said I looked like an old friend of yours? Won't that be weird for you?" Mara stared at him as if she couldn't believe what she was seeing.

He knew it was a gamble coming here, playing this game. But the way they'd met would always be a black mark against him.

"It's a weird coincidence for sure. I had to come up and meet you just out of curiosity. But now that I'm here, I find I want to talk to you just because I'm enjoying it so much."

Mara smiled tremulously. He could see how hard she was working to keep her emotions in check.

"I can't do this, Trent. Not again. I can't compete with your real life. For a really long time you couldn't face it all, and I understand that. I really do. But now that you've dealt with some stuff, you can go back to your life. Go back to the Upper East Side and the parties and summers in the Hamptons. Get back to where you would have been if Tia hadn't died."

"Is that what you want me to do?"

"I want you to be who you're supposed to be. But that doesn't mean it's easy for me."

"You keep talking about my real life, but *this is what's real.* The man I am with you is who I'm meant to be. All the rest is the lie."

She fell quiet and they walked a few minutes in silence, the only sound the wind in his ears and the calls of the gulls overheard.

"I can't just forget everything that happened, Trent. That would be like erasing history. I can't just pick up where we left off like my heart wasn't shattered. I can't marry you."

"Marry me? That would be awfully forward for our first date."

She wrinkled her nose at him. "Be serious."

Suddenly inspired, Trent turned to her and said, "I am serious. Tell me this, did you love me?"

She tried to tug her arm back. When he wouldn't let go, she narrowed her eyes at him. "Of course I loved you. I would have done *anything* for you. How could you even ask me that?"

"Did you want to be with me forever?"

"I wanted more than forever with you." Mara gave up trying to yank her hand back and settled for glaring at him instead. "I wanted us to die together and then be ghosts and haunt our grandchildren. Are you happy now?"

"Not nearly. I haven't been happy for a long time. Not since the day I came home to that half-empty closet and realized that I'd driven away the most extraordinary person I've ever known."

She sucked in a shocked breath, and then her hand clenched in his. "Oh, *damn it*. You're not allowed to do that. You can't just show up here and make me remember why I loved you."

He tugged her to one of the benches. She sat down and then pulled a tissue from her purse and dabbed her cheeks. He tipped her chin up and looked into her eyes.

"If you had this to do all over again, would you? I know I hurt you. I'll never be able to atone for that part, even though I'll try. But in the end, do you think our love was worth the pain? Did I make you that happy?"

He held his breath, waiting for her answer, sure she could tell by now how much her answers meant to him.

She seemed to have resigned herself to his strange line of questioning because this time she answered without any fuss.

"I'm clearly a masochist because yes, I would do it all over again. As much as this hurts, I can't imagine a world where I don't know you. A world where we could pass each other on the street and have no idea what we were missing."

His heart leaped at her answer. Her words perfectly captured everything he felt as well.

"Well then, Miss Simmons. I just have one more question for you." He leaned down, brushing a soft kiss over her forehead.

"What's that?" She leaned into his caress like she was as starved for touch as he was.

"Want to get a coffee with me sometime?"

TRENT'S EYES followed his fiancée as she wove her way through the room. Her curvy figure was wrapped in an elegant cream tea-length dress that Sophia had special ordered from some boutique they both loved.

Her dark hair was wound up on her head and woven through with white flowers and ribbons. She'd insisted their engagement party have a Midsummer Night's Dream feel to it, and he thought she looked every inch a sexy wood sprite.

She looked up and, when she caught his eye, winked. Trent had to smother a laugh as she was immediately drawn away by her mother, who no doubt wanted to bring up some new detail they needed to add to their wedding planning. Mara hadn't worked up the nerve to tell her mother that they were planning to elope. Trent voted for them not telling anyone. All he wanted was to make Mara his bride.

The sooner the better.

They'd spent every moment of the past few months together. Determined to move slowly, he'd gotten a small apartment in New Haven and commenced his courtship of the woman he loved.

They'd gone out to dinner, to the movies, had picnics in the park, and ridden a tandem bicycle on the boardwalk at Virginia Beach. He'd held her hand and kissed her chastely on their first few dates, and then they'd had marathon make-out sessions on her couch while the television played in the background.

He'd taken more cold showers that first month than during his entire adolescence, but it had been worth it.

He'd been determined to show Mara that he was with her *for her*. No other reason. And as time progressed and they got to know each other all over again, they'd fallen in love a second time. A love that was deep and true because it had the kind of roots that only come from heartache and forgiveness.

Over the past few months, he'd also had a chance to learn new things about all his friends. It was interesting that the guys he'd known for years had sides he'd never seen before.

Matt was still not fond of talking, but when Trent was having a hard day and just needed someone who got it, his friend was always up for hanging out or playing a game of pool at a local bar. And now when his mind was all twisted up, Mara understood because he wasn't shutting her out. She just kissed him on the nose, reminding him of what he was coming back to.

With her gentle love and encouragement, he had fewer bad days and more fantastic days.

"Stop staring at your future bride like that. There are children here." Jackson grinned, appearing at his left side.

Trent laughed.

He'd become particularly close to Jackson lately since his friend had also experienced the death of a woman he loved. He'd lost his first wife in a car accident when their children were just babies. An accident he'd blamed himself for. Talking to someone who understood about death and loss and guilt was invaluable.

Trent knew how lucky he was to have friends he could tell anything. More than all the money in his bank account, his friends were priceless.

Sophia stood up and ran after one of her children. His brother sat at the same table, bouncing Travis on his knee. The second DNA test had proven that James was Travis's father. James and Avery had been in counseling ever since.

He saw James and Travis at his parents' house, but he didn't visit them at home, something James understood. He was willing to be civil to Avery on holidays for his family's sake, but they would never be friends again.

He was okay with that.

His gaze settled on his parents, who looked slightly uncomfortable sitting at a table with Mara's extremely friendly and outgoing extended family. They had wanted them to have the engagement party in New York at some exclusive venue or another, something Trent had immediately dismissed. All he wanted was his friends and family right here, in the city he was proud to call home, surrounded by his family—both born and earned.

He looked up to see Mara waving at him. He turned to Jackson. "Looks like it's showtime. I have to go."

He joined her at the front of the room. Mara looked up from the notecards she held, her eyes bright. She held the microphone toward him. "Are you ready?"

He took the microphone and tapped it. The noise in the room subsided and everyone turned toward them.

"Welcome, everyone. Thank you for coming to celebrate my engagement to the most beautiful woman I've ever known."

A soft murmur went through the crowd, and he saw his mother and Mara's exchange approving glances. At his side Mara beamed, her cheeks flushed with pleasure. He turned back to the crowd.

"I want to tell you a story about the day we met."

———

I hope you enjoyed *Say You Will*! Tank Marshall and his brothers now have their own series! **One-click TANK now!**

Bonus Material: Want more? Eli & Kay's first kiss takes place in a special prequel that is only available directly from me. For a limited time, you can read *All I Want* (ebook or audio) for free!

The only gift Kaylee wants is for Elliott Alexander to stop treating her like she's invisible. When her car skids out of control on a snowy evening, she's forced to reach out to the only man she trusts to save her. Get your free copy HERE or at mmalone-books.com/alliwant

OR

Keep reading for a special excerpt of Eli's book.

ALL I NEED IS YOU

WHEN ELI LEAVES town after their steamy kiss, Kay decides it's time to stop pining for a man who doesn't want her. But when she's targeted by a stalker, Eli is the only one she can turn to. And Eli is willing to do whatever it takes to protect the one woman who gets under his skin.

Anything except fall in love...

All I Need is You **is Available Now at**

mmalonebooks.com/allineedisyou

KAYLEE SHOVED the books on her night table in the drawer. Her eyes swept over the rest of the room frantically. Hopefully she hadn't left anything embarrassing lying around. She wasn't used to having guys at her apartment. Especially not men like Elliott.

Big, masculine men that she fantasized about every night.

The hair on the back of her neck stood up and she didn't have to look to know that he was standing in the doorway. Her apartment wasn't that big, but it suddenly seemed exponentially smaller with Eli sucking up all her oxygen.

"Tank finished his assessment before we got here. We're all clear." Eli stepped in and looked around. "Where do you normally keep the figurine?"

Kay pointed to the top of her dresser. Eli walked over and looked down at her collection. He touched one and the sight of his thick fingers stroking the delicate china shouldn't have seemed erotic at all. But the image of this big, strong man handling tiny breakables with such care struck her as incredibly tender. Would that be how he treated a woman in bed? Like she was delicate, precious?

Or would he push her hard, demand things she didn't know how to give? Warmth spread to her face just thinking about it.

Not that you'll ever find out.

"There's an empty space here. He didn't even bother to push the others closer together to conceal what he took."

Kay hated to even think of it. Someone had been in her apartment, touching her things. Had he been here while she was home alone? While she was with her daughter?

While they were sleeping?

She shivered and grabbed the duffel bag she kept underneath her bed. Her favorite nightshirt was on top of the comforter, so she shoved that in the bag. Then she pulled open the drawers in her nightstand and added a big handful of underwear and bras. She didn't even look at how much she was taking, just grabbed blindly. Who cared, really, what she wore? All she cared about was getting out of here. Would she ever be able to relax in this room again without wondering if someone was watching?

She crossed to the dresser where Eli stood and yanked open the last drawer. In went several pairs of jeans, then she yanked open another drawer and added a big armful of sweaters.

"Kay, what are you doing?"

"Packing. I just want to get out of here."

She struggled with the zipper on the bag, almost breaking a nail on the metal teeth. Her breath came in harsh pants until little black spots danced in front of her eyes.

"Kay, calm down. Just hold on."

She struggled against his hold, but he held her securely in his grip, her back to his front. His arms wrapped around her, keeping her from moving but not holding her so tight as to cause pain. Eventually Kay stopped fighting and allowed her head to fall back against Eli's chest.

"Hey, hey. It's all right. Just calm down." He rubbed her arms gently, soothing her.

Kay finally stopped wrestling with him and allowed him to hold her. She closed her eyes and took a deep breath. It was a foolish moment of weakness, but for just a second, she soaked up the comfort and warmth of being in his arms.

"We're safe here. You've got a great security system. I already had Tank check it out and it hasn't been tampered with. I don't know how this guy got your figurine, but he didn't break in to do it."

Tears welled up, but she squeezed her eyes closed, swallowing back the sudden flood of emotion. There was no time for nonsense or feeling sorry for herself.

"Why would someone do this, Eli?"

"I don't know, angel." He spoke in a hush, the words flowing over her in a soft puff of breath.

His features tightened, and for the second time in recent memory, she allowed herself to soak up the masculine presence that was Elliott Alexander: the smooth dark skin, the high cheekbones, the long straight blade of his nose, and the sinfully full lips. It was a harsh face, not quite as elegantly hewn as his brothers' faces, but one that she vastly preferred. It looked like safety.

It looked like strength.

"I'm okay now. I promise I won't freak out on you again." She stood reluctantly. As wonderful as it felt to be held in his arms, there was only so much she could take before she lost all sense of propriety and threw herself at him again. She already knew he wasn't interested. When you kissed a guy and he responded by leaving town, that was plenty clear enough.

"It's okay to be freaked out, Kay. As long as you know that I won't let anything happen to you."

Kay nodded and dropped the duffel bag on her bed. She didn't have enough room to put him up in style, but at the very least she could rustle up some extra pillows and a blanket for him.

"I'm sorry I don't have a guest room. Or an air mattress."

Eli gave her one of his trademark *are you kidding* looks. "I'm not supposed to be on vacation, Kay. The couch is fine. Now, what about Hope?"

Kay gasped. Shame flooded her face. She'd told her mom that she'd pick up Hope by eight o'clock and she was already twenty minutes late. She pulled out her cell phone and hit the first speed dial.

Eli walked away to give her some privacy. Luckily, her father answered, so she was able to explain things with a minimum of fuss. As expected, her parents were thrilled to keep Hope overnight.

When she turned, Eli was watching her with an inscrutable expression. Unsure what to make of his sudden change in demeanor, Kay pushed past him and pulled open the door to the linen closet in the hallway. Several towels fell out and hit her in the face.

"Don't worry about that now." Eli took the towels from her arms and shoved them in the closet. "We need to talk first."

"About what?"

"Everything. Clearly I missed something when I was digging into your life last year. It's time to rectify that."

"But nothing has changed. I don't do anything interesting. So what's there to talk about?"

Eli stopped and nailed her with an intense look. "I need to know who you've been with since last summer." He moved closer and Kay inhaled, immediately assaulted by his unique scent—warm and rich and disarming. She looked up at him, her senses swirling from the intoxicating blend of reactions that only Eli could cause.

"We need to talk about your lovers."

All I Need is You **is Available Now at**
mmalonebooks.com/allineedisyou

also by m. malone

The Simmons

Birthday Cake : Ever since Mara walked into her brother's dorm room freshman year and came face to face with a shirtless Trent, she's known he was *The One*. She finally has a plan to get him exactly where she wants him. *In her bed.*

He's the Man : Matt Simmons is over Army doctors poking him until he sees his old babysitter, now a physical therapist, is h-o-t. Suddenly he's seeing the benefits of therapy.

Say You Will : Mara Simmons has always known Trent Townsend is *The One*. But when she suspects his frequent business trips have *nothing* to do with business, she sets in motion a chain of events bigger than she can imagine and discovers that the man she loves just might be a stranger.

The Alexanders

One More Day : "Good girl" Ridley has always attracted bad guys. Now she's on the run and has nowhere to hide. So when Jackson Alexander mistakes her for her twin, she decides to do something she knows is wrong. *She lies.*

The Things I Do for You : Nick Alexander finally has what the woman of his dreams needs. He'll give Raina a baby if she gives him what he wants. *Her.*

All I Want: The only gift Kaylee wants is for Elliott Alexander to stop treating her like she's invisible. When her car skids out of control on Christmas Eve, she's forced to reach out to the only man she trusts to save her. (**VIP List only**)

All I Need is You : When the man she loves leaves town after their steamy kiss, Kaylee Wilhelm is done. But when she's targeted by a stalker, Eli is the only one who can protect her.

Just One Thing : Bennett Alexander is a bona fide genius but he still can't figure out how to "get the girl". So he hires a dating tutor. What could go wrong? Other than falling for his teacher, of course.

One More Chance : Now that Ridley is expecting, everything is different. All she needs is for Jackson to pretend that he finds her as sexy as he used to, even if it's not true. But with a little advice from her meddlesome twin, she has a plan to seduce her own husband.

Bad Business (The Kingsleys)

Bad King: My parents just put a gold diggers target on my back. But if all they want is a wedding, I'll find the fiancee of their nightmares. *Who Wants to Marry a Billionaire? Must be completely inappropriate.*

Bad Blood : I'd do anything for my best friend's little sister. Until she asks for the one thing I can't give. One night. No rules. ***RITA® Award Winner!***

Mess with Me

Beg Me : My rooster is on strike. Yeah, I can't believe it either. But he'll only crow for one woman. Spoiler Alert *she hates me*

Ask Me : Am I arrogant? Maybe. Do women still want me? Abso-F'ing-lutely. Then I meet the one woman who isn't impressed.

Want Me : No strings attached. Sounds good, right? Except if I'm not her boyfriend ... the position is open for someone else.

Need Me : Crazy sh*t every day keeps relationships away. Except there's one guy who just *keeps* showing up. And if I'm not careful, I might get used to needing someone.

Blue-Collar Billionaires

Inheriting billions from the father they never knew sounds pretty sweet. Until they find out what he really wants in exchange.

Tank : Fake Dating the billionaire's son should have been easy. He's a bad boy and not my type. But he's also loyal and kind with an unexpected soft spot for rescue cats. Suddenly all I want is for this "fake" love to be real.

Finn : When she left me, I had nothing. Now I have it all: money, cars and most importantly, power. She's struggling to save her business, and I'm in the perfect position to save it. For a price.

Gabe : She thinks I'm arrogant and cocky as hell. She's right. A reformed con artist and a perfect little princess don't belong together. But I still can't leave her alone.

Zack : She's my brother's ex. Off limits. But she needs a nude model for her show so I'm taking one for the team. Turns out she needs more than just my picture...

Luke : My online BFF is the only hacker better than I am. Then I'm asked to consult on a hacking case for the FBI and the hauntingly beautiful suspect seems to know a lot about me. Things I've only told one other person...

* Join my VIP list for FREE books *

newsletter.mmalonebooks.com

M. Malone is a RITA® Award winner and a NYT & USA Today Bestselling author of completely inappropriate romantic comedy. She lives with her husband and their two sons in the picturesque mountains of Northern Virginia even though she is afraid of insects, birds, butterflies and other humans.

She also holds a Master's degree in Business from a prestigious college that would no doubt be scandalized at how she's using her expensive education.

instagram.com/minxmalone

bookbub.com/authors/m-malone

patreon.com/minxmalone

amazon.com/author/mmalone

tiktok.com/@minxmalone